BLACK ISLAND

David Forbes Brown

Cover: painting by Kenny Sloyer; title artwork, enhancement and
compositing by Scott A. Brown

CONTENTS

Prologue: Author's note

People forget. There are 4500 islands off the coast of Maine. A true archipelago. Some of the islands are miles long and support a winter community. Some span less than an acre and aren't the safest places to be in a storm.

Most of the islands are uninhabited.

In the summer, a few boating tourists dot these islands, landing on pristine pebble beaches to explore and take home shells and colorful beach glass, while lobstermen work offshore, tending to their traps.

But there are some islands visited by no one. Lobstermen don't set traps anywhere near them. Why? Deep water right off shore. No beach to land on. Cliffs jutting straight down into the murky depths. These islands are spikes of land, knifing up from the ancient deep. They are unappealing to visit, or to even look at for an extended period, I think... Or, I feel... People stay away.

BLACK ISLAND
David Forbes Brown

CHAPTER 1:   First Contact

1

Olias woke. He was outdoors?! He kept his eyes closed.

A sharp headache stung a new part of his mind and disappeared.

He opened his eyes. He lay nestled—rather comfortably, actually—atop a sea-strewn grassy ledge. He sat up and looked around. The small ledge was connected to a large wooded island by a thin tendril of beach rock. Ten feet below, waves crashed.

He slowly returned to consciousness as seagulls arced overhead and the sweet aroma of salt permeated his body. Strands of slowly-moving sea mist connected the many small islands. The red, bloated summer sun hung lazily on the horizon.

"Oh, that's right... I'm on Pond Island. I fell asleep?! At least I woke before dark."

He remembered sitting on the grassy perch an hour before dusk, drinking coffee, wondering about... something. He'd been getting ready to return to the boat and—

"The boat!"

He jumped up and hurried to the beach. There Ziggy was, still anchored off the southern shore.

"Whew... glad you're safe, guy." Boats are classically female, but Olias considered Ziggy male.

He looked at the yellowing sun. It had climbed in the sky—it was dawn, not dusk!

"How did this *happen?!* I finish a thermos of strong coffee, then sleep through a whole *night?!*"

He gathered his things and walked to the smaller boat— the tender—that was sitting calmly above the high tide line. He dragged it down the stony beach and rowed out to Ziggy.

He climbed aboard, put the tender in the stern and jetted toward his home on Mount Haven Island.

The odd headache returned. He remembered why he'd

fallen asleep!

He lost consciousness and fell headfirst onto the sharp rim of Ziggy's windshield, gashing his temple and crumpling to the deck.

Ziggy continued to whine at high speed, pointed at the open ocean, the next landfall unattainable—Africa.

2

An hour later, Olias and Ziggy were far out of the island cluster and deep into the Gulf of Maine.

Olias still lay unconscious, but somewhere in a previously unknown part of his mind was thought. "What's that island I can't see?"

Ziggy was almost out of gas, still heading full speed for Africa. Olias lay sprawled on the deck, his left leg draped lazily over the Captain's chair, his mouth marinating in a salty puddle.

Ziggy rocketed farther into deeper ocean, descending and climbing the mammoth ocean rollers.

The motor cut.

The boat slowed to a stop, and was turned by the wind and current in another direction—Nova Scotia—days away.

A black-back gull saw Ziggy from a distance. It circled lower and lower. It landed on the backseat. With black eyes, it studied Olias. After a few minutes, it flew back toward the islands.

An hour later, in a whisper, the bow slowly turned out of the current and wind until it faced Olias's home.

Ziggy began to *move.*

3

Kara was in the middle of the lunch shift at The See Food, Mount Haven Island's busiest summer restaurant, nestled in the little hamlet of Nor'easter Harbor called only "The Village."

She was slammed. Summer tourists filled the place. Only a few hardcore islander guys came in this day—they sat almost hidden at a little corner table, making fun of the summer people.

"Order up, Kara!" yelled someone from the kitchen.

"Okay, okay!" she yelled back.

"Excuse me, Miss? Check please. We're in a hurry," implored a man at one of her tables as the phone rang.

"Kara, can you get that?!!" asked Todd, the manager.

An angry woman who had been waiting three minutes for her check clapped her hands loudly. "Excuse me, Miss?!"

But Kara had already chosen her next action. There were four annoyed tourists standing at a dirty four-top table, waiting for it to be cleaned. She grabbed a washcloth and quickly wiped down the table. The phone was still ringing. Someone at a different table held up their empty soda glass. "Helloooo?!"

The phone stopped ringing. That felt good. She took some menus off the bar and handed them to the four-top.

From the kitchen came another yell. "Kara! Now ya got *two* orders up!"

"I'm busy!" she replied, hoping her frustration wasn't showing.

A party of eight walked in and stood in the doorway.

The phone started ringing again.

"Miss? Check!"

The party of eight looked lost, staring at her for guidance.

"Helloooo?! More soda?!" requested an old man at an adjacent table.

"Check!"

RINNNNGGGGGGG!

Kara ran to the phone. "See Food, how may I help you?"

"Hi Kara! Have you seen Olias?" It was Jon, Olias's best friend. "He didn't come in to work today, and he hasn't called!"

"No Jon, I haven't." A worry began in her gut, but she didn't have time for it and shrugged it off. "If you see him, tell him his girlfriend needs help at the restaurant!" She hung up and darted off.

"Three orders now, Kara!"

A party of six entered and stood behind the party of eight. The phone started ringing.

4

Jon tucked his cell away and got back to sanding the hull of the huge wooden sailboat that he and his fellow workers were restoring at Cranchet's Boatyard.

"Any word from Olias yet?" asked Old Man Cranchet.

"No, sir. Nothing."

Cranchet huffed while limping away with his cane.

"What the hell happened to him?" Jon wondered.

He heard a rumble of distant thunder and walked outside the warehouse building onto the dock. Far south, down East to West along the coast, clouds were darkening. A steady breeze kicked up off the water. A storm was coming.

He walked back inside and returned to sanding, hoping Olias was alright. "Maybe Ziggy's motor broke, and his phone went out?" After another few minutes of sanding, he called Olias's cell one more time. Voice mail.

A huge boom blasted outside. He ran out onto the dock. The storm was on top of them. The other boat workers followed. The waves were huge and the wind was swirling. The sky was so dark it was almost black. Lightning chains sliced into the ocean with exploding thunder.

"Haven't seen the sky this dark in years," Old Man Cranchet said before hobbling inside.

The other workers watched the storm with Jon as the rain came. The drops were so big, they hurt. "Shit!" They scampered inside, but Jon stayed out under a little awning, clutching his phone, looking into the storm, hoping his best friend was okay.

And then the hail came. At first, the hailstones were marble-sized. In fifteen seconds they were golf-ball-sized. In twenty-five seconds they were baseball-sized. One frozen baseball blasted through a boathouse window, just missing Old Man Cranchet's bad leg. The outside aluminum walls were being riddled with dents.

"It's gonna look like the Green Monster at Fenway!" Cranchet said.

Jon ran in and crouched behind a table saw, still able to peer out the big doors. It sounded like there was a huge drummer playing a fast timpani roll on the outside of the building. All the workers hunkered wide-eyed and still.

Then, like microwaved popcorn at the end of its cooking cycle, the hail slowed. The space between the hits grew—but the hail got bigger. Jon would never forget seeing basketball-sized chunks of ice torpedoing into the ocean.

And then it was over.

Silence.

One last splash!

The ocean calmed. Jon got up and went outside, hoping to

find one of the crazy basketball-sized hailstones so he could take a picture of it on his cell, get it viral and achieve his allotted fifteen minutes of fame; but the hugest ones had apparently all bee-lined into the ocean. There were still some baseball-sized ones lying around, and he snapped some shots as the other guys came out.

"Holy shit! I ain't never seen nuttin' like dat!" someone said.

The guys walked around in silence and assessed the damage. Cranchet stared at the smashed window. "Biggest hailstones I've ever seen!"

"Shit! My car!" exclaimed the oldest worker, an old seasoned boat builder named Hirum. The crew went to the parking lot to see Hirum's windshield completely smashed.

They walked around in a daze.

"You got insurance, Hirum?"

"No, I'm screwed."

"Okay guys, c'mon, back to work," Cranchet ordered.

Soon, sanders and saws roared back to life.

The sun came out and, in less than a minute, the temperature rose thirty degrees. Everything was suddenly baking in 110 degree heat, vaporizing the remaining hailstones.

The guys in the boathouse didn't feel the sting of the heat at first. Then the power went out.

Silence.

"What the hell, Bangor Hydro?!" hissed Cranchet.

The heat made its way inside.

"Holy damn, we got us a heat wave heeya!"

"I'm goin' swimmin', this keep up."

"Hey Jeffy, you got air conditionin' in your truck?"

"Yeah Joe, let's go."

"If the power doesn't come back in a half hour, that's it for the day, boys," Cranchet said.

"I'll call Bangor Hydro," Jon volunteered. He pulled out his phone and dialed, expecting their usual prerecorded message explaining that they know about the outages and are diligently repairing the grid, but there was no message. He hit #3, to talk to an actual person. He got one right away.

"Bangor Hydro, this is Julie, how may I help you?"

"Um, hi, I'd like to report an outage."

"Okay sir, what town?"

"Bass Harbor, on Mount Haven."

"I don't have that here. Let me look into that. Hold, please." She was gone less than a minute. "Sir? We have no outages in Bass Harbor. Do you have a pole down, with partial power?"

"No."

"Hmm... Well, what I can do—"

The phone went dead.

"What?!" Jon knew the battery was fully charged.

At the same time, Jeffy's truck stalled.

The guys wanted their air conditioning. "Hey! Jeffy, get 'er goin'!"

"I can't! She ain't turnin' over!"

The electricity, phone, truck, and a sander someone left on in the boathouse all fired up.

"Whoa!" exclaimed Jon, sprinting to the unattended sander and snapping it off.

"What idiot left that sander on?!" barked Cranchet.

"You gotta get this truck looked at, Jeffy!"

"Okay, back to work, people!" Cranchet yelled.

An ocean breeze kicked up and calmed the heat. Everyone returned to work. Jon dialed Olias one more time, and didn't even get the voice mail.

5

Ziggy sailed in silence—nobody knowing, no wind blowing. Olias still lay on the deck. The salt-water puddle at his mouth had gurgled away towards the stern as a result of the boat's momentum. Ziggy was quietly going forty miles an hour as he entered the island cluster en route to Penobscot Bay—home of Mount Haven—staying away from all other boats.

Olias woke. His first thought was, "No pain." He got to his feet, plopped into the captain's chair and rubbed his eyes. It was a perfectly calm summer day. Gulls called and arced in the above blue as gentle waves lapped at the boat.

He was back home, at his mooring!

"Did someone tow me back?"

Ziggy wasn't tied to the mooring, he just floated right off it. All Olias had to do was put out his hand and grab the line. He moored Ziggy and sat back in his chair, trying to make logic out of impossibility.

His mind grew less cloudy. "Shit! The boatyard!"

He fumbled for his phone and saw power with bars. "It's past five o'clock?!" He called Jon.

"Olias!"

"Jon, I don't know what happened! I just woke up in Ziggy, at my mooring."

"I'm glad you're safe. Old Man Cranchet was kinda being a dick about you not showing up and not calling, but he likes you, so... just say you're sorry and it'll-never-happen-again kinda thing."

"Yeah. I don't even know what happened."

"So, you went out in Ziggy and fell asleep at the mooring?"

"No, I went to Pond Island in the late afternoon yesterday and fell asleep there after drinking a full thermos of coffee. Then, on my way back, I fell and hit my head on the windshield!"

"Wow, how's the noggin?"

"It's fine. There's no pain. I'm sure there's a bruise—I need to get ashore and get in front of a mirror."

"How did you deal with those huge waves during the storm? Did you see that hail?!"

"What storm? Hail? Look, I have to call Kara and get to a mirror."

"Okay, call me when you're inside."

"K." He dialed Kara.

"Olias! Are you alright?!"

"Yes, luv. I fell asleep after a full thermos of coffee, and I'm trying to make sense of it... I missed work..."

"Oh luv, I'm just glad you're alright. I'm in the weeds here—four tables just sat at once. I'll call you when it calms down. I love you."

"I love you."

Olias slid the tender into the water, threw in the oars and gear, and rowed to his shore—a picturesque small-stoned beach overlooking many islands.

He had inherited his ocean-front house from his great-grandparents. As a young child, Olias drove up from Massachusetts with his parents to stay in this cottage every summer, and when it was time to leave he would cry and remain heartbroken for weeks. After graduating college, he was lucky enough to have the cottage willed solely to him. His family had lost interest in anything Maine. They were in love with their house in Florida's Keys. Olias moved straight from his dorm room to his cottage. He had lived on Mount Haven for five years.

He carefully brought the tender above the high-tide line and tied it to a tree. Walking up the steps, he felt surprisingly strong. "I guess I really needed that sleep."

Olias had never wanted a beer more than he wanted one at that moment. Luckily, he had an unopened thirty-pack in the fridge.

He dialed Jon. "Have beer, will drink."

"I'll be right there."

Olias had to see how bad a mark Ziggy's windshield rim had left on his face. He jogged to the bathroom mirror.

No mark!

He walked onto the porch, which overlooked Penobscot Bay, and sat down with a frosty beer. He knew Kara was still busy at work, so he texted her. "Luv, this first beer is for you!"

Soon Jon pulled up, having driven over from his apartment in the Village.

From his favorite chair on the porch, Olias heard Jon enter, walk to the fridge, grab a brew, walk through the living room—stepping around the drum set and band equipment, and emerge on the porch.

"Olias, you're alive!"

"Funny."

Jon cracked his brew and sat. "So, *what* the hell happened?"

6

At the See Food in Nor'easter Harbor, Kara got the text from Olias and chuckled, knowing it was his way of asking her to come over after work. She quickly texted him back, saying she couldn't because she was working a double.

The owner, Bob Lianelli—a 55-year-old, chubby, high-energy sort—bolted into his restaurant and sat at a table with two born-'n-bred islanders Kara didn't trust—Jimmy and Lenny, who were there at Lianelli's request.

Jimmy served in Desert Storm, but was discharged for reasons he never talked about. His face constantly twitched, a condition he picked up after too many bombs and guns went off near him. While he was serving in that war, Lenny was back on

Mount Haven, smoking pot and watching cartoons, awaiting his pal's return. Jimmy was a big muscular guy, whereas Lenny was a lumpy, nonathletic sort. Jimmy was the boss. He called the shots. Kara—also a lifelong islander—didn't trust either of them.

Bob Lianelli had bought the restaurant over the winter, naming it the See Food. "You gotta *see* the food before you eat it, right?!" he'd repeat. Bob was born in New York City to a mafia family in the garment district. He was as opposite a Maine islander as possible. He was brash, entitled and loud. He couldn't be trusted and, as a result, trusted no one.

"I wonder what that's about," Kara said under her breath. Jimmy and Lenny kept looking at her while they were talking. It made her skin crawl. She went into the kitchen to wait for an order.

Bob watched Kara go into the kitchen and said, "Look, I need you guys to break into his house and get onto his computer while he's at work."

"That's gonna cost an extra hundred," Jimmy said.

"Yeah, an extra hunnert each," chimed Lenny.

"Okay, you guys do what I tell ya, you get that. Now look, he works during the day, so you gotta break in when it's light out. But, he doesn't have any nearby neighbors, so it should be easy to get in and out without anyone seein' ya. The chump probably doesn't even lock his door."

"So, what are we lookin' for?"

"Everything. Look at everything he's got on his computer and make a copy for me with this," said Bob, pulling out a jump drive and plunking it into Jimmy's hand.

7

Mount Haven was one of the largest of the 4500 islands off the coast of Maine, comprising about eighty square miles with seventy miles of ragged shorefront, including three good harbors and many small coves, and lay ten miles offshore in a huge bay among clusters of smaller uninhabited islands and ledges. It was home to roughly 1500 year-round residents. In the summer, its population tripled to fill the summer cottages and mansions along the shore. Many tourists stayed in The Village Inn, the bed-and-breakfasts and the campground. Large numbers of day trippers emerged from the ferry to fill the few restaurants and shops and hike the trails that scaled the mountains and followed the shorelines.

Olias and Jon sat on Olias's porch, looking out over the islands dotting the bay.

"We should ask around the Village and see who towed you back, and ask 'em why they didn't try waking you up," Jon said.

"But that's just it. No one would do that!"

"True... very odd."

They were comfortable enough with each other to sit in silence for awhile. The only sounds were the drone of a far-off lobster boat setting its final traps for the day and the light patter of surf lapping at the beach stones. A seagull flew by with a protesting crab in its beak.

Jon sat upright. "So, you say you were on Pond thinking about something, and fell asleep. Do you remember what you were thinking about?"

"Well... I was thinking about what islands around here I haven't landed on in my life yet, and—"

Olias lost consciousness and fell out of his chair, hitting the porch with a thud as his beer spilled and foamed around him.

"Olias? Olias!"

Jon shook him. He seemed to be in a coma. Jon checked his pulse—fine. "Olias, wake up!"

Olias woke. "What happened?" he mumbled.

"You passed out right when you were about to say what islands around here you never landed on!"

In Olias's eyes was a dazed clarity that Jon would never forget. In those eyes he saw confusion and revelation.

"I... was... thinking that I never landed on *Black Island*." His eyes fluttered but he remained awake.

"I've never been either. I don't even consider that island. Don't even think about it, ever."

"That's just it, Jon. There's something about Black Island."

"Well, okay then. Let's go to Black Is—" Jon's body went limp as he fell, his face crashing into the coffee table.

"Jon! What's happening?! Jon! Wake up! There's something about Black Island!" Then, he had an idea. "Black Island, Jon! *Black Island!*"

Jon woke.

"Jon, you lost consciousness just like I did! It's all about Black Island! There's some really strong voodoo energy or something!"

"That's about the weirdest thing I ever heard of... Okay then, what do we do about it? What if this keeps happening?!"

"I guess it means we should go to Black Island? Or maybe never go?"

"But if we stay away, will we keep having these blackouts whenever we think about it?"

"Maybe we should go."

"Yes. I think we should."

"Let's test each other: LET'S LAND ON BLACK ISLAND, JON."

Nothing happened.

"LET'S LAND ON BLACK ISLAND, OLIAS."

Nothing.

8

Dan was born in the slums of Miami. When he was almost two years old, his parents were killed in a drug-war gunfight. He was raised in Florida orphanages and foster homes. Trouble always found Dan, especially when he went looking for it. From a very young age, Dan was the classic "have-not" hating the "haves."

As a child, he heard of a place called Maine, where there were thousands of uninhabited islands. His fantasies always included these almost-fictitious, mysterious-sounding islands.

When he was eighteen, he left the orphanage on foot and set out alone, even living in the woods for a time. He slowly made his way toward Maine—which seemed the polar opposite of the inner-city slums of Miami.

He spent almost two years in Roanoke, Virginia, immersed in the drug culture, with aspirations of becoming a drug lord, but when a friend of his was killed, he vowed then and there to never deal again and set off on his original course.

By age twenty-two, he had saved enough to buy himself a used car, and that's what finally got him to Maine. He'd never forget crossing the Maine border and seeing that big green sign on I-95 that declares, *"MAINE, THE WAY LIFE SHOULD BE."* "Damn straight!" he shouted while beeping his horn and flashing his lights.

He had been living on Mount Haven Island for almost a year. He had a respectable job working on the docks and had a modest apartment in the Village. There was even interest in a girl.

Today, he had decided to spend his lunch break eating in Mount Haven Park, where an elderly woman sat on a bench, smiling to passersby.

He plopped down on an adjacent bench and pulled a bagged lunch out of his knapsack. He started unwrapping a sandwich.

The elderly woman glanced over at him. "Excuse me, do you know what time it is, son?"

"Um, yeah. It's a few minutes before noon."

"Oh, thank you, son. You look like such a nice boy. Are you from around here?"

"No, I'm from Miami, but I always wanted to move to Maine, and that's what I did."

"Ohhhh, well I'm glad someone with a smile so cute has chosen to grace our island with his presence!"

Dan smiled and lifted his sandwich for pre-devouring inspection.

"What is your name, son?"

"Dan."

"Oh my goodness. My son's name *was* Dan!"

Silence.

He didn't know how to respond to this, nodding awkwardly and looking off into certain meaningless sections of the sky, scared that eating his sandwich would be rude. It certainly didn't feel right to start loudly crunching lettuce at this point. As a result, he felt insecure.

"Yes, my good-looking young friend, I'm afraid he was killed in a car accident many years ago."

"I'm sorry."

"Oh, thank you, you are such a sweet boy, just like he was. You've really made my day, Dan!"

He smiled and took a bite. He ate as they sat in silence, but no longer felt hungry—the sandwich didn't even taste good. Bologna? Why bologna?

"Dan, my name is Edna Black. I live only a few minutes from here. Do you happen to know anyone who is looking for some part-time work, doing some lawn-mowing and general yard maintenance? My yard is looking horrible and I just can't do it myself anymore."

"Hmmm. How big is your yard?"

"It's just an acre or so, on the ocean just out of the Village, an easy walk from here, even by me."

"Well hey, I think *I* could help you out!"

"Oh, Dan! You've made my day twice!"

She put her weathered hand on his shoulder, and something changed. His uneasy feeling disappeared. And his hunger was back.

He blushed and took a big bite as a warm smile came from deep inside—happy fuzzies growing and multiplying in his heart. The sandwich still didn't taste good, but it didn't matter.

CHAPTER 2:   The Wall

1

Olias woke seconds before his alarm sounded. It was Friday morning, and a big day: work at the boatyard after not showing up or calling the day before, followed by a trip with Jon to mysterious Black Island.

He got out of bed with the energy of someone who had been awake for hours, threw on some clothes, went downstairs to the kitchen and made coffee, knowing the aroma would wake Jon—who was draped over the sofa in a "happy-previous-night" stupor, with one leg dangling off the side, his head hidden in the pillows. Olias was starting to worry about Jon's drinking.

Olias inhaled half a mug before walking into the living room, where Jon's eyes were just starting to open. "Morning, Jon. Looks like you slept rather soundly."

"Mornin'. Wow. I think I had four too many," he moaned, finally moving the airborne leg onto the sofa. "I didn't get too drunk, did I?" he asked, rubbing his face.

"Well, we spent about forty-five minutes talking about how lonely you are and need a woman, but you didn't get angry, so, it wasn't a bad night. I'll tell you, it's going to feel a little weird going into work today, but I'm sure Old Man Cranchet will be cool."

"Yeah, he'll be cool."

They had showers, got ready and left for the boatyard.

"You need anything from your apartment?"

"Nope."

Olias had made sure to set the alarm earlier than usual, and they were the first ones there, even ahead of Cranchet. They sat on the dock, facing a small island cluster. Olias's mind was racing, whereas Jon's was still trying to wake up. Their silence was graced only by gull cries, foaming surf and a few chugging lobster boats leaving the harbor for a long day at sea. It was already hot.

Olias broke the quiet. "So, what will we need for the trip to Black Island?"

"Just the usual stuff. A flashlight—just in case. Nautical

charts, marine radio, food, mosquito spray, and I guess binoculars would be good."

"Definitely."

They heard Old Man Cranchet's truck, got up and walked over as he hobbled out. "Decided to join us today, huh Olias?"

"I'm really sorry, Mr. Cranchet. I got stranded out on the water and my phone went dead."

"It's okay, kiddo. I'm just glad you're here today. And, I'm glad you didn't get struck by lightning or belted in the head by that crazy hail out there! How's the boat?"

"Um, he's fine, thanks. I guess that storm didn't come right over me."

"It sure hit us here! Now today, what I need you boys to do—" Cranchet froze like a statue. His eyes rolled up into their sockets with a gurgle. His body shook for a few seconds and froze again. Olias and Jon stared, dumbfounded.

Cranchet's eyes returned and his body relaxed. He started walking to the boathouse as if nothing happened, stopped and turned towards them. "I think you men should go to Black Island today. We can handle the workload here. Be careful out there!" His eyes blazed and he laughed—a crackle-type laugh that sounded like it was from a completely different person.

Olias and Jon were in shock.

Cranchet stood facing them in an odd pose. He had his cane resting on his left shoulder, all his weight placed on his bad leg.

The three faced each other for half a minute as the ocean wind picked up.

Olias broke the silence. "Are you sure you want us to go to Black Island, Mr. Cranchet?!"

"Of course I'm sure. And I won't forget that I told you to go. Now get going! Time's 'a-wasting! We're done talking here. Go!"

Jon and Olias walked toward Olias's car as Cranchet watched, a strange smile stretching his lips.

"Hmm, let's go get our... supplies ready," said Olias.

"...Yup."

They got in and drove off.

2

Jimmy and Lenny drove slowly down the thin back road to Olias's.

"Lenny, you stay in the car while I break in and get this thing hooked up to his computer. Call me on the cell if you see *anyone*, got it?"

"Got it."

"But first, I gotta call Shep at the boatyard to make sure Olias is there. We can't fuck this up. We can't look bad in front of Lianelli. We do this job good, and he might have more paying shit for us."

"Yup."

Jimmy called his long-time drinking buddy Shep, who was just arriving at the boatyard for work.

"Shep, it's Jimmy. Is Olias there yet?"

"I don't see him, Jimmy. What do you care about that asshole transplant fag anyway?"

"On a job, Shep. Don't say nuthin.' Call me when he shows up."

"Ayuh."

"He ain't there yet," Jimmy said to a cartoonishly alert Lenny.

"Where the hell is he? He wasn't at work yesterday too. What a slacker pussy."

"Yup."

Meanwhile, Olias and Jon were parking at the Village's only market to buy flashlight batteries.

"How's your head, Jon? Still feelin' it?"

"Nope..."

"Let's get a new battery for the GPS tracker too."

"Good idea."

They bought batteries and headed to Olias's.

Jimmy and Lenny sat far up the dirt road, in sight of Olias's driveway. They were in Lenny's car—Jimmy wasn't stupid enough to have his truck anywhere near the crime scene—both munching on Doritos and burping Dr. Pepper. Jimmy's phone rang.

"Hey Shep."

"Hey Jimmy. Cranchet said he gave Olias and his buddy Jon the day off. I don't know what's wrong with the old senile asshole."

"Thanks, Bub," Jimmy said and put his phone away. "We're outta here. It's a no-go."

Lenny burped and turned the car around—almost scraping the paint on a tree—and drove in the direction they'd come. "So, what are we gonna do today then, Jimmy?"

"I don't know. Let's go to No-Name Point and get stoned."

"Sounds good. What's Elsa doing today?"

"I think she said she has the day off, I forget. After fucking her I fall asleep, I don't listen no more."

"Ha ha. Niiiiiice."

3

Olias and Jon came from the main road and pulled into Olias's dirt driveway. They gathered their supplies from the car and brought them down the path to the beach, walked back to the house and packed their usual island-hopping essentials.

"Let's bring the cooler."

"Definitely."

They brought everything to the beach, carried the tender down to the water's edge and loaded the supplies. Olias rowed out to Ziggy and transferred everything into him, rowed back and got Jon. They pulled the tender up into the stern.

It was a perfect summer day on the islands—a few white fluffy clouds floating in rich blue. Olias fired up Ziggy's engine, then brought it down to a low growl to warm it. He hit the bilge pump button as a little trickle of fresh rain water spurted into the sea. Jon turned on the weather radio as Olias unhooked Ziggy from the mooring.

Off they sped, the bright sun creating a brilliant sparkly wake stretching far behind the boat. A bald eagle followed them for a minute, before flying off in the direction of High Island to the south. Once past a few small islands and dangerous ledges, they turned in the same direction.

As they made their way toward the open ocean, the little wind-induced waves slowly transformed into gentle ocean rollers, each much taller than Ziggy. They climbed and fell over the huge hills of water.

Once past the southern face of wild, mountainous High Island, there it was in the distance...

Black Island.

Standing alone.

A last sentinel of land before the briny deep. Next stop, Africa or Europe.

Olias waited until they were past some dangerous ledge-strewn waters, and turned the wheel right at Black. In fifteen minutes they were close. He took Ziggy down to trolling speed and came in for a slow approach. "Let me see the nautical chart."

"Here."

Olias unfolded the chart and found Black Island. "Wow, there is absolutely *no* shallow water off this thing! It's just cliffs going straight down into the water. It's over a hundred feet deep right off every part of the island! How are we going to anchor?!"

"Hmm... we *can't* anchor."

Olias put the motor in neutral as they drifted two hundred feet off the island. "How about this... You see those little woods on the northern side, right near the water's edge? I say we bring Ziggy right up to those cliffs, climb up, and literally tie Ziggy to a tree."

"I think it could work, as long as the wind and current are pushing Ziggy away from the cliffs."

Olias nudged the engine into forward and motored slowly up to the cliffs.

"I got this!" proclaimed Jon, taking the main rope and climbing onto the bow. He tried to keep his balance on the slippery surface as Ziggy was carried far up and far down by the huge rollers. He knew he had to jump when they were at the highest point, so he wouldn't get ripped off the cliff by the next roller.

The next wave brought them up—Jon jumped. He landed tipsy on sharp rock, but recovered. "I'm on!" The next roller was a little taller, soaking his legs. He hung on. "The water's even colder this far out!"

He cautiously climbed up the jagged rock, testing each section for stability before putting any weight on it. One of the rocks was loose—he touched it with his foot and it broke off, plummeting into the ocean with a "ba-dooosh!"

"Be careful, Jon!" Olias yelled, backing Ziggy away from any falling rocks.

Jon got his hand around the trunk of a small juniper bush that just barely held its place in the soil as he pulled himself onto Black Island.

He stood and pumped his fist. "Wahooo!"

"Wahooooo!"

He tied the rope to a sturdy tree, securing Ziggy to the island.

"Here's another rope!" Olias yelled. "Tie it to the tree and throw it back!" He threw the rolled up rope to Jon, who caught it on the first try. Olias put out Ziggy's side fenders to keep him safe from the sharp cliffs. "I hope the wind and current don't change direction!"

Jon nodded while making sure they had a strong and stable climbing rope from the island to the boat.

"Jon, let's take the tender out of Ziggy and bring it up onto the island, as a just-in-case kinda move."

"Good idea."

Olias climbed onto Black Island.

It took some painstaking maneuvering to pull the tender onto the island without badly scratching its hull on the jagged cliff. They carried it into the woods.

Olias exhaled. "I say we even tie the tender tightly to a tree. This place is already giving me the creeps."

"Same here. I could go for a drink!"

"This isn't the time, Jon. You didn't bring any, did you?"

"I... might've..."

"Don't pull out your flask. Don't drink. I need you sober."

"Okay..."

After getting all the gear out of the boat and making sure everything was secure, they sat at the cliff's edge for a breather.

"I feel like I'm being watched," Jon said.

"I feel it too."

"So, which way do we go?"

"I think we should go through these little woods to that grassy higher ground, and then climb up to that *very* high ground. See it? Let's try and get to the top. From there, I bet we can get a good look at this island and decide where to go from there."

"Sounds good."

They drank limeade as a lone cricket's chirp mixed with the sound of the breaking surf below.

Soon it was time. They zipped up their backpacks and started off through the sparse woods, which opened up into a field that slowly and gracefully arced upward. Wild flowers painted the land a mélange of color.

"This doesn't look like some weird island. It looks normal,"

Jon said.

They came to the bottom of the hill. "Here we go," Olias said.

They ascended the rocky rise and soon found themselves above the tree tops. They stopped to imbibe the view.

"Wow! The bay looks different. What a great view," Olias said, searching for his binoculars.

"Olias, this seems like just a regular Maine island. No special magical powers, or whatever."

"But don't you feel like you're being watched?"

"Not anymore, no."

They reached the top—a prime vantage point to see the island in full.

Black Island was roughly the shape of a crescent moon, stretching from north to south. There were two peaks. Olias and Jon were standing on the northern, lower one. The taller was on the other side of "the moon," covered by thick forest. The two peaks were separated by a large, low-lying field.

Jon pointed. "Look at that forest on the other peak! Gimme the binoculars."

Olias handed them over.

"Holy shit, look at that tree at the foot of the forest!" Jon said while handing them back.

Olias saw it. "That's not a Maine tree! That looks like some kind of... African tree."

"Yeah, like a baobab."

"There's your magic! Let's go!"

Jon smiled.

As they descended toward the low-lying field, the sky seemed to brighten.

They reached the field to see that its plants were much bigger than they looked from afar. The weeds and reeds were over fifteen feet high. They could no longer see either island peak.

"This is pretty weird, not a normal island, huh Jon?"

"Agreed. Are we even going in the right direction?"

"Just watch your shadow from the sun, and keep it right in that spot while walking. I have a compass, but we don't need it yet."

A deep, growling "*SNORT!*" sounded in the thick scrub to their right.

"What was *that?!*" Jon jumped.

24

"I don't know, but it sounds strong—maybe a large badger? Let's just keep going. Shhh."

They heard scuffling from all angles and felt animal eyes watching—a growing number. Jon shook off a shiver. "What *are* these animals? That snort sounded weird!"

"I don't know." Olias stopped and pulled off his backpack.

"Dude, what are you doing?!! We gotta keep moving!"

Olias took two sharp knives out of his pack and handed one to Jon. "I have to remember to buy a gun. This is all we have. Something charges, slash it in the face. Preferably the eyes."

"...Sure."

"We're in this together. If we get surrounded, we touch backs and fight."

Olias threw his backpack on and they continued. The scuffling noises grew.

A thick sweat moistened Jon's hair. "These things are surrounding us!"

"I know, keep moving. We should be able to see the trees of the high forest soon."

"I could *really* go for a drink!"

Olias let this go. After a few minutes, they saw the tops of spruce trees high in the sky.

"Finally!" Jon whispered.

"Okay, look for the baobab," Olias said.

"There it is!"

They reached the hill and climbed. It became steep and rocky, forcing them to climb with their arms as well. The field—with its snorting and scuffling animals—fell away as they made quick work of the gradient.

"I'm glad you're not drinking, Jon," Olias huffed.

Jon let this go. Soon, they reached the plateau of the ancient woodland.

Before them stood the oddest tree they'd ever seen. It towered over the surrounding pines with an impenetrably thick trunk that looked like it was made of woolly-mammoth hide. It had only a few branches—each more fat than long—and on the ends of these stubby "arms" protruded plumes of palm leaves. It stood stalwart at the foot of the forest like a sentinel, marking the way into dark, hidden depths. The forest itself was very thick; it looked as though almost no sunlight penetrated inside.

"Look!" Olias said.

They turned to see an even more beautiful view of the bay—the deep greens and blues of the Maine island archipelago.

"Let's go into the forest here," Olias said.

They went in, leaving the sunlight behind. It was shady and cool, almost damp.

"I like the cooler temp in here," Jon said, wiping sweat from his forehead.

"Do you see anything else weird?"

"I don't."

"Let's continue in this direction, farther in. It's really dark in there, maybe there's something weird."

The forest got thicker and darker as they went. The trees became closer together and tougher to navigate. Soon, the sunlight barely permeated the canopy—it only trickled down in thin tendrils. Where those wisps of sun hit the forest floor, little pockets of mist rose.

"Trippy..."

They came across something they would never forget, and stopped dead in their tracks.

Sitting before them on the forest floor was an immense purple mushroom. A thin thread of bright sunlight snaked down through the blackness, hitting the mushroom like a lone stage light in a darkened theatre. The beam was cutting into the mushroom—slicing it—opening up a painful-looking wound. There was a soft hissssssssss as smoky mist rose from the infected area.

"That's... gross."

They stared at the giant mushroom as the light slowly moved off it, leaving a hideous, smoking scar. The hissing stopped. The mushroom's open wound bled viscous purple goo.

"Gross!"

"Let's go," Olias said.

They continued into the growing darkness.

"Oh, shit! I gotta get a picture of that mushroom!" Jon said.

They went back, but the scar on the mushroom was completely gone. "What the-?"

"Put your flash on, it's dark."

Jon took a picture of it without its wound, and they continued. As they went, the trees thickened. They had to start crawling on the forest floor just to move forward, at times having to contort their bodies around branches and trunks.

"Should we go back?" wondered Jon.

"This is too weird. It's so dark in here. I've never seen a thick island forest be *this* dark. Let's go a little farther."

"In that direction?" Jon pointed.

When they peered as far ahead as possible, they saw only black. Olias and Jon had *kind* of seen this before, on many islands. Often on an island with a thick spruce forest—even on a bright sunny day—there were pockets of black woods devoid of sunlight, but what they saw ahead trumped anything they'd ever seen.

"Oh. My. God," stammered Olias, "Look how *black* that is!"

They crawled on all fours, then stopped, stunned.

"Olias, that's a *wall* of BLACK..."

"I've never seen black so... *black.*"

They inched cautiously up to the wall. There was nothing visible beyond it.

"This is not possible," Olias said.

4

Dan stood with a shovel at the end of a float as the surf rocked him up and down. He finished shoveling bait into a little shed and his work for the day on the docks was complete. Reeking of fish and low-tide scum, he got in his car and opened all the windows. He drove home, showered and put on fresh clothes.

He got back in his car—which had mostly aired out—and drove to Edna Black's seacoast cottage. It was easy to find, right off the main road in the Village. He drove down the short dirt driveway and parked in front of a dilapidated old shed.

"That's like a Bob Ross shed," he mused.

Parked in front of the house was an antique car from the fifties or sixties. "Looks like a Batmobile," he chuckled, then walked up to the door and knocked.

Silence, save for the patter of light surf on the beach from the other side of the house.

"Hello?"

Nothing. A giant black-back gull—the king of the gulls—arced overhead, let out a guttural "gack" and banked over the house before flying out to sea. Dan knocked again. "Hello?!"

He walked around the house and saw an ancient well. He

peered down it, and saw no bottom. "Wow, that's deep." He searched and found a rock, held it over the center of the well—making sure it wouldn't hit the sides—and let go. The rock dropped into the black and disappeared without a sound. "Must have hit soft ground," he told himself.

He saw a little path leading to the beach. "Hello?!" He walked to the ocean. Village boats dotted the harbor. A seal kept popping its head out of the water not far offshore, curious. A few arctic terns flew by only inches over the small breaking surf, quarrelling.

He sat on the beach for a few minutes, then went back to look at Edna Black's yard. The grass was badly overgrown—weeds invaded from all fronts. "She sure *does* need some yard work."

He knocked on the door again, this time with more authority. "Hellllooooo?!!" Nothing.

He walked back to the beach and sat, figuring she must be on a walk. The lapping of the small waves lulled him into a slight trance. His eyelids got heavy and closed. When he opened them, she was standing next to him.

"Hello, Dan."

"What?!"

"Looks like you were getting a little shuteye?"

"Um, yeah, pretty nice beach you have here, Mrs. Black."

"Thank you, son. Sorry to make you wait, I was visiting my neighbor. Would you like to get started? The old mower and tools are in the shed. I'll be inside making some phone calls if you need me. Would you like some lemonade?"

"Not right now, maybe a little later."

"That's fine, dear, I'm so *glad* you are here, Dan!" She lightly patted his back. He stood and followed her up the path.

"No need to knock, son, just come in when you want something cold to drink."

He walked around the old car to the shed. The decrepit door was barely resting on one hinge—the whole structure looked on the verge of collapse.

He carefully creaked the door open. Inside, it was musty and dank with aromas of kerosene, turpentine and dirt. There were old tools hanging on the walls and cobwebs everywhere. "It's like the set of *The Munsters* in here," he joked.

He saw the mower. It was one of those old, no-gasoline push mowers. "I can't mow a lawn with this thing!"

He exhumed the ancient relic from the shed and propped it up in the daylight to get a better look. Mini ropes of thick spider webs kept it connected to the inside. "Jeeeeeesh..." He pulled it farther out, snapping the webs.

The blades were sharp enough to *maybe* get the job done after passing over the same patch of grass two or three times. He wished he had a real mower, but figured she was paying him and he could use the extra cash.

He started "mowing." The situation was indeed as he'd predicted—it took three passes over every patch to get the job done. Luckily, the yard wasn't very big. He set about mowing the entire lawn. The weeds would come later.

After finishing a small section, he neared the old well, which he'd have to mow around. As he rattled the old machine past it, he heard a voice.

A voice from the well.

He froze. It had sounded like "Hello." His skin prickled. He stood still and listened.

Nothing, just the sound of birds, insects and sea. He cautiously looked down into the well. Black.

"I really must be tired," he said out loud, needing to hear his voice for some reason, and continued mowing.

5

Olias and Jon stared at the wall of black. It was completely quiet there—the sounds of the ocean, wind and birds a memory.

Olias looked for a branch—or even a twig—on the forest floor, but couldn't find one. "How can there be no sticks on the ground? That's impossible."

"Let's just take one of these living ones in our way," Jon said while breaking off the nearest small branch and handing it over. "Here's your stick."

"Thanks. Let's get right up to the wall, okay?"

"Okay."

They crawled to within a couple feet. Olias held up the branch and slowly inched it closer and closer.

"Touch the stick to it!" Jon said.

Olias *touched* the wall of black with the branch—but there was nothing to touch. He put half the branch right through it.

"Wow!" he exclaimed, pulling the branch back out.

"Do you think we could crawl through that wall and see if there's something on the other side?!"

"I don't know. I think so. The stick was unaffected…"

"Try throwing the stick into it, and let's listen for it hitting something. Throw it hard!"

"Okay." Olias crept back and got ready to fling the branch into the wall as if he was throwing a Frisbee from his knees. "Here goes." He flung it with all his might. They listened. They heard it hit the ground about sixty feet away.

"What?! There aren't thick trees on the other side!" Jon said.

"I'm going to try putting my hand into it."

"Be careful."

Olias slowly brought his hand up to the wall, extending his pointer finger. He jabbed it in and out.

"Well?"

"Nothing. It felt like there was nothing there at all!"

Jon put his hand into the black and quickly pulled it out. "Wow!"

"Next step, we put our heads through."

"I don't know, Olias, that's… I don't know."

"Look, I'll do it. If anything happens to me, pull me out of there, okay?"

"Alright. And if you don't have a head when I pull you out?"

"Then I won't curse you out," he retorted, feeling newfound sweat running in rivulets down his back. This was all so crazy. He felt faint but recovered.

"You sure you wanna do this, Olias?"

"Yes." He brought his face right up to the wall. It was some kind of void—an optical illusion that didn't make sense. Having his face almost against it was inexplicable. He looked to the left and right, and could see that it was a sharp boundry—a *wall*. It stretched into the dark forest with no visible ending. Looking up, he saw that it also stretched into the dark canopy with no discernible border. "Okay, here goes!" He held his breath and put his face into the wall of black.

"Olias, can you hear me?"

"Yes."

"What do you see?"

"Nothing, just more blackness." He breathed in and out.

"It's like a really dark room, and there's no smell." He took his face out. "Give me one of the flashlights."

Jon fumbled through his pack and found one. Olias took it and faced the abyss. "Grab hold of my belt, and pull me back at any sign of trouble."

"You got it."

Olias clicked on the flashlight and stuck his head and his right arm into the black. He shone the light all around. "Weird!"

"What?"

"The light starts out normal for a couple feet, but then the beam bends to the ground and dies!"

"Wow, that's... what is that?!"

"No clue."

"Does some of the light get to the ground? What's the ground look like?"

Olias got onto his knees and beamed the flashlight at the ground. "Wow. It's rocky sand, like a desert! It's nothing like the forest." He crawled back out. "You want to check it out? I'll hold one of your arms."

"Alright." Jon took the flashlight as Olias held onto his arm. He went in. "Holy crap! What the hell *is* this place?!" He returned. "So what do we do now?!"

"Good question, my friend. Hold on." Olias put his head and both arms through the wall, shined the light on the ground, picked up a rock and came out holding it. "Look!"

They stared at the rock, which was flat and had a sharp end. "Looks like a normal rock, but wow," Jon said.

They sat in silence, staring at it. Only the sound of their breathing existed in that moment. Time froze. The world froze. Existence, in its knowable, familiar structure, was forever turned upside down for Olias and Jon.

Olias put the rock in his pocket. "The rabbit hole, ay?"

"Yup."

"We need a long-ass rope."

6

Kara darted into the See Food bathroom and looked in the mirror. Three doubles in a row had left her with little bags under her pretty eyes. She undid the ponytail on her thick, golden mane and shook her hair out. "You need sleep, deary," she scolded herself.

She tied her hair back and dialed Olias, and again got voicemail. "Olias, please call me! I'm starting to worry." She figured he must have gotten out of work early and was out on the boat with Jon. She dialed Jon. Voicemail. She hung up.

There was a knock at the door. "Kara? Are you in there?" It was Stacy, another waitress.

Kara wasn't close friends with Stacy—and certainly wasn't in the mood to listen to her problems—but knew Stacy had no one else to talk to. "Come in," she said while applying a little makeup under her eyes.

Stacy opened the door quickly and darted in. "I really need to talk, Kara!"

"Well, what about Todd? That's what good boyfriends are for. Have you talked to him?"

"Um, it's kind of about him... I mean, you and I are pretty close, right?"

"Well—"

"I mean, I'm sorry, but, you are my best girl friend on the island. I know Tawny is your best friend, and you have others, but... I guess I'm not as good at making girl friends. I always hang out with the boys, you know?"

"I know. Some girls are like that."

"If you don't mind, can I tell you a secret?"

"Sure."

"I kind of have a thing for... Bob."

"Bob Lianelli?! Stacy, he's like twenty years older than you!"

"I know, I can't believe it myself! But he's just got something, you know?"

"No, I really don't."

"He's strong, you know?"

"Stacy, Todd is young and cute."

"Yes, but he's like a boy compared to Bob. Bob owns real estate all over the country. He's a businessman, a mover and a shaker. A *real* man."

"My advice is to stop these thoughts from growing or break up with Todd."

"But I can't! I don't want to hurt his feelings."

"Also, Bob is married!"

"Yes, but they are getting a divorce."

"Look, Stacy, we have orders up."

"Can we hang out tonight, Kara? I really need to talk."

"I'm sorry, Stacy, but I have plans."

"How about tomorrow?"

"...I'll let you know."

A forced happiness flooded Stacy's eyes. "Great!" she said, bounding out the door.

Kara took out her cell and dialed her best friend since age three, Tawny.

"Kay-Kay!"

"Hi Tawns. Stacy is really coming on strong and trying to force a friendship, and I just don't trust her."

"Neither do I. Stay strong, Kay-Kay."

Kara smiled—the first real smile she'd had all day. "Thanks, I will. Okay, got to go, just wanted to hear your voice."

"Hang in there, deary."

"Ha ha, I will, deary, see ya." Kara hung up, looked back in the mirror and applied a little more makeup under her eyes. "Get it together, deary." She walked out into the restaurant.

"Order up, Kara!" yelled Scott the cook.

She felt only half alive. The constant chatter and clinking of silverware on plates was starting to turn her mind foggy, and she fought a fainting feeling. "Only two more hours, two more hours..."

Jimmy and Lenny sauntered in like they owned the place and sat at the bar. Lenny spoke in hushed tones. "So, when are we gonna go back?"

Jimmy answered out of the side of his mouth. "Whenever he's at work, and we *know* he's at work, we'll go back." He saw Kara and straightened up on the bar stool, flexing his arms. "Hey, a little service here?!"

Kara put napkins and silverware in front of them. "What'll you have?"

"Um, I don't know. What're you gonna have, Lenny? Gettin' somethin' to eat, or what?"

"I don't know."

She was annoyed, but tried with all her might not to show it. "Well, let me know when you figure it out."

She started walking away to refill someone's soda when Lenny barked, "Whoa whoa! Hey! A little service here!"

She stopped in her tracks, still looking in the other direction, and slowly turned to face them. This made them chuckle.

"Look, darlin', how 'bout some waters to start, huh? Run

along now."

They smirked at each other.

"Sure," she said, biting down on her lip so hard she almost tasted blood.

"And hurry up," said Jimmy. "You don't want us going to the owner and complaining, now do you, you little wench?"

"Funny stuff, guys."

She got their waters. They pushed the glasses off to the side.

Jimmy was just getting started. "So, where's that boyfriend 'a yours, don't he ever come in here no more?"

She wanted to say that he was about to show up with all his friends, but she hated lying. "He comes in."

"Will he bring his boyfriend with him?"

"Don't know." She was too tired for comebacks. She just wanted to relax on her sofa and watch TV. Close her eyes whenever she wanted. Fall into a deep, dark, black sleep...

"I seen them two skippin' around town together. Ain't you worried? You might lose him."

"Worried, yup."

"I hear they're doin' it every night. They're gonna get a place together and leave it all behind."

"Uh huh. So, are you guys eating today?"

"Woah, woah, don't rush us or we'll tell the owner, little lady."

"Cool." She walked into the beverage area where Stacy stood at the soda fountain pouring a ginger ale for one of her tables. "Stacy, these two assholes at the bar are really pushing me, could you take them?"

"Sure!" she replied, "I'll do it right away!"

As Kara retreated farther into the kitchen, she could make out Lenny at the bar loudly saying to Stacy, "Ohhh heyyy, where's—" She walked out the back door into the fresh ocean air and spied someone's pack of cigarettes and lighter sitting on an empty beer keg. "Must be Stacy's," she thought.

She uncharacteristically took a cigarette out of the pack and lit it, exhaling her frustration. "I have tomorrow off, tomorrow off..." She sat on the empty beer keg and stared off into nothing, hoping Olias and Jon were safe.

7

Bob Lianelli had been eyeing Stacy since he hired her. Eyeing her ass, mostly. And he noticed that whenever he talked about his real estate deals and restaurant ownership, she perked right up as if it was an aphrodisiac. "Chicks dig power," he thought. Sure, she was dating Todd, one of his managers, but he knew how to woo her away from him: money. "Throw money at a bitch and she'll come around. Show her who the big man is." And this big man had a secret plan.

Sure, he was married. But he left "that bitch" with the kids in California all summer to run this seasonal restaurant in Maine. He needed a "summer-only bitch."

He was in his office near the kitchen doing some paperwork when Stacy and Todd walked by his open door. "Look at that ass, that's gon' be miiiine," he smarmed.

He strode out of his office right behind them. "Todd! C'mon over here, buddy."

Stacy kissed Todd on the cheek and went back to her tables. Todd walked over. "What's up, boss?"

"I need you to run an errand for me."

"Oh, I'm on duty on the floor right now, Bob. Can you take over for me while I'm gone?"

"Ohhhh, riiiight... hmmm... Well, I guess it's finally time for my big announcement! Go get Stacy in here, will ya?"

"Sure." Todd left and brought Stacy with him to the office.

"What's up, Mr. Man?" she flirted.

"Stacy, I think it's time that you got promoted. You've done a great job for me, and I think you're manager material!"

Todd and Stacy were wide-eyed. "Wow! Thanks Bob!" she said, and gave Bob the big hug he'd been itching for.

Todd was happy for her. "Congrats, Stacy!"

Bob turned to Todd and spoke in a commanding tone. "Todd, go take over Stacy's tables. She has to come in my office and fill out some forms." Bob knew he didn't have to remind Todd to give the tips to Stacy, knowing Todd was the kind of man who would.

"Sure, boss." Todd went out onto the floor and took over the four tables—they all had their food already, so it was a low-maintenance task.

Five minutes later, Bob and Stacy came out, Stacy giddily hanging on his arm.

Todd's smile was forced. "So, how's the new manager

feeling?"

"On top of the worrrrrld!"

Bob walked in between them. "Todd, we're going to go run those errands I need done, so hold down the fort, big guy, okay?"

"...You got it, boss."

"And maybe we'll get a nice gift to celebrate the promotion of our new manager!"

Stacy hugged Bob.

Todd walked to Stacy and forced a hug. She giggled flirtatiously while batting her eyes at Bob.

Bob looked at Todd and gave a thumbs up. "Hold down the fort, big guy!"

As they bounded out the door, Todd's smile immediately caved into something resembling shock.

"Check, please!"

While he was printing out a check, Kara walked up behind him. "Where'd Stacy and Bob go?"

"Oh, they're just out doing some errands for the restaurant." He paused, then added, "And he just made her a manager."

"What?!"

"Yup, it's a great day!"

Todd's fake smile was back. Kara recognized it for what it was, and said, "Well, I hope she learns a lot from you. You're a great manager."

Todd's smile flickered as Kara touched his arm in a consoling gesture. "Thanks, Kara, you're always so nice."

Kara had a bearable end to her work day, especially because she had the night and the following day—a Saturday—off.

She drove home in late afternoon and relaxed in front of the television, quickly falling into a blissful sleep. Two hours later, Olias called.

"Hello, luv!"

"Hi luv! I'm in the boat with Jon. We're coming home from visiting Black Island, and man, do we have a story for you!"

"What? Black Is—" She lost consciousness, dropping her cell on the hardwood floor and falling on top of it.

"Kara? Kara?!!"

Ziggy rocketed through Penobscot Bay toward Mount Haven Island.

"We didn't get cut off, she just stopped talking!" cried Olias in a panic.

"Olias, you mentioned Black Island to her!"

"Oh, shit!"

It seemed like forever until they saw Mount Haven. They nervously stood up in the boat as if at attention. "God, please let her be alright!"

Ziggy blasted into Olias's cove. Olias cut the engine and the boat whooshed up to the mooring. Jon grabbed the mooring line and ran it out to the bow. They threw the tender in the water and jumped in. Olias hurriedly rowed them ashore. They carried the tender above the high-tide line and ran to Jon's car, which was blocking Olias's. They sped off toward Kara's apartment in the Village.

"I hope she didn't hit her head when she fell..."

They raced right by the See Food, where Bob and Stacy had just parked out front and were getting out of the car. In one hand, Stacy was holding a bag of presents Bob had bought her, and her other arm was locked with his.

Bob didn't get a look at who sped by. "Who the hell are those assholes?!"

"Oh, that's Kara's boyfriend and his buddy."

"Assholes."

Olias and Jon reached Kara's and ran inside. "Kara?!"

She was sprawled on the floor.

"Kara!" They lifted her carefully onto the sofa. Jon put her phone on the table. Olias gently took her hair and folded it behind her head on the sofa pillow.

"What now?" asked Jon.

"Kara? Kara?! Hmmm... Kara—*BLACK ISLAND!*"

She woke. "...Huh? Black?" Her eyes were in an inner-spiral daze. "Olias!" They hugged. "What happened?"

"Well, that's a long story, luv."

Kara smiled at him, glad he was finally with her. "I missed you, luv."

"Me too, luv."

They let her lie in silence.

"Would you like anything from the fridge, Kara?" offered

Jon.

She cocked her head slightly as her lips formed a little smile. "Yes... a glass of water, and... a glass of wine."

"You got it." He got her the water first.

She quickly drank half a glassful. "Olias, what just happened to me? How long was I out?"

"You were out for almost an hour. Jon and I booked it back to get here. You're not going to believe this, but there's an island in the bay that has some type of.... mystical powers."

She could tell he wasn't joking—his eyes had an intense look of conviction she'd seen only a few times in their three-year relationship. "Powers?"

"Yes. I was the first one to faint, just like you did here. I was thinking about Black Island, and..."

Her eyes fluttered, but she remained lucid.

"...and I fell asleep on Pond Island for a whole night. I woke at sunrise. Then, while taking Ziggy home at top speed, I thought of Black Island and fainted *again.* I woke up in Ziggy, drifting right off my mooring, which is impossible, because I was heading around some other islands and going in the wrong direction when I dropped."

"You mean, you are saying that Black Island"—eye flutter—"makes us faint?"

"Yes. The same thing happened to Jon on my porch while we were talking about Black. But that's not all. Jon and I went into work this morning, and Old Man Cranchet got all weird and gave us the day off, saying we should go to Black Island! It was like someone else was speaking through him. After we'd already both fainted more than once due to Black, it didn't seem so crazy, so, that's what we did. We went to Black Island today."

"Isn't it impossible to land on that one? There's no beach."

"Right. We tied Ziggy to a tree and let him drift off the island."

"So, what happened there?!"

"After walking to some high ground, we saw a tree at the foot of a high-ground forest—a tree that looked *really weird.* It looked like an African baobab, kind of, in the binoculars. We decided to check it out. We climbed back down to almost sea level, and walked through a weird field with weeds over fifteen feet tall, and there were grunting animals following us that we couldn't see! We climbed up the taller hill that leads to the high-ground forest. We finally got to the weird tree. It has palm leaves!"

"What?! A tree in Maine has palm leaves?!"

"Yup. Then we walked into the dark forest."

Jon chugged a glass of pinot grigio while they weren't looking, then poured Kara a glass and handed it to her. "Here, Kara."

"Thanks, Jon."

"Olias, you want one?"

"No, thanks. So, we walked into the forest. At first, it was just a regular Maine spruce woods, but the farther in we went, the thicker and darker it got."

"Tell her about the mushroom!"

"Yes, we came across this crazy-huge purple mushroom! There was this dot of sunlight hitting it—slowly moving across it— and where it was hitting, there was a hissing sound, and smoke! It was being ripped into, like a cutting wound—it was gross! Then we walked away, but returned in less than a minute, and it was completely healed."

"Hold on! I have it here!" Jon whipped out his phone and found the shot.

She stared at the picture. "Wow..."

"Then, we walked farther into the darkening forest. We had to get on our hands and knees to move forward, because it's so thick in there. And... we actually came to... a *WALL OF BLACK!*"

"What do you mean, a wall of black?"

"Well, it's not solid... You can't even feel it, but it's a wall... It's a visual wall. And, you can pass through it like it's air! When we stuck our faces in to see what's on the other side, we only saw more blackness. Even the flashlight couldn't penetrate it. It bends the light to the ground! And the ground in there is like a rocky, sandy desert, with no trees. Right on the other side!"

Kara sat in silence, trying to process all this. She looked down at the floor as Olias and Jon let her have as much time as she needed. She looked up. "So what did you do?"

"Well, it was getting late and we didn't want to just walk into it and get lost forever or faint or die, so we decided to leave the island and regroup with a better plan. My phone finally worked when we were in Ziggy on our way back, and that's when I called you."

Her eyes changed to playful warmth. "Okay, c'mon guys, joke's over..."

Olias and Jon stared into her eyes. She stared back, then

sat bolt upright. "So, when are we leaving for Black Island tomorrow?!"

CHAPTER 3:   And Then There Were Three

1

Dan finished mowing the lawn and pushed the ancient mower back into its web-laden crypt. He walked cautiously toward the well and leaned over the lip, peering into the black. "Just a well, what the hell's wrong with me?"

He walked to Edna's door and knocked, remembered she said there was never a need to, and walked inside. "Hello?"

Nothing. He walked through the kitchen into the living room, which overlooked the bay and some of the Village. "Hello?"

He started walking around the room aimlessly, looking at pictures on the walls. All were pretty standard—pedestrian paintings of ships at sea and quaint harbor scenes—but there was one odd one. It was a crude drawing of an island, an island shaped like a crescent moon. On one section of the island was drawn a large "X" that reminded him of a treasure map. For some reason, he couldn't stop staring at it. His eyes glazed over.

"I like that one too."

He whirled to see Edna standing behind him. "Oh! Mrs. Black! Um, hi..."

"Such a good job on the lawn, Dan! You make me soooo happy!" she said, touching his shoulder. Her hand was so warm.

He blushed, surprised at how much this woman's praises meant. "It feels good to help."

"I see you are admiring my old family drawing."

"Yes, it reminds me of a treasure map, like when I was a kid."

"Ha ha haaa! Yes, this is *indeed* a treasure map, Dan. That is an island not far from here. And there is *indeed* treasure there! But I hear there are rich, evil people planning to go to the island and find the treasure."

"What?! What type of treasure is it?"

"Jewels! The type of which are so rare, that anyone who has possession of them will have extreme power. And, it is rich and already-powerful people who are planning on taking it! The 'haves' Dan, are once again going to take all the power from the 'have-nots.' What do you think about that? That doesn't sound very fair, does it?"

"Of course not. Rich snobs. The people with money don't deserve it, ever."

"That's true. That is why the 'have-nots' must rise up! The meek shall inherit the Earth, Dan."

"Yes, they will!"

"But not the meek of spirit... Dan, what if I told you that I know exactly where this treasure is?"

"What?! Really?!"

"Yes. The rich want to take control of it, but the valiant working class of people like us want to give it to all the people. What if I told you I was one of those people working to get the treasure?"

"Really?!"

"Yes, son. And if you're ever interested in joining our cause, you are certainly invited."

"Of course I'll help!"

"Alright then. Dan? *BLACK ISLAND.*"

He crumpled to the floor.

2

The purple mushroom sat alone on the dark forest floor. It was currently wound-free. It had gotten used to enduring the biting wounds from the sunbeams epochs ago. Its name was Gumtooo. It was very surprised to see people again. It hadn't seen people since the Third Destruction, back when the Main Peak fell to the ocean and the Great Crystal was put to sleep. It had even been alive long before that, back when there was only one big continent on Earth and the Main Peak towered over high mountainous desert—the Great Crystal's magnificence overseeing the land, supplying power to the people.

Gumtooo couldn't remember its earliest times. All it knew was that at one time it was something else. It came into this Earth reality and melded with a plant, and now it was stuck as a plant-like life form that could not die—timeless life giving infinite life to a type of life that grows from death... It once *loved* the feeling of being a plant. The inner peace was soothing to its spirit. But that was so long ago. It was taxing to even try retrieving those memories.

Things were different now. Sunbeams cut into it, now that it was a dark and wet being. It was once a dry and contented being with a reason to exist—as a guard, a highly telepathic sentinel for the security of the Great Crystal. But now, it was lucky that the plant part of it was good at weathering loneliness and time, able to shut down its thoughts, not even interrupted by the wounds inflicted by the Sun. Ironic... The Sun, which once gave it and the Great Crystal life, now hurt it.

But these new people... Who were they? They must have meaning. They must have been invited, because Gumtooo's alerts to the Chamber were readily accepted and no ancient security measures had been activated. That meant that these people would be back. Maybe it was time for the next Age. Maybe it was time for the Great Crystal to once again thrum the hum of the ancient Rescue Souls, who stood in this world with one foot remaining in the Higher Dimension, staying over a thousand years at a time before returning Home.

Gumtooo never got to go Home. Gumtooo was still here on Earth, wet and lonely. But maybe not for much longer...

3

Kara decisively plopped her glass on the coffee table. "I'd rather be drinking with a view."

Olias looked at Jon, who was quickly sucking down a full glass. "Jon, you have to drive, tone it down, huh? At least until we get to my place."

"Yeah, of course," he said as he walked to the sink and carefully poured half the glass of wine back into the bottle.

They gathered their things, got into Jon's car and drove to Olias's cottage.

Kara went through the fridge and saw there wasn't enough for dinner. "Olias? Maybe you could go down to the See Food and pick up some food?"

"...Oh," he hesitated. "Sure." He knew there was no way she was going back there until she absolutely *had* to. "You got it, luv. Call in the order. I'll get going."

"Thank you, luv," she said, wrapping her arms around him in a *very* warm embrace that prompted Jon to look away. Jon wasn't jealous of Kara and Olias, but the love they shared made him feel lonely. Ironically, he had *them* to keep his loneliness at bay. He couldn't imagine a life without them.

Olias left for the restaurant as Kara and Jon ordered take-out from Stacy.

Olias walked in and up to the bar, where Stacy was changing TV channels, trying to find something to her liking.

"Hi, Olias!" she greeted him happily. "Did you hear the news?"

"The news?"

"I've been promoted to manager!"

"Oh, nice!"

"Yup. Bob said I have 'what it takes.' Now Todd and I are *both* managers!"

"Very cool, but won't you miss seeing him at work?"

"What do you mean?"

"There's only one manager on duty at a time, so you'll now be working opposite hours."

"Oh, right..."

"And now you can't really hang out away from work either, because one of you always has to be on duty."

"Oh, right..." she said, her eyes glazing over.

"I take it Kara called in our order?"

"...Yes, it'll be up very soon." She walked off in a directionless daze, still holding the TV clicker, having accidentally left the TV on the channel-choices menu.

Olias sat at the bar as Jimmy and Lenny sauntered in and sat near him. Jimmy stared at Olias and puffed out his chest, his face twitching wildly. "Hey there, big guy."

"Hey."

"Sittin' at the bar without a drink, huh?"

"Yup, same as you."

Lenny, under his breath to Jimmy, whispered, "Lookit his arms. Looks like he got some guns under that shirt there."

Olias tried to ignore them.

Lenny giggled. "Hey Olias, you know Jimmy here boxes an' spars wit' a major professional wrestler in Ellsworth. Bet you couldn't do that."

"Yup, cool, not my thing, whatever."

Lenny whispered under his breath to Jimmy, "We be seein' what's on his computer soon."

Olias pretended to read the channel choices.

Stacy finally came out of the kitchen with the bag of food. "Tell Kara this is on the house—my first management decision!"

"Nice! Thanks, Stacy!" Olias took the bag and bolted for the door as Jimmy started saying something to him. Olias got out quickly and the words stuck in Jimmy's throat.

Lenny looked at Jimmy. "Transplant fag." Jimmy nodded.

Olias couldn't get to his car fast enough, and raced home while breathing in the delicious aroma. He pulled into his driveway and went inside to find Kara and Jon in the kitchen waiting. "Free food here! Come-'n-get-it!"

Kara took the bag and pulled out a fried scallop basket, three lobster rolls, a crab roll, shrimp scampi, crispy french fries, even-crispier onion rings and three slices of homemade blueberry pie. "Thank you, *Stacy!*"

Jon poured three glasses of pinot grigio as Kara got some plates and silverware, and they walked to the porch. Olias floated some classical music from the living room and they happily munched in the salt air. They stayed on the porch well into night, listening to a great Red Sox win on the radio, highlighted by a Big Papi walk-off bomb. They cheered, drank and laughed.

By eleven o'clock, Jon was extremely drunk. Kara leaned into Olias and whispered, "Luckily, the Sox won and he's happy tonight."

Jon leaned over in his chair. "Heyyyyy, Oliashh, I got suh ropes! To tie 'agether!"

"Cool, we'll need the longest rope chain we can make, just in case the inside of this black dimension is really... vast."

"What's the rope for?" asked Kara.

"We'll tie it to the person who passes through the wall of black, so they'll at least know which way they came, and so we can pull them out if there's any trouble."

"But, why even go in there? Maybe there's a way we can find answers to Black Island without going in?"

"Maybe. But so far, all we've seen is the weird tree and this wall, so we should plan for that."

"That makes sense, I guess. I just don't want any of us to get hurt!"

"I 'gree with th' hot chick!" Jon slurred while staring at her body.

"Oh, Jon," she said, smiling. "Are you going to be able to wake up tomorrow at all?"

"Yesh, I will waish up, hottie patooty!"

"I hope so... Olias, should we set the alarm?"

"Hmmm, I say no. Let's get as much sleep as we can, and plan to leave by eight o'clock. Sound good?"

"That works for me," she said.

"I..." Jon started, then fell asleep and began snoring.

"Olias, can you get him to the sofa?"

"Yup. I'm getting used to this. "Jon? Jon?"

"Hmmphhhh. Don't touch me."

"Time for bed, my friend."

Kara cleaned up as Olias helped Jon to the sofa.

4

"Black Island."

Dan's eyes fluttered. He was on Edna Black's couch. "Wha?"

"Dan, I think the excitement of going on the treasure hunt made you light-headed. I know I get light-headed sometimes, thinking about the possibilities!"

"Oh, yes, it seems, exciting."

"You must be parched, can I get you something to drink, son?"

"Um, sure, some water would be great."

"I'll be *right* back, son."

He moved from a lying to a sitting position on the couch and looked across the room at the drawing of the crescent island. It didn't look crudely drawn anymore, and above it, it now said "Black Island."

"I don't remember it saying the name of the island on the drawing," he thought as a piercing itch began below his navel.

Edna returned with a glass of water. "Here, this will make you feel better. I have great well water here at the house."

He took the glass from her outstretched hand and froze. "The well?!"

"Yes, I had a new well installed last year under the house. The water is absolutely delightful! Drink up!"

Dan hesitated, then took a sip. It was nice and clean. "Mmmm, yes, this is good water."

"Oh do drink up, water is so healthy."

He drank his water in silence as she stared at him. It was an odd moment. He burped. "Excuse me."

"I won't tell."

"So, that treasure island is called... Black Island, I see."

"Yes, Dan, Black Island. The legends say that the treasure is hidden somewhere in the forest where the 'X' is on the map."

"Can we get to Black Island?"

"Yes, my son."

"When can we go?!"

"Very soon, my Dan." She leapt upon him in an overly loving embrace. Something about her touch stung. He started to scream, but his body relaxed and he stood still. His eyes rolled up in their sockets with a little gurgle.

"Dan, you are now *mine*. Do you agree, Dan?"

"I am… yours."

"You hesitated. Please don't hurt me like that again."

"Yes'm."

"You may have your eyes back now."

His eyes rolled wetly out. He teetered on his feet for a moment, and sat on the couch facing the Black Island map.

"Now Dan, would you like some more water?"

"Yes, please!"

As she walked into the kitchen, he felt a big itch below his navel. He scratched it, digging into his flesh so hard it produced blood.

She returned with more water. "Oh do drink up, my Dan!"

"Thanks!"

He drank deeply. "What kind of treasure is it, Mrs. Black?"

"Well, son, it's the kind of treasure us 'have-nots' don't have, and all the controlling 'haves' already own. It's not fair that they have all the money and all the jewels and all the power, is it?"

"Of course not. I hate those kinds of people."

"Yes, son. And this is our chance to take the power and the jewels from those horrible people. Take it no matter what. In any way we can. They don't deserve it. We do."

"We do. We are better than them."

"Yes, Dan. Some of my old friends have their ears to the wind, and the word is that some people on this island—some 'haves'—are going to try and get the remaining Black Island treasure first, before us, and they are those kind of people we hate who are already rich!"

"Really?!! Well let's go out to the island first and get the treasure before they do!"

"I like the way you think, my son."

"Do you know where we can get a boat? I'm sure people like them already have a boat."

"Yes, I believe I can ask some favors from old friends

around town. We'll get a boat and go take the treasure. But first, we have to stop those 'haves' from using their means to hurt us. We have to take their power from them."

"Yes! Let's take what's ours!"

"I like how you think, my son."

5

Olias woke in the middle of the night and saw that the covers had fallen off Kara. He pulled them gently around her, got out of bed and quietly walked down the stairs, past a loudly snoring Jon, and out onto the porch.

It was a bright night. The moon was almost full, and it cast a long sparkly streak of light across the bay. A lone cricket chirped a song to the small waves tinkling the beach stones. A dark bird flew across the moon.

Olias couldn't sleep. So much craziness... What was behind that wall of black? What *was* that wall of black?! Who—or what—built it? How many more otherworldly things would they find? Why did it want Olias, Jon and Kara's help? They were just average people with good parents who came from middle-class upbringings. They weren't special... They weren't rich or powerful. Wouldn't powerful people be the ones to help this island or whatever it was?

Would they get hurt out there, or could the odd powers help them? The voice that spoke through Cranchet said to be careful out there. Careful of what? Why be so cryptic?! Careful of those scary-sounding animals in the brush? Something worse? Were there other people who knew about Black Island? Would they also visit the island? Would they be kindred souls or enemies?

He walked off the porch, down the front path to the beach and sat at the water's edge. It was a very high tide—a full-moon high tide—and there was almost no beach at all. He sat with his back touching some beach-pea plants. He broke off a couple pea pods, gently extracted their peas and popped them into his mouth, wondering if he was going to be able to get any more sleep.

Three minutes later, he rolled onto his side and slept soundly in the soft, billowing beach-pea plants.

6

At first light, Old Man Cranchet pulled into the boatyard and hobbled out of his truck carrying a thermos of coffee and a small bag of donuts in one hand, his cane in the other. He fumbled for his keys, jingled one into the lock and gimped inside the main boathouse.

He was anxious, because the boat they were working on needed to be finished yesterday. He figured he'd have to call in some workers and pay them overtime. He took out his little notebook of employee phone numbers and dropped it by the phone. After some coffee and donuts, he'd begin calling.

He wondered whom he'd call first. "Jon and Olias had the day off yesterday," he said out loud in an authoritative tone, "so they should be the first ones I ca—" His eyes rolled up in their sockets with a gurgle. A hunk of donut sat in his mouth unchewed. No saliva mixed with the donut—it stayed perfectly dry. He twitched. He stayed frozen for five minutes, and his eyes returned.

He stood, spit the dry donut hunk onto the floor, put the employee-phone-number notebook away, left the steaming coffee sitting on his desk and walked back to his truck. He didn't hobble. He walked normally. He threw his cane into the passenger seat, roared the truck to life and drove home.

He parked in front of his house, grabbed the cane, strode inside—straight to the bedroom, undressed and got into bed. He slept the soundest sleep of his life, living through myriad wonder-filled dreams.

He slept until 5:00 PM. When he woke, he pulled a phone/address book out of a drawer.

He wondered whom he'd call first. He started calling people.

He spent the night with his oldest friends on the island. They hadn't hung out in years.

They had one of the most meaningful nights of their lives. Many shared memories relived made them feel young and whole, emboldened and brash. Timeless. They had revelations about their lives. It's as if they never lost touch. The ol' buds were back. Connected. Forever.

7

Kara was sleeping soundly in Olias's bed when her eyes started rapidly moving under their lids. She was dreaming. Her dreams were more vivid this night than they'd ever been in her life.

In the final dream, she was on top of a huge mountain, looking down over a lush, green valley. She was a boy? Weird... She was with another boy. He was a couple years younger than her (him). They were brothers.

It had taken so long to climb to the top. It was hot and barren, like a desert. The sun baked down on her (him) and her (his) brother, as they snuck around a very important building. Trespassing was not allowed, but here they were, on a secret mission. They loved how naughty they were being. And they were getting away with it! No adults knew they were up here!

And they were so close to the big humming thing!

They knew to keep hidden so the flying machines wouldn't detect them.

"Tine, we have to run from this rock to those monument rocks, then stop under them and stay very still, okay?"

"Okay, Aing!"

"Ready, set... *run!*"

They darted from their hiding place into plain sight and ran their little legs as fast as they could toward an ancient monument—four huge vertical granite monoliths supporting two even larger horizontal granite monoliths. "This is some old-person boring thing, probably made by Mommy or Daddy like a thousand years ago or something. So boring," she (he) thought.

They reached the monument and ran into its shadows. No one saw! Their breathing was heavy. They crouched down as their panting slowed.

"What now, Aing?!"

"Hmm... we have one more run to go and we'll be at the humming building!"

"I can do it, Aing! I can *do* it!"

"Good."

They crouched, noticing many complex symbols etched into the granite. They were used to seeing symbols like this— their parents cared so much about that stuff. It had something to do with how they made stuff float or whatever.

Tine followed Aing to the monolith facing the humming

building. From there, they'd only have to run about a hundred feet—by that funny purple plant—and be right at the humming building! Where no one was allowed to go! They'd tell all their friends in school the next day! Heroes for all time! They would do something that no other kids could ever do!

But the hum was so loud... It pulsated through their bones. No kids ever got this far. They were so close. They would tell this story to the other kids *forever!*

"Are you ready, Tine?"

"Ready!" Tine whispered excitedly.

"Go!"

They bolted for the main building, running right by the purple plant—that thing was weird.

They got there! They made it! They were standing right at the stone structure that housed a bright, white, extremely powerful, pulsating, humming thing.

"What is it, Aing?!"

"It's the Great Crystal! Can you feel its power?"

"Yes! It's so strong, the strongest thing ever!"

"It's a huge diamond crystal thing!"

The thick, dense rock surrounding the Great Crystal wasn't strong enough to keep the raw pulsating power from flowing through them in all directions, and it made them light-headed.

Then they heard something. It wasn't loud. It sounded like a bicycle flying in the air—the sound of a bike being pedaled mixed with a slight whine and hum.

They saw it. A small winged flying ship. There were no people aboard. It passed right over their heads and then off the mountain peak, banked, and came around for another pass. They were caught!

A loud voice entered their minds, saying, "You should not be up here."

Fear struck Aing as he—as she—Kara woke in a sweat.

She lay in bed a few minutes, taking stock of what she'd just lived through. It had felt so real, so familiar...

She noticed she was alone in bed. She got up and walked around the house—ignoring Jon's loud snoring. She checked the porch. Olias was nowhere. She called quietly from the porch, "Olias?! Olias?!" She heard only waves.

She walked back to the bedroom and put on more clothes, grabbed a flashlight and headed for the beach. A light ocean

51

breeze had kicked up and the surf had grown loud. "Olias?!"

There he was, sleeping soundly in the beach-pea plants. She chuckled, not knowing if she should wake him. She plopped down softly beside him and whispered, "You need sleep, Tine, get some rest." That she said this surprised her. She figured it was only because the funny dream was so fresh in her mind. The realistic dream. The most memorable dream of her life.

She softly snuggled into him, and was soon asleep at his side.

8

While Old Man Cranchet was beginning his long slumber—the precursor to his memorable night with his old buds—the sun crested the horizon and began its climb. Olias woke to find Kara by his side in the pea plants, sleeping. A warm feeling came over him. He knew her so well and loved her so much. A few tears welled in his eyes as he gazed up from her to the sun, the tears making it look like a huge crystal in the sky.

"Kara?"

"Olias."

They held each other. They kissed. Ever so slowly, his kisses descended down from her lips. She moaned and took off her shirt and shorts as he kissed her chin. Deep warm kisses moved slowly down her neck and beyond... They finally reached her breasts, then her bellybutton. She fell over backward into the pea plants as he kissed her where he would slip into her. He kissed her all over her body as her heart raced. She moved underneath him, nestled softly in the billowy plants. He slipped inside her. The waves drowned out the cries of passion. They were one.

They held each other as the waves—now farther down the beach—gently crashed. The wind had stopped.

"I guess we should go see what time it is," Olias said.

"I'll leave that to you, luv. I'll make us some breakfast."

They put their clothes on and walked up to the house. Olias peeked in on Jon, who was just waking up.

"Morning, Olias. Wow, did I have some funky dreams. What time is it?"

"It's about six o'clock. We're way ahead of schedule. Go back to sleep."

"No, I actually feel good, I'm gettin' up."

"Cool. Kara's making breakfast. I'll go make sure we have all the supplies we need."

"Mmmmm, sounds good," Jon said as he closed his eyes and lay still, remembering a huge, beautiful chandelier from a dream.

Olias made sure all the supplies were ready to carry to the boat, and helped Kara with the bacon, eggs, toast and home fries. They ate on the porch as classical music wafted from the living room.

An hour later, they set off for the beach. Olias rowed the supplies out, then taxied Kara and Jon.

They were off. The water was calm. The open-ocean rollers were large and gentle. Ziggy climbed up and down them as Olias avoided dangerous ledges off High Island, then turned toward Black.

When they were about three-hundred feet away, Olias took the motor down to trolling speed. They went in slowly, back to the spot they had landed. The ropes were still hanging against the cliff. "Still there!" proclaimed Jon.

"So, where's the forest with the weird baobab-type tree?" asked Kara.

"It's on the other side of the island," Jon replied.

She stiffened. "Luv, will we have to walk through that scary field with the hungry animals you told me about?!"

"I'm afraid so, luv."

"Well, okay then. Let's do this thing."

Olias and Jon looked at each other and smiled, pleased with their new Black Island partner's bravery.

Olias brought Ziggy's bow up to the ropes. Jon jumped onto the bow and grabbed one. He tied it to Ziggy, then climbed onto the island. "Okay Kara, your turn!"

Kara climbed onto the island. "Hello, Black Island," she said, smiling. "I feel like we're being watched..."

Olias fastened one of the ropes to the tender and climbed up to join them. They worked together, pulling the tender up onto the island, making sure not to scratch its hull. Once it was on land, Olias and Jon carried it farther into the island and hid it in some scrub. Kara broke out some sodas from her pack and handed them out. "Here's to Black Island!"

"BLACK ISLAND!" they toasted. They drank and looked across the bay.

"I can feel the other side of the island pulling at me... Do you *feel* that?" Kara asked.

"Yes," said Olias.

"Totally," agreed Jon.

It was time. They set off through the little woods to the lower field with the large weeds.

They reached the field. "Look!" Kara said, pointing. Three great blue herons flew over their heads. They watched the herons disappear behind a hill to the left.

"Here we go," Olias said. He was in the lead, Kara in the middle and Jon the rear. Olias stopped. "Hold up." He pulled off his backpack, took out knives and handed them out. "It's all we have. I don't think we'll need them, but, just in case. Let's go."

They entered the field. "The Field of Unseen Beasts," Jon said.

The weeds soon rose fifteen feet over their heads.

There was a scuffling sound to their right. Kara jumped. "What's that?!"

Olias kept walking. "It's nothing. There'll be more of that. Just keep going."

A guttural snort blatted behind them. Kara screamed. They froze. "Luv, that was *big!*" she whispered.

They looked and saw nothing. Olias shook his head. "You know, we haven't actually *seen* these animals. They stay in the brush. Maybe we're protected from them."

"Well, let's think about that when we're out of this damn field!" whispered Jon.

"Yup." Olias continued with Kara and Jon almost touching him.

Something dead ahead—some animal laughed. It sounded like a hyena—laughing at them.

"Keep moving, keep moving!"

"Right *toward* it?!" Kara whispered.

"Yes, slowly."

Their knees felt weak. They reached the spot where the animal had laughed. There was nothing there.

They pushed on. Soon they saw a tall weed up ahead get flattened and heard a very large animal grunt. Kara grabbed Olias. They stopped. "Luv, we can't go toward *that!*" she said, shaking.

"We have to. Just wait."

The animal grunted and stomped.

"Can you see what it looks like?!" Jon asked.

They couldn't. They stood still.

The animal ran away.

"C'mon," said Olias, and started walking. Kara clung to his shirt.

They finally reached the rocky hill. "Hallelujah!" Jon said.

They began their ascent. The field with its grunts fell away. Kara saw the odd tree looming at the foot of the forest. "That's... wow."

They reached it. Kara touched it. "It's like a huge dog or something!" She petted it. "It has fur!"

"C'mon, let's go," Olias said.

They walked into the forest. It got thicker and darker as they went.

"Wow, it really is *dark* in here," Kara said. "And quiet."

They walked into night as the trees got so close together that they had to contort their bodies around the trunks and branches to keep moving.

"I think we're getting close to the wall," Olias said.

"Look!" Jon exclaimed.

They came to a little clearing.

They stood before Gumtooo.

CHAPTER 4:   Grammie

1

Bob Lianelli's mind was drifting. He was doing paperwork in his office—midst constant phone calls to vendors and local fishermen selling their catches—but he just wanted that blond bitch's hot ass. Where was that bitch? The phone rang again. But this time it was his wife in California. The other bitch. "Hello?"

"Hi, hon! Whatcha up to in Maine today?"

"Oh, hey there. You know, same old. Making money for the wife and rugrats down in my lovely wine state of California."

"When are we going to see you? We miss you! The kids' summer vacations are going to be over soon. School starts up in early September this year. We haven't seen you in soooo looooong! When can we see you?!"

"I don't know, my managers are assholes and I have to do everything myself." Bob cupped the phone with his hand and peered out the office door, scared for a second that Todd or Stacy or anyone heard that lie. He dropped his voice. "These inbred hicks in Maine don't know what the hell they're doing, it's a wonder any one of them can finish high school."

"Oh gee, that's a shame. But, I was thinking... Why don't the kids and I come visit? It's so hot here, and we'd really enjoy some Maine time."

He was ready for this. "That sounds *great!* I'll get right on it! I'll find you some plane tickets!"

"Oh! I'm so excited!"

"Look, I have to go, some new idiot I just made manager is fucking everything up. I'll call you back in a day or so when I get the tickets."

"Oh Bob, I love you!"

"Yeah, love you, bye." He put the phone down and leaned back in his chair. It was time for some damage control. He smiled. Child's play. He'd say that he really misses California, and will want to visit there instead, but he needs to find a time when he can. That'd hold the bitch for two weeks. Stupid bitch.

Todd knocked. "Bob? Got a minute?"

"Yeah buddy, c'mon in! What's up, buddy?"

"Heyyyyy, well... I was wondering, can I maybe get a

bartending shift or a wait shift sometime?"

Bob was waiting for this. He'd planned for it before he'd made Stacy manager. Child's play. "Of course, buddy! I don't want to take anyone else's shifts away from them, but as soon as one comes up, it's yours."

"Thanks! It's tough, I never see Stacy anymore, now that we are working opposite hours."

"Ohhhhh riiiiiight... Well, don't worry buddy, I'm on it!"

"Thanks, Bob!" Todd left happy.

"Stupid asshole hick," Bob hissed. He got back to his paperwork as Randy, a waiter, popped his head in the office.

"Hey, Bob? Some guy named Jimmy is at the bar asking to see you."

"Okay Randy, thanks." Bob walked out into the house and motioned to Jimmy to follow him. They sat at an empty table in the corner.

"Bob, we'll be breaking into Olias's house this week. I need to know somethin'... why do you want to go through this guy's personal shit?"

"I've been approached by a third party to get as much info on that little wimp as I can. That's all you need to know. You do a good job, you get a bonus."

"Works for me." Jimmy stood and walked out.

"Stupid hick," Bob thought, as he walked back through the kitchen to his office. Scott, the cook working the fry-o-later, thought he heard Bob snort like a pig.

Bob entered the office and closed the door. He picked up the phone and dialed. "Hello, Mrs. Black?"

"Why hello, Bob. It's always so *good* to hear your voice!"

This made him so happy he almost blushed. He couldn't believe how whole this old woman made him feel. It was as though she was his loving grandmother, back from the dead. He'd do anything for her. "Always good to hear your voice as well, Mrs. Black."

"So tell me, Bob, have you gotten any information from Olias's house?"

"No, not yet, ma'am. But this week I hope to have as much information as you'll need about everything in his life. Hell, you'll know his hopes, dreams and every dirty little secret the sicko has by the time I'm done with him."

"Oh good, son."

Bob glowed. "Of course, ma'am."

"I wish I didn't have to ask you to do this, but I can't get near that house, due to neighbors I know who live nearby."

"Of course, I understand. Can I ask you why this punk is so important?"

"Yes, of course. Some people I know in local power are scared that he's a threat to island security and our way of life. I just need to make sure it's true. If it *is* true, I might ask some more favors of you."

"The price is certainly right! You keep paying me *this* much dough and I'll do whatever ya want!"

"Oh ha ha Bob, you're cute."

Bob's face turned pink. "Thank you, ma'am."

"No, thank *you,* son, you always make my day. Call me as soon as you get any information on that horrible boy."

"I certainly will, ma'am. Talk to you soon."

"Goodbye, Bob."

Bob hung up and sat in silence as waves of happy fuzzies climbed down his veins, swam through his synapses and glided through his lower intestinal tract. He felt young again. He leaned back in his chair, smiling. He didn't notice that he'd begun drooling out of the left side of his mouth.

2

Dan sat in his apartment eating a grilled-cheese sandwich while fantasizing about jewels, treasure hunting on Black Island and fighting the evil "haves." He felt his body getting taller every time he thought about hurting those bastards, even killing them. Beating them. Showing who was stronger. "Fuck them to hell. Go all aggressive apeshit on their spoiled asses." Oh yeah, he was really enjoying that sandwich.

He wanted to go to Edna Black's in the morning—he needed her—but she had said to come in the afternoon, and that was still a few hours away. He could wait. Wait while fantasizing about killing the "haves" and showing who was stronger and better. "*More* better. Great grilled-cheese." Dan also knew he was way smarter than all those college-educated money dumbass "haves," because he had street smarts. "They're all dumb fucks anyway. They think they're better than me." He was ten times the man those puny fucks were. And he could beat all of them the fuck up. Each and every one. Wasn't Olias a college boy? He was. "Kill him. Show him who's the fucking boss around here. Fuck him to hell. Great grilled-cheese." Dan felt like he was actually getting taller. His anger was justified! His wish to kill was just! He would honor this by doing just that—taking whatever was Olias's and making it his own, then killing Olias. "Fucking little wimpy piece of shit. Kill him. Kill him. Kill him. Great grilled-cheese!"

Dan knew he was really clever because he could always fool the college boys—those fucking "haves"—tell some bullshit fact and they'd go "oohhhhh" to be nice, and the whole time he knew it was bullshit, the thing he said! He was so much smarter than them! Being that clever is very rare and hard to do! He never seen no one do that before! He was the fucking *man*. "Kill Olias. Kill Olias. Kill Olias. Great grilled-cheese!"

He stopped. "Wait... *who's* Olias?"

A huge itch began under his navel. Heartburn set in—it was wicked. He doubled over. A piercing headache stabbed his brain. He tasted acid while soiling himself.

3

Lenny's little apartment in Nor'easter Harbor smelled like stinky feet in a used port-o-potty. Lenny sat on his ratty couch, eating Funyuns and watching The Suite Life On Deck, which aired on one of those tween channels. People didn't need to know, but Lenny liked the little boys on those shows. He liked to watch them run and frolic and overact, and their feathered Hollywood hair gave him little tingles. People didn't need to know. This was Lenny's Lair, Castle a' la Lenny, Lennington Manor. "Ain't no one seen the things I do here. And ain't no one gonna. 'Cuz it's *my* place. I'm the big man around here. In fact," he mused, while watching a certain little boy, "it might just be time to do a little sum-um sum-um—"

There was a knock on the door. He froze, turned off the TV and walked to the door.

"Lenny, it's Jimmy, lemme in."

"Oh, ah, yeah, Jimmy," he said, opening the door.

Jimmy walked in. "Damn dude, ever hear of air freshener?"

"Oh, ah, yeah, Jimmy, I'll go buy some 'a that real soon, like today even."

"Good." Jimmy thought about sitting on the couch, but decided against it and grabbed a lawn chair from Lenny's plastic kitchen set. He placed it near the door, where the air was freshest. But damn did it stink. "Lenny, Lianelli says he's gonna pay us the big bucks to get as much info on that transplant fag Olias as we can, right?"

"Right Jimmy, right."

"So, are we on for Monday then?"

"Whatever you say, Jimmy."

"Yeah, well I know you have to work the docks on Monday. Have you thought about how you're gonna get off 'a work?"

"I'll think 'a somethin' Jimmy, sure I will, is all."

"Oh yeah? Like think of what?"

"Ummm... you know, somethin'."

"Lenny, you already had Friday off saying you were sick, so you can't say you're still sick, that's three days later. You'd have to get a doctor's note for that, I bet."

"Oh, so, you know a doctor, Jimmy?"

"No, I don't know a doctor, Lenny. Look, I can get outta work, but we gotta think of something to get you outta work, or we can't break into his house, and if we can't break into his house, we can't get paid by Lianelli. So whatta we say to get you outta work?"

"Um... that I got... um..."

"See? It ain't so easy, is it?"

"No, it ain't so easy."

"I ain't come up with nothin' neither. This is a real problem, Lenny."

"I know, Jimmy, I know."

"Maybe we could break into his house at night, if he ever goes somewhere. But I hear he's so boring, he never leaves his fucking house. And night is better for breaking in, too."

"Great idea, Jimmy!"

"Well, maybe not so great. Who knows when he'll go out at night next. And we don't have a guy to watch him at night, the way my buddy at the boatyard can watch him in the day, making sure where he is when we break in. We'd be taking a chance there... a chance he'd show up while we were there."

"That would suck, Jimmy."

"I know. So, we'll have to play this by ear. I know that Stacy chick down at the See Food is friends with Olias's girlfriend, so maybe if we keep our ears open down there, we'll find somethin' out."

"I like going there!" Lenny just wished Jimmy would leave, seeing as he had urgent things to attend to. "When should we go next?"

"Let's go tonight. It's Saturday night, maybe we'll get lucky!"

Lenny thought, "I'm trying to get lucky *now*." He noticed he paused and quickly retorted "Yeah! Lucky!" He hoped he didn't sound too stupid.

Jimmy looked at him with that expression he so often had, that said "idiot." Jimmy got up, returned the lawn chair to the kitchen set and strode quickly for the door. "And air this place out, Lenny, huh?"

"Ha, you got it, Jimmy. See ya tonight."

"Meet me there around eight o'clock, okay?"

"Eight, got it."

Jimmy all but ran from the stench. Lenny bolted out of his chair, locked the door and jumped to the TV. The Suite Life was over, and now a Hannah Montana repeat was showing. "Damn!" But he wasn't deterred, seeing as he had many episodes of The Suite Life on old, grubby VHS tapes. "Where are my Zack and Cody?" he sang.

4

Olias, Kara and Jon stood in awe of Gumtooo. "Wow, you guys weren't kidding," Kara whispered.

"I know, that is one weird-ass mushroom," agreed Jon.

"Is there a sunbeam anywhere near it?"

"I don't see one."

"If there was, I'd block it from hitting the poor thing," she said.

As they stared at Gumtooo in reverent silence, a fleeting voice blew through their minds and was gone: "ahh"—a part of a word—someone else's voice.

"What?! Did anyone *hear* that?!" Kara asked.

"It sounded like someone was trying to speak inside my head!" Olias exclaimed.

"I heard it too!" Jon chimed.

Kara's eyes turned to slits as she studied the mushroom.

"Maybe this is more than just a plant?"

"What do you mean, maybe *the mushroom* spoke to us?"

"Maybe."

"Then I think we should see if it happens again," Jon said.

"Okay," they agreed.

They stood silently for five minutes in a vacuum of sound, facing Gumtooo in anticipation.

Nothing.

"Maybe the voice came from something else? Something behind the wall of black?" Jon wondered.

They waited a little longer.

"Alright, let's get to the wall," Olias said.

They continued. The woods got thicker and they had to inch their way forward. Soon, they were crawling. The wall of black became visible through a dense thicket.

Kara saw it. "Oh my *God* that is *weird!*"

"Tell me about it. Wild. Totally wild," Olias said.

They reached the wall.

"This isn't *real*," Kara whispered with her head cocked to the side, eyes ablaze. "This cannot exist..."

"But it does," Olias said. "Jon, hand me the end of that rope."

Jon gave him the rope and Olias tied it to the back of his belt.

"Be careful, luv."

"I shall, luv. I love you."

"I love you."

Olias pulled out his high-grade flashlight and clicked it on. "Be right back." He crawled into the black and onto rocky sand. There was no more choking thicket. He stood upright.

Jon squeezed the rope.

Olias was in the blackest darkness possible. The flashlight beam shone only two feet before bending to the ground and disappearing. "It's so weird how the light bends down!" he yelled.

"Luv, we're right here, right next to you. There's no need to yell."

"Oh, right..." He pointed the light at his feet and saw the ground. There was no smell. He deliberately kicked up some dust and inhaled an ancient, dirt-dust cloud. While inching forward, he extended his left hand fully out in front so he wouldn't walk into anything. The other hand pointed the flashlight toward the ground. "Can you guys hear me?!" he asked nervously.

"Yes luv, you're still right here."

"Wow. Okay. There are no trees in here. I'm moving forward now. I'm going to try and walk in a straight line, if I can."

"Be careful luv, please!"

"I will. Jon, hold on to that rope. Keep it taut."

Jon made sure the rope hung in the air. Olias proceeded, petrified he might fall into an abyss. He tested each step.

After twenty paces, he felt alone and far away. "Can you guys still hear me?!"

"Yes luv, you're farther away, but we can easily still hear you!"

"Luv? Can you whistle a happy ditty for me?"

"I can." Kara began whistling an improvised, happy melody.

That eased his fear. "Okay, going forward. Making sure every step is safe before taking it."

The rope was now pulling on the back of his pants. "The rope's almost at the end!" cautioned Jon.

"I really like your whistling, Kara!" he said, gaining confidence. He moved faster.

"Only a couple feet of rope left!" Jon warned.

Olias stopped. There was still nothing to be seen ahead of him, but his wishful nature and curiosity urged him to leave the rope behind and keep inching forward.

Kara knew him all too well. "Olias! Come back! You are *not* untying yourself from that rope!"

"Yes, of course not, luv."

"So, there's nothing else we can do?!" Jon asked.

Olias frowned. "I don't know, my friend. I guess not. Let's bring this puppy to its end. Hold tight!"

"Holding!"

Olias crept forward another two feet, and detected a barely audible hum coming from straight ahead. "I hear something!"

"What is it, luv?!"

"Some kind of low hum—I think I'm really close to it!"

"But Olias, the rope's at its end!" Jon warned.

Olias went back to considering...

"Luv! Get back here! We'll come back with more rope. Get back out here now!" she ordered.

Olias knew she was right. And that hum was intimidating.

What if he lost consciousness all over again? Jon and Kara would hopefully be able to pull him out, but he'd get horribly scratched up, being dragged through all the sharp rocks in the sand. And what if the humming thing was so powerful it could kill someone who only approached it? What if he died? "Coming back out!"

He turned around and faced the rope and his footsteps in the sand. "Walking back now!" He walked at a more normal pace, holding the flashlight's shunted beam right on the footprints.

"Remember to get on your knees when coming back out!" cautioned Jon.

"Oh, right." Olias made it to the barrier and got on his knees.

His head appeared from the wall first, then he crawled out. Kara grabbed him and hugged him tight. "Luv…"

Jon pulled the rest of the rope out of the dark zone and coiled it up. "So, we found something out. There is something humming in there! Maybe it's some alien spacecraft that's been affecting our minds and Cranchet's body and moving Ziggy?!"

"Perhaps," Olias offered.

Kara raised her hands. "So, what now?"

Olias peered back the way they'd come. "Well, we need to come back here with a lot more rope. I guess it's time to go home and regroup. Have a fun porch night, what do you say?"

"Sounds great. I could use a drink or ten," Jon said.

"Of course we are going home, that's just a given," Kara said, "but I meant, what are we going to do about coming back here?"

Olias pondered. "Well, we could conceivably come back here tomorrow. It's Sunday, and we have off—" He tried to swallow the rest of the sentence as Kara glared at him with her "duh, Olias" look. "Oh, right, you have to work tomorrow…"

"Yes, I have to work tomorrow! And I don't want you two coming out here without me! What if something happens to both of you? I'd be the one to save your asses!"

"She does have a point," Jon said.

"When's your next day off?" Olias asked.

"I think Wednesday or Thursday."

"That dicks the whole thing over then. Until we have a day when we *all* have off, we can't come back."

Jon put on his backpack. "Who's as hungry as I am right now?"

"Me," Olias and Kara answered in unison.

"Well then, let's get going."

They gathered their island exploration items and got underway.

"Wait!" blurted Olias.

"What is it, luv?"

Olias crawled back to the wall of black, reached his hand into the bottom of it, felt around in the rocky sand and grabbed a sharp rock. He brought it out and held it up. "Look."

Kara and Jon stared at the foreign rock in wonder. They passed it around. Olias put it in his backpack. "Why not, right? I'll start a collection."

"Why not, luv."

Olias looked in the direction they'd have to go to exit the dark forest. "Okay, my luv and my bestie, let's get out of here."

They muddled through the thickest and darkest section, and soon were able to walk upright.

They stopped to stare at Gumtooo for a few minutes.

They continued. The forest thinned and more sunlight flooded through the canopy.

"I never look forward to those hungry-sounding animals," Jon said as they made their way out of the forest and came to the baobab-type tree. The sunlit big-weed field lay beneath them as they stood squinting, their eyes adjusting to the sunlight.

"Wow is it *bright* out," exclaimed Kara while petting the tree. "Such a cute tree, can we keep him?"

The guys chuckled and pet the tree with her. They stood in silence, letting their eyes adjust, listening to the island sounds: birdsong, light wind wafting through the leaves of the deciduous trees, far-off waves crashing on cliffs and red squirrels chirping their territorial warnings.

Suddenly, a huge STOMP! sounded in the field below, followed by a loud "*SNORT!*"

"Oh my God," shivered Kara, "We're going right where that thing is!"

"That thing sounds like a freakin' ra-raptor," Jon stammered.

Olias was determined. "Look, we've been through this! We never *see* these animals, right?! They have always stayed *away* from us, right?!"

Jon wasn't convinced. "Yeah, but what makes you think that won't change? Maybe now is their feeding time! Maybe they'll finally eat the crap out of us!"

"What are our alternatives? I mean, we could try going around the black forest, staying on the ocean cliffs, but that'll take a good three hours, easy. Probably more. We might even come up to some terrain that'll be next to impossible to get through. Hell, for that matter, we might come to a field just like this, with the same kind of animals in it."

Kara and Jon considered these points.

"Let's just go," Olias said.

They climbed down the rocky hill and reached the field of colossal weeds.

They stood at the bottom of the hill, unwilling to move any farther, every instinct telling them not to.

A huge beast stomped right where they needed to walk.

"This just *sucks!*" whispered Jon.

"That it does," agreed Kara.

They stood indecisively still, their knees weak. Olias said, "Let's sit for a second and gather our thoughts." This made sense, so they sat down at the foot of the field and listened to the occasional grunts, snorts, blats and stomps.

"Are we waiting for our hunger to outweigh our fear?" asked Jon.

"Apparently so," answered Olias.

"Let's just go. Let's just get this over with," Kara said as she stood.

The guys stood. Quivering, in they went.

5

Dan lay shivering on his bed. He hoped he had gotten everything out of his body that demanded evacuation—namely that grilled-cheese. He had to go to Edna Black's. At this point, he might even be late. He needed to feel her love. He needed that treasure of jewels and power. He needed to kill the "haves." He needed... Grandmother. Yes, she really *was* his grandmother. He felt it. It was so real. He couldn't *call* her Grandmother, but he could feel it in his heart, and he *knew* she felt that she was his Grammie. "I love you, Grammie!"

He softly rolled off the bed, testing himself. "I feel better. I must get cleaned up and go to Grammie's." He walked shakily to the bathroom and started the shower. "That fucking asshole spoiled piece of shit Olias," he mumbled to himself while stepping under the water.

The shower gave him new life. But that's when he noticed the huge boil just above his pubic hair, under his navel. "Oh, God!!!"

He stared in disbelief at the huge zit. He jumped out of the shower—the water still running—and looked at himself in the mirror.

He stared at the boil, then poked it. It itched. He scratched. Gunk came out.

He jumped back into the cascading, healing water. He lathered, rinsed and repeated five times. Afterward, he felt better, his newfound decisions to hurt others somehow more manageable.

He had some zit cream in his medicine cabinet, and slathered some over the boil. "Time for you to go the fuck away." He topped it off with a big band-aid, got dressed and put a few extra band-aids in his pocket.

"I'm coming, Grammie," he said out loud, as if talking to someone in the room. He heard a scuffling in the corner.

He got in his car and sped to Edna Black's.

He pulled into her dirt driveway and saw an unknown car parked by the house—right on some of the grass he'd mowed. "Who the fuck is that?!" An intense feeling of jealousy shot through him. He parked aggressively next to the car, got out and jogged to the door.

He walked right in. No more knocking for him. He bet that the new person had to knock, not like him—not like Grandson—who had the run of everything around here.

"Helloooo?" Nothing. "Always nothing at first," he thought. "That's odd." The boil under his navel became painfully itchy. He scratched as goo seeped into the bandage.

"Hellooo?!" He walked to the picture of Black Island and stared, mesmerized. "I wants me some 'a what belongs to me, I wants me treasure!" he sang happily. "Mrs. Black?!"

He heard someone walking onto the path from the beach stones, and ran to the window to see a young man walking toward the house. He fought an urge to run outdoors, but his protective side wanted to stay in the house, hoping this person would knock, and Dan would be the one to open the door for him—it being Dan's place now. Grandson's place.

He stayed in the living room, waiting to hear a knock. He was going to say, "I'll be right there!" then make the guy wait a minute or so before allowing him entrance.

The guy walked right in! Right into the living room! The audacity! The nerve! The taunting! The declaration of war! "Or, it's someone she's known longer than she's known me," a diminishing part of him thought. The boil itched more. He scratched harder.

The guy had the nerve to walk right up to him. He looked about thirty-five or so—ten years older. He was muscularly built and sure of himself. "Hello. I'm Seth, and you are?"

This alpha-male attitude really pissed Dan off, but he kept a smile on his face. "Hi, I'm Dan, a *very* good friend of Edna's. How do *you* know her?"

"I've hung out here with her a couple times. She came to me, asking if I could find a boat for a special trip out to a special island. My dad has a boat. She said she'd pay me for getting the boat and going on the 'mission' as she called it. She's so nice, isn't she?"

"Yes, she's very *very* nice."

"Do you know where she is?"

"No. She's usually visiting neighbors, I think."

"Well, she told me I could just come in without knocking and wait for her."

A volcanic anger erupted inside Dan. He tried to hide it with a fake smile. The boil stopped itching. "She of course said the same thing to *me.*"

"So, are you going on this 'mission' with us, Dan?"

"Of *course* I am!" he retorted.

"Oh, okay. Um, cool."

"So where *is* this boat, Seth?"

"It's in the Village. It's my dad's boat. I promised I'd keep it safe. If anything happens to it, I'll be spending the next few years paying for it!"

Dan wished the boat would break apart on a jagged ledge, but remembered he'd be *on* the boat. "Oh, that wouldn't be good."

"No, it wouldn't. Do you know where we're going on this 'mission,' Dan?"

This filled him with confidence. *He* knew they were going to Black Island for the treasure and to keep the evil rich people from getting it. "Ha ha, of course, we're going to Bl—"

"Hello, boys!"

They whirled to see Edna Black standing a few feet away,

gazing at them with loving eyes.

"Mrs. Black!" Dan cooed.

"Hello, Mrs. Black," Seth said.

"Helloooo my boys!"

This cut Dan like a knife. Edna placed a hand on him. Her hand instantaneously acted as a salve on his jealousy, which was replaced by warm feelings that tickled, the boil a distant memory.

"We are a team, boys."

She wanted to get Seth away from the Black Island picture, and she didn't want Dan to witness Seth fainting. That might precipitate too much thought. The last thing she wanted was Dan thinking. He was best when he was just reacting—much more controllable. "Oh boys, let's go to the beach and talk about our mission!"

They happily followed her out the door and down the path. Dan was surprised to see three beach chairs placed at the water's edge.

"Oh *do* sit, boys."

They made themselves comfortable as a few working lobster boats droned not far offshore, a sailboat quietly navigated by and a curious seal intermittently popped its head out of the water.

"Hey, look at the seal!" Dan exclaimed.

Edna ignored this. "Dan, I will tell Seth all about the island we are going to, but later. I don't want to get into that right now, alright?"

"Of course, Mrs. Black," Dan said with a smarmy glance at Seth.

"So, our mission. We are going to an island to find a treasure. Jewels. Diamonds. There are evil people who also want this treasure, and we may have a little bit of a fight on our hands. Can you boys handle that?"

"Of course!" declared Dan, fighting the urge to stand at attention.

Seth's main concern was his dad's boat. "Will the boat be in danger? I'm worried about anything happening to my dad's boat, Mrs. Black."

This made Dan's innards dance. He was the chosen boy! He was much closer to Grammie than this douchebag asswipe. He was ready to help her without a thought, while this ass was holding out! And to top off his victory, Dan knew about Black

Island wayyyy before this guy! Ha, what a dick this guy was!

She smiled. "Seth, I feel your concern, and I also want nothing to happen to your father's boat. But, if anything happens to it, I can cover the full expense, son."

"Oh! Okay then!"

"Now boys, we may have to take some measures to assure that this evil enemy of ours does not take the treasure."

"What kind of measures?" Seth asked. "I mean, I don't want to hurt anyone."

"What a wimp," Dan thought as his smile grew.

"Oh, of course, my young Seth. I think we can creatively stop this man and his evil team from getting the treasure without hurting them physically."

"Well... okay, and we all get some treasure when this is all over?"

"Yes, Seth! Yes!"

Seth was decided. The mission was on. He figured this treasure business was probably bullshit concocted by a senile old woman. "But if she wants to go out boating and is willing to pay handsomely for it, why the hell not?" he thought while extending his hand to her. She shook it. "Sounds good to me, Mrs. Black. The mission is on. Dan? Are you in?"

"What a completely clueless tool," Dan thought. "I already said yes, Seth."

"Oh," Seth responded, not really caring.

Edna put her hand on Dan's leg. "Dan, my son, will you please trim the hedges in front of the house?"

"Of course!" Dan bolted up and obediently jogged to the dilapidated shed to get the clippers.

Edna was pleased. "Seth, please come inside, I want to show you a map of the island where the treasure is."

"Sounds great."

They walked up the path. When they got to the kitchen door, Dan was already walking past them with the clippers, smiling right at Seth—a smile that said, "This is *my* domain, dude." Seth didn't notice.

Edna brought Seth into the living room and showed him the picture on the wall. "This is the island where we are going, son."

"Looks like a moon. Where is it in the bay?"

"It's southwest of High Island, son. You are going to BLACK ISLAND."

Seth fell to the floor, landing in an awkward, contorted heap. Edna stared down at his sprawled body, pleased.

Dan clipped the hedges in ecstasy. "This is the *life!*" he announced, hoping Grammie could hear him.

Meanwhile, Edna lifted Seth with ease and dumped him onto the sofa. "Seth... *Black Island.*"

Seth woke. "Huh?"

"It's alright, son, you fainted for a second, probably the excitement of this whole treasure hunt."

"Ummm, okay..."

"Would you like some water? It's from my well, son."

"That sounds great, thank you."

Edna walked out of the room as Seth's eyes were pulled to the picture of Black Island. "Weird, I didn't notice that it says 'Black Island' on top..."

Edna returned with a glass of water. "Here son, drink up."

Seth imbibed as Edna put her hands on his shoulders. "There, that's good, son, that's good. You make me soooo happy! I am soooo glad you are on our team!"

This somehow rocketed Seth into a state of euphoria, as his feelings for this old woman grew. Her warmth felt like little fuzzies caressing his very essence, multiplying in his heart. "Thank you soooooo much yourself, Mrs. Black!"

"Yes, my son. You make me soooo happy!"

Seth's smile seemed to be ripping at his face. "Meeee toooooo!"

"I need to be alone now for my nap. Please procure that boat for us tomorrow?"

"I certainly will, ma'am!" He obediently walked out of the house, got in his car and drove off.

Edna figured Dan was finally ready for remote control, so she planted a thought in his head. "Go home now, grandson."

Dan stopped clipping, ran the clippers back to the shed, jumped in his car and drove off.

Edna Black walked out the door and up to the ancient well. She looked down into it with a grotesque smile. "I looooove my boys."

She dove into the well, disappearing into its abyss.

6

Jimmy had a girlfriend named Elsa. He couldn't tell her that he did illegal things. She wouldn't have respected him if she knew. And they already argued enough...

Jimmy and Elsa were shopping in the Nor'easter Harbor grocery store for their evening meal.

"Is spaghetti okay again?"

"Yes, Elsa, whatever you want."

"So, where were you earlier?"

"I... went to Lenny's place."

"Why do you hang out with that dork? I don't get it."

"I told ya, he's a childhood friend, is all."

"Some people say that if you hang out with losers, you become a loser."

"So that's what your girlfriends are sayin', huh?"

"Well, yeah. But there's something creepy about Lenny. Dawna actually calls him 'Creeepy'."

"Hey, I agree, the guy's a douche, whatever."

"But you actually spend a lot of time with him, honey. Why?"

"Just an old friend is all."

"Hmmm."

"Hey, do we got some time for me to work out, babe? Before dinner? Gotta get these guns flexin', babe."

She smiled. "Oh Jimmy, hee hee, I'm sure there is."

7

On the other side of the island, Seth pulled into his parents' driveway. Both their cars were parked in front of the house. He parked them in and went inside. They were in the living room watching *The Price Is Right.*

His mom was the first to tear her eyes away from the screen. "Hi Seth, so, will you be making some money with the boat?"

"Yup, it's a go! And Mrs. Black said that if anything happens to the boat, she will compensate us in full."

"Excellent!" his dad declared, eyes never leaving the television.

"So, this Mrs. Black is an islander, from the Village?"

"Yes, Mom. I was just at her beachfront house."

"Hmm. I'm very surprised I don't know who she is. This is a small island."

"True. I think she must have lived somewhere else for a long time, while her old family house was vacant?"

"Hmmm, yes, that must be it. I *have* heard of a Black family on the island. I think Hazel Calderwood's maiden name is Black."

"Uh huh." Seth sat down and watched with them.

When the commercials came, his dad finally looked up. "So, when do you need the boat?"

"Tomorrow."

"That means you need to stop at Foy's in the Village and gas her up on your way to Mrs. Black's." He reached into his wallet and pulled out two hundred-dollar bills. "This should almost fill the tank."

"Thanks, Dad."

His Mom patted him lightly on the shoulder. "So, what is this whole boat trip, anyway?"

"Well, we are going to Bl—" Something inside him absolutely *refused* to say the name of the island. He didn't consciously notice and kept speaking. "—some nearby island to look for treasure or something."

Even though *The Price Is Right* was back from commercials, his parents both looked at him. "What?! A treasure hunt?" his dad asked.

"Yes, I don't know… she says there are hidden jewels and diamonds out there… I think she's just lonely. Or misses being out on the water. I mean, we get paid no matter what."

His dad laughed. "She's probably a senile old biddy with too much money to spend before she dies! Ha ha ha!"

"Oh now, dear, be nice," his mom added. "She's probably very lonely and just wants a boating day with company. She wants people to listen to her old stories."

"Yeah, that's probably all it is, Mom. But she's really nice, she reminds me of Nana."

"That's sweet, dear."

8

Olias, Kara and Jon entered the Field of Unseen Beasts. Their knees were weak and started to buckle, but they pushed forward. The hyena-thing laughed off to their right. A huge guttural growl from dead ahead froze them.

"I can't *do* this!" cried Kara and fainted.

Olias caught her as she fell.

Jon stood his ground, shivering. "Please stop, please stop!"

"Kara! Kara! Wake up!"

Her eyes opened. There she was, still in this damn field, still hearing animal grunts. For a moment she felt like she wasn't even in her body. "Luv, do we have to?"

"Yes. Come on." He helped her to her feet. She almost fell again, but he held her. "I think we are being protected. We haven't seen even *one* of these animals yet," he reminded her.

Jon was the first to start moving again, and marched forward. "I need to get back to Mount Haven and my beer. Let's go."

Olias, partially holding Kara up, followed.

"SNORT!"

Eventually, they reached the end of the field. They walked up to the little woods and plopped down in the soft grass, where they rested in silence. The debilitating fear now over, the relief they felt was equally debilitating. They closed their eyes and slept as the sounds of the waves and gulls caressed them.

CHAPTER 5:   Carved In Stone

1

Jimmy and Elsa were eating their spaghetti dinner at the dining room table. The TV was on and a little loud. It was tuned to professional wrestling, which Jimmy loved and Elsa hated. He was sitting and facing the TV, while she was sitting and facing the opposite direction—which happened to be at him.

He was loudly slurping his pasta. "Mmmm, love the sauce, babe."

"Thanks, honey. It's Prego."

"That's some good bread there," he said while mesmerized by one of the wrestlers putting his counterpart in a choreographed choke hold.

"Yes, it is. So, what do you want to do after dinner, Jim?"

"Um, I'm supposed to meet some buds, at the See Food."

"Oh? Can I come?"

"No one's bringing their girlfriends, babe, sorry. It's a guys' night thing."

"So I'll be alone *again* on a Saturday night?!"

"Hey heyyy, sorry there, babe. How 'bout you call some 'a yer girlfriends? Huh?"

"Hmph... I'll call Linda and see what she's up to, I guess."

"There ya go, babe," he said while glued to the entertainment.

She finished her dinner while he scarfed seconds, found her phone and dialed Linda.

"Hi, Elsa."

"Hey Linds, so what are you doing tonight? Want to hang?"

"Oh, sorry Els, Johnny and I are going out tonight. We're going to watch a romantic vampire movie, followed by a late, candlelit dinner back here. I can't wait!"

"Oh... glad, to, hear, that... Okay, talk to you soon..."

"Bye."

"Bye..."

Her head started to ache.

"So babe, yooz two gettin' together tonight?"

"No... and I think you should stay home with me, Jim. I'm getting sick and tired of you always doing things without me. We're a couple, we live together, and we're supposed to be *sharing* our lives for God's sake!"

She was becoming irate. Jimmy had dealt with this before, and tried calming her down. He didn't need the bitch yelling so that the neighbors could hear. "Baaaaabe, baaaabe... look, it's just one night, huh?"

"It's every *fucking* night!"

She was already yelling. Loudly. Now the neighbors could hear, and Jimmy didn't want to deal with that. "Shhh! Shhh! Keep it down, babe! You don't want the neighbors to hear you!"

She yelled even louder. "I don't care *who* hears me! FUCK YOOOOOOOU, JIMMY!"

He put his head down in defeat, then bolted to the bathroom and closed the door.

"You can't hide from me in there, you asshole! Come out of there! Get the fuck out here, you coward!"

He brushed his teeth and applied a little deodorant (in case he saw any hot chicks at the See Food bar he could flirt with), and combed his hair. He rinsed with mouthwash and came out, walking briskly to the door.

"Come the fuck back here, you asshole piece of shit!"

"Look babe, I'll be back soon, okay? Love you!" He shut the door and started jogging to his truck.

She ran after him. "I might not be here when you get back, you cock-sucking son of a bitch!"

An elderly woman and her five-year-old grandson were walking by, and they found themselves in the crossfire—between Jimmy at his truck and Elsa screaming on the sidewalk.

"Jimmy, you son of a fucking cock-in-the-mouth! GET BACK HERE! GET THE FUUUUUUCK BACK HERE!!!"

Jimmy jumped in and rolled down the window.

The elderly woman put her hands over her grandson's ears and shuffled him quickly down the street—literally pushing him. Through a nearby open window, an infant started crying.

Now Jimmy was yelling just as loudly. "FUCK YOU, BIIIIIIITCH!!! Maybe I won't fucking come fucking back at fucking all!!!" He gunned the engine and peeled away from the curb. Two dogs started barking.

Elsa had to get the last word. "I FUUUUCKING HOPE YOU DON'T COME BAAAAAAAACK!!!"

He was gone. The stench of a too-revved engine hung in the thick summer air as the dogs were barking and the infant was crying. Elsa looked around to see if anyone was asshole enough to be showing their face to her at that moment, because she wasn't done yelling.

No one. Empty street. Some shades and windows closed in the homes around her, including the one with the baby.

She was still shaking from the exchange as she sat down on the stoop, put her head in her hands and started bawling.

2

Dinner time was over at the See Food and drinking time had begun. The place was packed. There were more people than chairs, and every available bit of floor space was covered by someone holding a drink and talking loudly over the music. It was a typical summer Saturday night.

Lenny had a rough time saving a seat at the bar for Jimmy, who was late. Where was he? Lenny was annoyed, because he could have stayed home longer and watched another *Suite Life On Deck*.

"Is this seat taken?" asked a young, well-to-do summer socialite.

"Yeah, my buddy's in the bathroom, get away!" cried Lenny over a loud Billy Ocean song.

"Calm down, my man, calm down, jeeeesh."

Jimmy walked in, saw Lenny and went over. "Thanks for saving me a seat, Lenny."

"Oh yeah, no sweat, Jimmy."

"Any news yet about Olias or Kara?"

"No, nothin' Jimmy, just loud music and rich summer snobs."

"Any hot chicks tonight?"

"Um, I didn't see any, is all."

Jimmy assessed the situation. He saw that Stacy was managing, and Manuel—a seasonal bartender—was tending bar. Jimmy hated Manuel. "That idiot hick," he thought, "just in town for a summer job, some spic or something. What a dick! He thinks he's so fuckin' hot." Jimmy stared at Manuel's opened shirt, rippling muscles and washboard abs. He watched as Manuel flirted with girls and they flirted back. "All of 'em are stupid bitches."

Jimmy hated everything about Manuel, even though he had never spoken a word to him or knew the first thing about him. Because, as a child, Jimmy was taught to distrust anyone who wasn't from the island. He was taught that island rumors were all he needed for an opinion about "those from away." Most of his fellow islanders wouldn't judge someone unless they met them first, but Jimmy thought those islanders were idiots. They were nothing like his family. "My family done raised me right!" Jimmy sometimes wondered why his family was so wise. "Maybe it was the inbreeding," he considered. He heard that kings, queens and royalty do that. It must be how a smart family can stay smart—don't let any lesser genes into the gene pool. "Yup. That's why some islanders know how to hate outsiders so good," he thought. "And know how dirty them jungle-bunny blacks are."

He saw that Lenny was drinking a Budweiser and put his hand up to Manuel, who didn't see it for a good thirty seconds. "Heyyy yoooou!" he yelled over a loud Duran Duran tune.

Manuel came over. "What can I get you?"

This asshole even came complete with a Spanish accent! Jimmy's chest puffed way out. "I'll have a beer."

"What kind of beer?"

"A beer."

"Excuse me, sir? What type of beer would you like?"

"You ain't been on this island too long, huh there, Chico?"

"Excuse me sir, my name is Manuel."

Lenny started to laugh.

"That's what I said—'Chico.' Now give me a beer. Now."

"What brand of beer do you want, friend?"

"Well *friend*, when someone on this island tells you he wants a beer, he means a fucking Budweiser, you stupid hick foreigner."

Manuel was a black belt and could have killed Jimmy in 1.5 seconds, but was a sensitive man and felt that violence wasn't honorable, let alone legal. "I'll get you a Budweiser, sir."

"Yeah, you do that, Chico. Hop along now."

At this point, Lenny was laughing so hard he thought he was going to pee his pants.

"You see that, Lenny? These people think they're so worldly, but they're just stupid foreigners."

"Ha ha ha yup, Jimmy. So true!"

Manuel quickly got the beer and placed it on the bar in front of him, then moved on to more pressing matters—there were some hot girls standing near the entrance and beckoning him to shake some margaritas.

"I'm tipping Chico here in pennies," Jimmy riffed.

Lenny's laughing culminated in a near choke as two bar stools next to him opened up and two pretty, born-'n-bred islander girls, Maura and Hessie, jumped into them. This pleased Jimmy. He always flirted with Hessie, and as far as he was concerned, Lenny could flirt with Maura if he wanted. The math was good here. "Xy = xy, or some chromosome joke shit like that," he thought. "Hi there, Hessie, what you girls doin'? Out and about the town, are ya?"

"Hee hee, yes, Jimmy. Where's Elsa?"

"Oh she's... with friends. So, what can Chico here get you?"

Lenny started laughing all over again.

Hessie looked at Maura, giving her a knowing look that said "lust". "Oh, you mean *Manuel?* He can get me *anything* he wants!"

Jimmy's face started twitching wildly. "Aw, he's just a spic. Do you know how stupid he is? Have you actually *spoken* to the guy? I think he's a half retard."

"Jimmy, he's a pre-med student at Johns Hopkins."

"Well, that don't mean he's no brain."

Lenny stopped laughing as Jimmy caved into himself and sat in silence, angry as hell, wanting to punch Manuel.

Hessie and Maura didn't notice—their eyes were only on Manuel, and Manuel's muscles, and Manuel's abs...

"Manuel! Manuel! Thirsty girls! Thirrrrrrsty girls here!"

Jimmy had reached his limit. "Hey Lenny, let's get the fuck outta here and go for a ride."

"Sounds good, Jimmy!"

With a loud crack, Jimmy slapped three singles down on the bar—the exact price of the beer without a tip—and angrily stood. He had already decided he was going to leave without saying goodbye to those bitches Hessie and Maura. "Learn them a fucking thing or two," he thought. "C'mon, Lenny!"

Jimmy stomped out, Lenny navigating his wake. Their seats were filled immediately. Maura didn't notice they were gone until ten minutes later, and Hessie never noticed.

Jimmy floored it and they rocketed out of the Village towards the North Shore Road.

There were three main roads on the island of Mount Haven: the North Shore Road, the South Shore Road, and the Middle Road. The Village was on the center bottom of the island, where those three roads converged and became Main Street.

Jimmy screeched his truck off of Main Street onto the North Shore Road, gravel and dust shooting into roadside pine.

"There ain't a cop on the island tonight, is there Lenny?"

"I don't know. I seen that one come over on the ferry a few days ago, so he's probably gone."

"Well fuck him, he doesn't know No-Name Point. Let him fucking try and stop us from getting there!"

"Yeah! You go, Jimmy!" Lenny hadn't felt young in awhile, and this made him feel eighteen again. "Fuckin' let's riiiiide!"

There was indeed no cop on the island that night. Police officers who came over on the ferry in their patrol cars had to stay awake on a long shift, with only their car to house them, and thus couldn't be on the island for longer than twenty four hours at a time. The island had no police station and no bed for an officer. The only available toilet was at the ferry terminal, which was closed at night.

Most islanders didn't take kindly to cops on the island. Referring to the breakwater in Rockport—where the ferry left daily for Mount Haven—islanders would tell you, "There's no law past the breakwater. We have our own rules, people follow them. If there's a problem, we handle it in-house." The end result of these traditional island values? Many secrets stayed hidden on the island.

Jimmy pumped the accelerator regardless, hoping there *was* a cop. He needed a good fight to vent his rage.

They sped up the North Shore Road and came to the hidden dirt entrance to No-Name Point, where Jimmy turned onto the thin road and proceeded to drive recklessly, sparking dust clouds into the surrounding scrub.

They passed the high cliffs of Great Head and reached the highest and final peak, No-Name Point.

Jimmy pumped the brakes hard as the truck skidded to a stop right at the drop. A few tiny stones from his skid plummeted over the lip of the cliff. Below—almost three hundred feet straight down—jagged ledges were pounded by ocean rollers.

"Fuckin' right!" cried Lenny into the night.

Jimmy, very pleased with himself, coolly said, "Fuckin' right..."

They sat in silence for a minute. Lenny farted. "Whoops... quite a ride."

Jimmy was so in his own head he didn't even consider giving Lenny the "idiot" look. "I say we bring Manuel up here and drop him."

"Yeah man, fuck that douche." (Lenny didn't mention it, but he thought Manuel's hair was fluffy and rather pretty.) "Hey Jimmy, we need some beer."

"Yeah we do."

"So, you got some back at your place?"

"I ain't goin' back there! The Bitch From Hell is there! You got any?"

"No, I ain't got none."

They knew the store was closed.

"The only beer is back at the See Food, Jimmy..."

"Well we ain't goin' back *there* either."

3

Gumtooo thought about its attempts at communication with the new people. They had barely heard it. Only part of a word... "Perhaps I can improve." Gumtooo felt alive again, but that made the cutting sun tendrils hurt more. It wondered how it could ever get back to its old strength, when it lived under the sun. The thick plate-like outer layer of its skin had become painfully soft after epochs in the wet shade. Where once it was on a high sunny mountain, now it was almost at sea level in this wet, gushy place. Gumtooo had never moved since its "birth" but now, for the first time ever, wondered if it *should* be moved, moved behind the wall of black, back onto the rocky sand from its Strong Time. But Gumtooo had deep roots stretching fifteen feet down in this now-wet soil. Being able to move was probably just a fantasy. At least it was probably going to be able to help these new people and once again have purpose. Gumtooo finally felt hope.

4

Earlier on Saturday night, Bob Lianelli stood outside the See Food in the warm, salty air, holding menus and approaching all summer tourist passersby. "Heyyyyyyy, buddy! C'mon into the *See* Food and *see* the exact kind of food you wanna *see* from the *sea!"* Every now and then he'd offer a free drink and this would snare customers.

Stacy was managing, which entailed troubleshooting computer problems for servers and the bartender, and making sure everything generally ran smoothly.

She saw Bob on the street doing his shtick, smiled, and poked her head out the front door. "Hey there, Mr. Mannnn," she flirted, "How long are you going to keep harassing our summer tourists?"

"Until they make me enough money to retire, Stacy!"

"Ha ha haaaa!" She was enthralled by his confidence and flipped her blond locks. "Well, everything's running fine inside your restaurant, Mr. Mannnnnn!"

"Thanks, Stacy! I knew I hired the right person to be my next manager!"

This made her blush. "Well, I just want to do my best for you, Sir Bob."

He cartoonishly pretended to wield a sword. "I am Sir Bob, and I shalt Knight thee!"

"Oh! Ha ha ha ha haaaa!"

"Listen, Stacy, I got to tell ya... You keep doing this well, and I'm going to have to give you a promotion! You can be the... Queen of the World!"

The blood in her veins accelerated and her body warmed.

Stacy grew up poor. Her father was a hippie deadbeat. If there was one thing her mother had taught her, it was to find a man with money. "A real man has money, little girl."

Her expression became serious. She looked Bob up and down, and with a slight batting of her eyes, cooed, "But I'm already right where I want to be..."

Bob knew it was all coming together. "Yes, you are..."

A family of Mount Haven summer mansion owners were walking on the other side of the street, and Bob ran over to them, yelling, "Come be Knighted at the See Food Bar and Grill! A free Knighting with every entree!"

Stacy started laughing so hard she lost her grip on the door handle and fell to one knee.

The old-money Boston family—uncomfortable with Bob's aggressive invasion of their personal space—smiled politely and continued walking down the street.

Manuel came to the door. "Stacy, there's a phone call for you, it's Todd."

"Okay, thanks Manuel."

Bob noticed Stacy getting a good look at Manuel's body, and it ripped a hole in his ego. "You go take your call, Stacy, and I'll keep trying to get some more tourists into our restaurant and bar. And have something to eat on the house, anything, you've earned it!"

"Well, Mr. Mannnnnn, I'm partial to anything chocolate!"

"I think there's some homemade chocolate cake left. It's yours! Keep up the good work!"

She was flirting at a heightened level now, and batted her eyes while softly uttering, "Thank you, Bob..."

His demeanor softened—he knew just the right time to deliver his rehearsed line, and that time was now. "Thank *you*, Girlie..."

She hung out the door staring at him for a few seconds, then let her ass do the talking as she walked inside. This made him very happy. "Have a great talk with your big, big man, Stacy," Bob cackled.

Manuel was shaking a margarita on the rocks as tourist girls ogled. He'd left the phone sitting upended on the bar and Stacy grabbed it. She was in a very good mood—channeling her Bob-induced giddiness into talking to her boyfriend. "Hi, Todd! How're things?!"

"Hi. Well, not so good. I never get to see you, honey, and I was wondering if you want to do something after work tonight."

"But Todd, I won't get out of here until almost two o'clock!"

"I know, I know. It's just... I miss you, Stacy. I never see you anymore."

"Yes, honey, I know. But I'm going to be dog tired after work. It's really hopping here. Last call might not be until one o'clock. And then, you know how it goes. I have to make sure the bussers are tipped and go through all the server checkouts and finalize all the books and credit card statements and well, you know."

"Yeah, I know. Why doesn't Bob ever help us with that? Shouldn't he help us with some of that?"

"Hey! Don't talk like that! Bob is doing a great job, he's got a lot to do just running this place, and that's why he hired us, to do these things for him!"

This caught Todd off guard. Stacy used to always agree with him about things like this. "Um, yeah, Bob is great, you're right, Stacy."

"Look, I've got to go, Todd. I don't want to be slacking on Bob's dime."

"Yeah, sorry, um, love you—"

"Talk to you later." She hung up and walked away from the phone, not caring if she saw him tomorrow or the next day or the day after.

Bob had been watching from the street through a big bay window in the front of the restaurant, right over table six—where an elderly couple sat, eating their lobsters uncomfortably, because Bob was effectively the third person at their table, ignoring them, looking between them, staring at Stacy on the phone, watching to see if she glanced at Manuel's body again.

When Bob saw Stacy leave the phone on the bar in a huff, he knew it was a good sign. He walked away from the window in the mood to dance a little jig.

The elderly woman looked at her husband while cracking a lobster tail and said, "We're *never* coming back to this restaurant again, Herbert."

Herbert looked up from his browned butter and said what he always said. "Yes, dear."

Todd put the phone down. Something felt very wrong with Stacy. Something was different. Something bad. He walked like a beaten man into the living room, where he kept a framed picture of her hugging him and laughing. He stared at this happy moment in their relationship, hoping it was their destiny. But there was something wrong... He stepped outside and started walking down the street with no destination.

She had never talked to him like that. They had been together for almost a year. It was the longest relationship he'd ever had, and she was his first love. He couldn't lose her, he just couldn't. So he kept walking, in the direction of the restaurant. In twenty minutes he got within eyeshot of the See Food, and saw Bob outside loudly soliciting patronage.

Todd's first reaction to seeing Bob's antics was to smile, and he started walking toward him, but stopped. He couldn't let Stacy see him. He turned and walked home.

Meanwhile, Bob kept sneaking glances through the big bay windows at Stacy, who was now standing at the bar and enjoying her slice of homemade chocolate cake. "That bitch's ass gon' be miiiine!" he sung.

His cell phone rang. He playfully flipped it open—just like Captain Kirk flipped his communicator on the old Star Trek series—without even looking to see who it was. He was in a very playful mood and knew he could deal with anyone at that moment. "Bring 'em on!" He saw it was his wife. Child's play—he'd channel his Stacy's-ass-induced giddiness into talking to his wife. "Enterprise?! Helllllllooooo? Captain Kirk here! Enterprise? Spock?!"

"Ha ha hi, Bob, you sound like you're in a good mood."

"Hey, babe. Yup, we're hoppin' here tonight, gonna make you and the rugrats some serious coin this summer, I think. And I'm gettin' the managers better at their jobs—they'll be able to run the place on their own when I... come... to... see... yooooooou!"

"What?! I thought we were going to enjoy some Maine time! Did you call about the plane tickets?!"

"Look babe, I'm sick of Maine, I miss California, and I really really want to see you. So, I've decided to go there. And it'll cost me a lot less to buy just one plane ticket."

She hesitated. "But, we really had our hearts set on visiting Maine, honey."

"Look, there's nothin' going on here. Maine is just pine trees, inbred hicks and water. Who cares about that crap. And fog everywhere. It's as cold as an old witch's tit up here. I hate it here. I'm so sick of it. And I want to see you soooo much!"

"Oh Bob, I want to see you too."

"Okay, it's settled then. I'm going to be looking for a plane ticket after I make sure my managers can run this place while I'm away. I'll call you as soon as I know when that'll be."

"Oh, alright, Bob... So, how have you been? I've been thinking about you a lot. I really love you, and I miss you."

"Yeah, I've been great. Oh, shit! Some idiot server just messed up an order and I got a table full of pissed tourists, got to go!"

"Okay, bye Bob, I lov—"

He hung up and walked away from the restaurant, now even happier, his gait becoming bouncy. He moved into the shadows of Main Street and danced. He considered himself a pretty good dancer. He didn't know it, but no one else considered him a pretty good dancer. To everyone else, Bob had a complete lack of rhythm. He couldn't even clap his hands correctly to a beat. But Bob believed that if he were ever to star in one of those "dancing with celebrities" shows, he could hold his own for sure. "What is rhythm, really? It's just moving around," thought Bob. "Any idiot can move around." He sang off-key while he danced, "The bitch is oooout of the waaayyyyy!"

After his personal performance was completed, he sauntered back into the light of Main Street and up to the big bay window that touched table six, where now two young African-American couples from Manhattan were sitting. Bob ignored them, looking over their table at Stacy's ass. He sang under his breath, "You're the next biiiiiitch! Giiiiiive me some-'a that aaaaaaasssssssss!"

The couples were highly offended. They exchanged words and stood, leaving the restaurant before ordering.

Bob watched them leave and walk down the street, and did a little jig behind them, singing, "Fuuuuck yooooou! Thaaaaat 'gon be myyyyyy bitch-aaaasssss!"

Stacy looked out the window, saw Bob dancing and started laughing, thinking, "He's so much fun, and really sweet. He's improved my life. Where would I be without him? And he's so confident and strong—he really *is* cute." She watched him, trying to convince herself that he was sexy. It took effort, due to his paunch, prominent jowls and nose.

5

Dan stayed in the shower for over an hour, trying to scrub away his new hate. Maybe another twenty minutes... "Seth better watch the fuck out, 'cuz *I'm* the main man. *I'm* Grammie's main man. *No* one gonna fuck with *that!*"

His periods of intense hate seemed to go in cycles. At the height of it, he had no problem wanting to kill another. But at the other end of the cycle, a little voice of doubt said that hurting others in any way wasn't what a hero would do—wasn't what a real man would do... That voice said he was a tool, a puppet—and those were the times that pain shot through his boil.

Seth didn't seem to care about Grammie... Seth was no threat. Yet Dan screamed under the water, "*I* am the chosen son!" He shut off the shower and got out. He dressed and walked outside into the summer night. A sea breeze blew through his wet hair, making his head cold. He walked down the street, ignoring a few passersby.

He came upon a dock in the Village, near the Mount Haven ferry terminal, and sat at the water's edge. He remembered how he wasn't *always* angry. Why was he so angry now? His boil itched. He scratched. It wasn't Grammie, she was the only thing *good* in his life. Was it Seth? Was he some bad guy that Dan was meant to kill? No, because Grammie trusts Seth. "No... it's someone named... *OLIAS!!! KILL HIM!!! KILL HIM!!! KILL HIM!!!*"

6

Olias, Kara and Jon hiked the rest of Black Island's upper crescent, getting back to Ziggy without incident.

After enjoying a relaxed trip home, they found themselves on Olias's porch for yet another fun night of food, drink, Red Sox on the radio, music and good talk in the salt air. Olias had the barbeque grill sizzling, and the Sox were tied with the Yanks in the eighth inning at Fenway. A low-hanging moon spilled sparkles across the bay. A few porpoise blow holes sounded near shore, but out of earshot due to the radio—Dan Castiglione's play-by-play.

From a nearby tree, a gull was watching. It had black eyes and was very still.

"C'mon, Wakefield!" championed Kara. "Find the force and float that knuckleball!"

Olias smiled. "These are not the pitches you are looking for..."

Wakefield struck out A-Rod. "Ha!" laughed Jon and fell out of his chair while trying to chug the rest of his beer—some of it ending up in his lap.

Olias and Kara shared a look of concern. "Jon, I think you've had enough," she said.

"Oh Karrer you're so hot so you can shay tha'. So, guyshh, whennn are we goin' back t' Black?"

Olias and Kara shared a different look. Olias said, "Whenever we can *all* go next. So, let's figure that out."

Kara said, "I can ask off for next Sunday, unless I find someone to work for me on Saturday."

"Well, they have a full summer staff right now, right?" Olias asked with widened eyes.

"Perhaps. I'll do what I can, luv."

"Of course. Thanks, luv."

Olias and Kara melted into an embrace. Jon watched. He fought jealousy and looked away while chugging half a fresh beer, then looked back. They were still hugging. He stood and threw his half-empty beer into the night. It shattered on the beach rocks.

"Whoa!" Kara said, looking up.

"Dude, what was that?!" Olias asked.

"Ha! I jusht wanted t' make shum beach glass, ha ha! Goin' t' pee," he said as he stumbled off the porch.

"He did that when we were hugging," Olias said.

"Yup. He's very lonely. And very drunk."

"He's always very drunk."

They sat in silence, listening to the game. Soon Jon returned. Kara looked at him as he popped a fresh beer. "Jon, next time we go to Black, I'm bringing a huge coil of rope on *my* belt as well!"

"Yes, me too," agreed Olias. "We need as much rope as we can bring. Jon, do you have some rope at home?"

"A li'll. I shay we buy more."

"Definitely."

Jon put his beer down on the table. "Maybe I coul' wait t' finn'sh this'n."

Mike Lowell blasted a go-ahead wall-ball scraper double off the Monster. "Yayyy!"

The black-eyed gull sat in the spruce tree and studied them. A seal, contentedly beached on an exposed ledge not far away, wondered what that thing in the tree was, that thing watching those people.

On the other side of the house, Dan approached from the dark driveway. He had walked from the dock in the Village, which had taken over an hour. He had to remember to thank Grammie for telling him where Olias lived. When did she tell him? His boil flared. It didn't matter when she told him! It was what she wanted.

He carefully approached. "Fucking spoiled rich piece of shit." He snuck into bushes on the side of the house and peered in the windows. Nothing. Then he heard laughter from the ocean side. "Shit, that puny, clueless, goody-goody fuck-shoes has company."

He crept to a tree line on the side of the property to get a look at the porch. The black-eyed gull watched, amused. He positioned himself behind a large spruce with a perfect view of the action. "Who's that hot chick?" he wondered. He remembered seeing her in town. The bitch had acted out of his league when he'd talked to her at the See Food bar last year, even though she had been nice. "Fucking stuck-up bitch."

"And who's that other guy?" He remembered also seeing that guy around town. "He's always driving around the island and acting all superior and shit. Fuckin' thinks he's better than everyone. Fucking asshole. Bunch of fucking assholes. Look at them. Don't they know I'm going to steal their energy and make it *mine?*"

"Oliash, you want 'nother burger?" asked Jon.

"No thanks, the beer is filling me up. You should have one."

"Stuck up assholes," seethed Dan.

Kara smiled and said, "Jon, you're so cute, you should have a little chef hat on!"

"Fucking whore," thought Dan.

"I think the next time we go to Black Island, we should bring a cooler full of sandwiches and drinks," suggested Olias.

"Yeshh!"

"Could we even camp there?" wondered Kara.

"What a great idea! Bring supplies for spending the night. Nice idea, luv."

Dan said very softly, "They better stay the fuck off Grammie's and *my* island!"

The Red Sox beat the Yankees 9-8.

"Hey, lesh put on some tunesh!" Jon said.

"Sounds good," Kara agreed.

Jon almost fell getting out of his chair, then stumbled indoors and started looking for a CD. Olias and Kara gave each other another concerned look.

"Oliash! Where'sh th' Yes albumsh?!"

"Hold on, I'll show you."

Olias walked in, leaving Kara alone on the porch. She walked to the railing holding her wine glass, swirled the wine and sniffed its nose. A puff of sea breeze caught her hair. Dan stared.

He was amazed at how beautiful she was. His boil pain flared. "She's just a stupid bitch."

The Yes album *Tales of Topographic Oceans* started playing from the living room as Olias and Jon returned. For some reason, that particular music made Dan's anger unbearable. He shook with rage. He clawed his fingernails into the tree—breaking them as they left marks in its trunk. A piercing headache plowed into his skull. He almost fell to the ground, but caught himself. If the music hadn't been playing, he would have been heard. He held onto the tree. Had the three looked closely, they would have seen his hands on either side of the trunk. The huge boil started to pulse with stabbing pain, producing a pungent stench that reached his nose. He knew it was time to go, but he couldn't move.

Extreme pain has an element of *blank*: no past, no future—just hell. He was forced to hold onto the trunk in agony as Olias, Kara and Jon joked, laughed and sang along to the music. He knew then and there that it was either him or them. Whatever ride they were all on together, either he would be standing at the end, or they would. He would die trying to kill them, no matter what.

He heard a rustle in the brush next to him, and was startled to see a gull standing still, staring at him. He couldn't tell in the dim light, but it looked as though it had black eyes. As he stared back, his pain diminished.

After ten minutes, he felt much better. A half hour later, the gull walked away and he was able to let go of the tree.

He followed the gull back toward his apartment. He had a big day tomorrow—he was going to Black Island. He couldn't wait to tell Grammie that the evil Olias and crew had already been there. "But maybe the gull will tell her first," he absently said aloud while teetering on the dark road. "That asshole Olias."

After listening to the full two-disk album, Olias and crew were sleepy. Soon the music was turned off—replaced by the sound of lapping waves. The grill was put away and the lights in the house went out. Olias, Kara and Jon slept soundly.

7

　　Jimmy and Lenny pulled up to Jimmy's apartment and sat in the truck. The lights were on—Elsa was home.

　　"Fuck," assessed Jimmy. "I was hopin' she would 'a gone out wit' someone. Ain't she got no friends?!"

　　"You want *me* to go get the beers?" offered Lenny.

　　"No, that's okay, I gotta do this. But come with me."

　　They got out and walked to the door. It was locked. Jimmy took out his key and unlocked it. They quietly entered. Jimmy walked to the fridge and started taking out beers and handing them to Lenny.

　　"Shouldn't we get a bag, Jimmy?"

　　"Shhhh!"

　　"Hello?!" Elsa walked down the stairs and into the kitchen. "I see the Two Stooges are thirsty."

　　"Fuck you. We're just here to get my beers. You and I will talk later."

　　"Not if I'm not here, we won't."

　　"Well where the fuck're *you* going?"

　　"I could go back to my mother's, Jim."

　　"Ooooooo! Just 'cuz we had a little fight?"

　　"The tenth fight this month, Jim."

　　"Yeah well... couples fight, is all."

　　"Not like us, Jim."

　　"Sure they do. Right, Lenny?"

　　"Um, yeah, everyone fights. Should I get a bag for them beers, Jimmy?"

　　"Wait."

　　Elsa stared incredulously at them, then laughed. "Look at you two... Ha ha! I now pronounce you asshole and dickhead, ha ha ha!"

　　"Fuck you, Elsa."

　　She became calm, her voice soft. "No, fuck *you* Jimmy. Fuck you to hell."

　　Jimmy was caught off guard by her calmness. She turned and walked back up the steps without a word.

　　"We got us a bag for these, Jimmy?"

　　"Shut up. Here." Jimmy handed him a few condensation-laden beers, then grabbed a few himself and started walking for the door.

　　Lenny followed. "No bag, Jimmy?!"

　　"Shut the fuck up! No fucking bag! Let's go!"

Lenny didn't say a word and obediently followed. Jimmy bolted across the road. Lenny tried to keep up as one of the wet bottles in his left hand fell to the sidewalk with a smash.

"You fucking *idiot!*" Jimmy screamed.

They got in the truck. Jimmy gunned the engine and roared off.

Upstairs, Elsa sat on their double bed with a peaceful look on her face. Two small tears gathered weight in her eyes and fell onto the pillow.

Jimmy and Lenny gunned it out of town, back toward No-Name Point. They cracked their beers and drove in silence. Lenny wished they had gotten a bag and taken *all* the beers.

This time, Jimmy didn't feel the need to show off his skidding prowess, and came to a normal stop atop No-Name Point.

They drank in silence for fifteen minutes. Lenny's slurping sounded like a thirsty dog lapping at a bowl and it started grating on Jimmy's nerves. "Lenny! You sound like a fucking dog!"

"Oh, um, sorry, Jimmy." Lenny drank quietly.

"I guess I gotta go apologize to the bitch, Lenny."

"Yeah."

"But *she's* the ass. It ain't fair. Why do *I* gotta say sorry when it's *her* that's a bitch?!"

"I don't know, Jimmy."

"She don't got enough friends! Maybe I should just say *fuck you* to the bitch and go live somewhere else!"

This scared Lenny. He didn't want anyone infringing on his *Suite Life* home. "Well, you have such a *nice* place there, Jimmy."

"Yeah, I guess, but if that bitch starts yelling one more time for the neighbors to hear, I swear I'll kill her!"

"Ha ha! I'll tell ya, Jimmy, I got some real asshole neighbors too—*really* bad, much worse than yours!"

"What? Really? What do they do?"

"Um, they constantly knock on the door and tell me to take out garbage and... they *hate* any kind of noise, like when I watch *wrestling!* They hate when I watch wrestling and constantly knock on my door and tell me to turn it the fuck down and shit!"

"Wow, you should *move!*"

Appeased, Lenny relaxed with his final beer.

Jimmy sat in silence, scared about what he'd have to say this time to shut her up.

Lenny pulled a little baggie of pot from his pocket. They got stoned in silence as the waves crashed on the sharp cliffs below. They faced out the dark windshield at a vivid star field, but didn't notice it or the intermittent shooting stars that ripped across it.

Every now and then Jimmy would say something about his relationship and Lenny would lend him moral support. "Fucking bitches. They're all fucking bitches."

"Yup."

When their final bowl of pot was smoked to a fine gray ash, it was past two o'clock. Jimmy turned the bowl upside down and drummed it on the dashboard, then stuffed the pipe in his pocket. "Thing is, Lenny, I need to break up with the bitch. She's holdin' me back. I can't stand her. I should 'a never gone out with her."

"I hear ya, Jimmy."

"But there's no way the bitch is gonna leave! She needs me, Lenny. But I don't need her, ya know?"

"Sure, Jimmy."

"Man, it's gonna take everything I got on the inside to get rid of her, Lenny. Even though she's an extreme fuckin' bitch, she's all way fuckin' into me and shit. Ya know?"

"Oh yeah, Jimmy."

"I think if I even *hit* her she'd stay with me!"

"Ha ha."

"Oh *man...* I gotta get *rid* 'a her!!"

"Yeah you do, Jimmy, yeah you do."

Jimmy was tired. He really wanted his bed. To hell with the bitch. He'd tell her whatever she wanted to hear tonight so he could just get some sleep. "Well Lenny, what say we go home and go to bed, huh?"

He roared the truck to life—startling a fox in the bushes—and drove normally back to the North Shore Road. Once in the Village, he dropped Lenny off at the stinky apartment and drove home.

He parked and walked gingerly to the door, figuring he'd be as quiet as he could so she wouldn't wake up. Luckily, the bitch had left the kitchen light on for him.

He put his key in the door and turned—it was already unlocked. "Stupid bitch!" he hissed under his breath, but then remembered it was *he* who had left it unlocked, when he left with

Lenny. "Oh, right…" He made a mental note to *not* yell at her about the unlocked door.

He quietly entered the apartment and took off his shoes, pants and shirt in the kitchen, so as not to make any noise once upstairs. He took off his socks, and the smell reminded him of Lenny.

Now only in his tighty-whities, he set about his mission and approached the creaky staircase. He ascended the stairs painstakingly—putting slight weight on each step at first, then slowly easing his full weight onto it. This was the only way to keep them from creaking loudly. He did pretty well, but it took a while, and he was really tired—he really needed that bitch to stay quiet once he got into the room and into bed. "Just stay the fuck asleep!" He finally reached the top of the stairs, where there was a rug. He quietly tiptoed to the bedroom door and opened it slowly. "I'm gettin' pretty fuckin' good at this," he thought.

The room was pitch dark. He slowly made his way to the bed, lifted up the covers on his side and slid underneath. "Ahhhhhhhh…"

His mission was a success. His body fully relaxed, and sleep started to overtake him. As his eyes adjusted to the dark, he looked over at Elsa, which he liked to do right before falling asleep—she looked pretty sexy when she slept, even though she was a bitch.

But she wasn't there. He was alone in the bed.

"What?!" He bolted up and turned on the bedside lamp. "Where the fuck *are* you?! Elsa?! *Elsa?!!*"

He got up and turned on the light. He bolted out of the room and ran around the apartment. She was gone.

It started to hit him. "What the fuck, Elsa… Elsa?"

He put his shirt and pants back on and ran outside to see if her car was parked on the street. It was not.

It was three o'clock and the rest of the island slept. The only sound was the wind. He walked slowly back inside.

He found it in the kitchen. A note.

"Dear Jim, I think we both know this is it. This is the end. We just don't work anymore, and we never will. What we had, especially in the beginning, was so special. I'll never forget those times. So, let's remember those times when we think about us. I know I will. I've taken everything I want from the apartment, the

rest is yours. Goodbye Jim, and please remember the good times.   Elsa"

After reading the letter over and over, he carefully placed it on the table and stood up.

And then Jimmy cried. He cried on and off all night, and into the sunlight of the new day, wishing to God that Elsa was still with him. He figured out that he was largely at fault.

Around ten o'clock in the morning he felt cried out, and that is when he vowed to get her back no matter what he had to do. It was decided. He would win her back. No matter what.

8

Seth woke up in his old room, to his childhood alarm clock. Bright sunbeams shot through the window. It was easy to wake—he was excited. He walked downstairs. His parents were still sleeping as he quietly made his toast and coffee. He showered, made sure to grab any boat gear that wasn't already on board, and walked down to his parents' dock.

The boat was roughly the size of a lobster boat. He rowed to it in the tender.

He tied the tender to the stern with a tow-rope and turned the keys in the ignitions. The two four-cycle engines roared to life as small streams of cooling sea water jettisoned out their sides. He climbed to the bow and unhooked the mooring line, jumped back to the captain's console and quickly cracked her into reverse—moving the boat's whirring motors away from the mooring line and buoy, while turning her in the direction of the Village, toward Foy's Boatyard—the biggest boatyard on the island, and the only place a boat could gas up.

He gunned her full-speed ahead. It was a perfect summer morning and the ocean was calm.

When he had the boat docked and tied at the boatyard, Foy walked out and gave him the gas pump nozzle.

They stood together as the tank filled. "I'm up for two hundred today, Foy."

"Sounds good. So, where are you headed?"

"Oh, to... just out with friends, toolin' around, is all."

"Nice day for it." Foy saw that Seth was lying, but figured it was none of his business. He finished putting exactly two hundred dollars worth of gas in the tank, collected payment, and went back inside to work on a wooden skiff he was building from scratch.

Seth untied the boat from the dock and set out for Edna Black's, amazed at how much he was looking forward to seeing her. "Such a nice lady," he thought. "Nicer than Nana even!"

CHAPTER 6:   Waiting

1

Dan hadn't gone home. He'd trudged painfully to Edna Black's beach in the dark of night, taken off his clothes and dragged his pulsating head into the cold ocean. He floated in the water just offshore, hoping the headache would dissipate. The black-eyed gull stood on the beach staring. He stared back into its sharp eyes.

After two hours, his headache began to diminish. When the first light of dawn splashed the eastern sky, the gull flew off. Dan's pain seemed to fly off with it. He swam to shore and walked out of the frigid water.

He looked down at his boil—it had gotten smaller. "Ahh, the healing power of salt water," he said aloud while looking up at Edna's house for any sign of life. Nothing.

He let his naked body dry as he sat on the smooth beach stones. When he heard the first lobster boat leaving the Village for a long day at sea, he threw his clothes on and walked to Edna's kitchen door. He put his hand up to knock, then thought otherwise and quietly walked in.

Shadowless pre-dawn light lit the inside of the house as he shuffled around the living room aimlessly, eventually planting himself in front of the Black Island picture. He stared at it for an hour.

The whirring sound of an approaching motorboat knocked him out of his trance. He walked to the front windows and saw the boat was already anchored and Seth was rowing the tender to shore.

He walked to the foot of the staircase and called, "Gra— Mrs. Black?!! Mrs. Black?!" Nothing. He ran through the kitchen and outside into already-hot morning sunbeams. "Mrs. Black?!!" Nothing.

He sprinted to the beach as Seth was landing the tender. "Hi Seth! I don't know where Mrs. Black is, I can't find her!"

"Oh, she's already in the boat, I just brought her out. I came back for you."

Dan saw Edna in the stern, waving. He waved back as happy little fuzzies caressed his innards.

"Let's go, Dan," Seth said.

Dan got in the stern as Seth shoved off and rowed them out.

Edna walked to the port side. "Dan! So nice you are coming! I am always so glad to see you!"

Dan's heart melted. He had a Grammie. His life finally felt whole.

"So nice to be going on this mission with you, ma'am!"

Seth was in "git-'er-done" mode. "Okay Dan, climb aboard and grab this rope."

"Got it."

Seth threw him the other end of the tow rope, secured his end to the eye of the tender and climbed into the main boat. He took the rope from Dan, who stood still, not knowing what to do—he was more in the way than anything. Seth adeptly tied the tow-rope to the stern, then went to the bow and pulled up the anchor by hand. He gunned the engines and they set off for Black Island.

A wind had kicked up while they were anchored, producing burgeoning whitecaps in the deeper waters—where they were headed. It was still a nice day, however, and Seth kept the boat pointed towards High Island, where he'd have to negotiate around dangerous ledges before turning toward Black.

Dan sat next to Mrs. Black. "I didn't see you inside, Gra, Mrs. Black."

"Oh Dan, I saw you staring at the picture of Black Island and didn't want to disturb you."

She was so grandmotherly and perfect! Dan blushed redder than his boil. "Thank you, ma'am."

Seth started to look concerned. "Mrs. Black?"

"Yes, son?"

"The wind is picking up, and it's going to be pretty rough water out by High Island, and even rougher at Black."

"That's alright, son, I have been on boats my whole life. I can take it."

"Okay then. This boat is great in rough water."

The wind blew harder. Clouds began to fill the sky in the direction they were heading. Seth navigated around the dangerous ledges off the southern face of High, and turned straight toward Black.

Edna pointed at Black Island. "There it is, boys! Black Island, here we come! Oh please do something for me, boys, won't you?"

"Of course, ma'am!" Dan replied. "Sure," Seth said.

"I want you boys to picture us landing on Black Island. I want you to picture it in your minds! Picture us walking on Black Island, boys. Can you do that?"

Dan and Seth focused on these images. She studied them intently. "Gooooooood... Very good, boys. We are going to Black Island!"

As they stared at Black, dark clouds formed behind them. Edna was the first to notice. She whipped her head around with the dexterity of a teenager and saw clouds growing directly above them.

Seth and Dan finally turned around and saw the swirling vortex. "Oh, God! We have to turn around, Mrs. Black!" yelled Seth.

"No, son, stay on course."

"But, Mrs..." Seth kept the boat pointed at Black Island, but growing fears and images of being struck by lightning started to dominate his mind. Dan's as well.

"Boys, pleeeease! Picture us landing on Black Island, on a sunny day... Please? For *me?!*"

"Yes, ma'am..." They tried, but thunder cracked right over the boat. "Oh my God! We're going to be killed!"

A huge lightning chain sliced into the ocean fifty feet off starboard. Dan and Seth screamed as Seth turned the boat away from the storm, to the north.

Dan saw the expression on Mrs. Black's face. Was it... anger? "Sorry, ma'am, but us getting killed out here isn't going to help our mission!" he cried over the storm, scratching his boil.

She sat with a stoic expression, as if her face were carved in stone. At that moment, Dan was sure it *was* stone. He involuntarily looked away.

More lightning chains lit into the water behind them. Huge waves tried to topple the boat. It was hard for Dan and Seth to remain upright. They held onto the railings for dear life.

Edna sat.

Seth had navigated in dangerously rough water before, and knew how to keep them afloat by cutting through each attacking wave at the proper angle. But even with his boating prowess, they almost capsized. Edna stayed completely still in her seat, her face as frozen as the Sphinx.

Seth moved the boat away from the storm, toward the other side of Mount Haven.

The waves diminished and the sunlight returned. Seth cut the engines. "Well, that was close…"

The stone-carved expression melted from Edna's face, and a warm, loving expression bloomed. "Oh, boys! That was so exciting!"

Dan and Seth felt so happy and excited. "It sure was!" Dan said, hazily picturing the favorite toys he used to play with in the orphanage.

"What now?" asked Seth.

"Well boys, it's too volatile of a day to try and land on Black Island, so let's head home."

"Yes, ma'am." Seth decided he'd bring the boat around the other side of Mount Haven to Nor'easter Harbor and the Village, then to Edna's; so he pointed it toward an old stone structure called The Monument, which emerged from a swath of dangerous ledges.

The Monument was an ancient warning to all sea vessels of the sharp, hidden ledges surrounding it. Not even the old timers in the Village knew when The Monument was built or who built it, because their grandparents hadn't known. There were many harrowing tales, campfire yarns and myths about The Monument; one was a nursery rhyme still sung to the island children.

Edna knew the true history of The Monument, but didn't care. The only thing that mattered to her was getting onto Black Island and, after her boating experiment with Dan and Seth, she now knew there was only one way to set foot on that "blasphemous" peak.

2

While the black-eyed gull was staring at a submerged Dan in the predawn light, Jon woke on Olias's sofa. He heard something. Something upstairs. "Uh oh…"

He discerned in his half-awake state that it was Olias and Kara making love. He tried covering his ears with pillows and getting back to sleep, but his mind was too active.

He got up—still fully clothed—and walked outdoors. The new day was barely bright enough to read by.

He walked to the beach. A sweet salt aroma hung heavily. He sat at the water's edge and thought about the last few days. He couldn't believe the magnitude of it all. Phenomena that directly defied modern space-age science! Some type of "Star Trek-y" wall of black! Was this a job for Mulder and Scully? For Walternate? For the cast of Haven? Should Stephen King be notified?

Should they go to a national news team with this information, or was it meant only for them? It felt personal... What was the intelligence behind it? "Something that can make other people say whatever it wants, like it did to Old Man Cranchet, is some serious shit," he whispered aloud.

And did it keep those scary-sounding animals from attacking them? What kind of animals are they? What happens to them in the winter?

Jon sat on a flat granite slab that stretched lazily into the Atlantic. Gossiping gulls arced against the blue sky above. One of the gulls saw fit to angrily "nook-nook" at him. "Hey, this is a communal beach!" The gull flew away.

Far off, a lone lobster boat meandered through strands of sea mist connecting the smaller islands. Jon dreamily looked down the coast at the old houses—built in the 1800s—that dotted the shores of Mount Haven, their upstairs windows like knowing eyes, peering across the harbor. And then there were the oldest houses on the island, perched atop the highest cliffs, their topmost attic slit windows gazing outward across the bay like sentinels—watching, knowing, scrutinizing, keeping score.

His eyes melded with these upper-window eyes as he went in and out of a dream state. Odd images and sounds started to flood his mind, then intensify. He went further, reaching his inner self, that place where the conscious mind can't remember what happens while there.

The tide was rising, and a little wave brought cold water under his rear end, shocking him awake. He stood and walked up the beach a little and sat back down. It didn't take long. He fell back asleep.

When he woke, the sun was well up in the sky. He saw dark clouds in the direction of High Island. "I wonder what time it is." He stood, stretched and walked up the beach path to the house, where he found Olias and Kara in the kitchen making breakfast.

Kara smiled. "Good morning, Jon! Like some eggs?"

"Definitely."

"So how long were you down on the beach?" Olias asked.

"A few hours I guess... I fell asleep. Did you guys see those dark clouds off High Island?"

Kara and Olias were surprised. "No!" they replied in union.

They all hurried to the porch and saw the small, far-off patch of blackening sky.

"It's all blue sky everywhere else," Olias said. "That *must* be a Black Island thing!"

At that moment, someone speaking clear as a bell rung through a new, different part of their minds: "—mtooo reports storm crea—" And then it was gone.

"Did you *hear* that?!" Kara asked.

"What *was* that?" Jon wondered.

Olias tried to do the exact impression of what he'd just heard, "Two Reports Storm Creea—!!"

"Maybe the voice has something to do with the storm at Black Island!" Jon said.

Olias turned to Kara and Jon. "Let's get in Ziggy quickly and get a better look!"

Kara turned off the stove. They ran to the beach and hurried out to Ziggy. They left the tender tied to the mooring and jetted off towards High Island. The sky was blue, but dark only in the direction of Black. "Holy crap!"

As they got closer, the storm dissipated and the black clouds turned gray, then white. The storm was completely gone in twenty minutes.

"Do you guys see that boat way out there?!" asked Olias.

Kara grabbed the binoculars. "It looks like a lobster boat. But there are so many boats that look like that."

"Olias, how much gas do we have in Ziggy's tank?" Jon asked.

"Oh, shit! I forgot!" Olias took Ziggy's engine down to trolling speed and pointed him back toward the house. "Thanks for reminding me, Jon. We're going to have to go very slow on the way back."

3

Seth brought his father's boat around the point on Mount Haven that led to Nor'easter Harbor and Edna's beach. Edna, Dan and Seth sat quietly as the motor droned. Dan couldn't resist the occasional glance at his "Grammie," who sat perfectly still with a little smile. Oh, how he loved her.

By the time they rounded the point, there wasn't a cloud in the sky.

For Dan and Seth, it felt right to be quiet, because Edna made sure they didn't talk and annoy her. She was angry. She wanted to kill weak human Olias and his little friends. She wanted the power of the Great Crystal. She should have ruled the Earth with its power epochs ago, and this time she would.

She spoke as an old, feeble, human woman would speak. "Oh, boys, help me into the tender when we are anchored off my beach, please."

"Of course, ma'am." Seth brought the boat to Edna's beach and threw anchor. They helped her stand up and disembark into the small boat, then rowed her ashore.

"Boys, I wish to be alone to phone old friends. I will call you when we need to go out in the boat next, okay?" They agreed without a thought.

She walked up the path and into the house as Dan robotically marched to his car and drove off. Seth rowed back out, pulled up the anchor to see he'd caught a starfish, threw the starfish back into the sea, fired the engines and set course for his parents'.

Edna walked out of the house and jumped down the well.

When Dan walked into his apartment and looked around at all the pictures he'd put on the walls over the past year, he felt a piercing soreness below his navel. He ran for the bathroom. The boil had doubled in size and was throbbing. Gelatinous goo festered off in sheets. It smelled like rotten eggs and burning flesh. A monstrous headache stabbed his brain as he lurched into the shower. He stayed under the water for hours, long after the hot water was gone.

4

Gumtooo knew it was able to send a few *more* words into the minds of the new people, but still considered itself a failure, because its telepathic abilities had grown so weak. Perhaps it could send a full sentence in its next attempt.

Gumtooo was pleased that the weather-security-forces of the Great Crystal still worked. The threat from the Oldest Evil had been easily averted. At least, this time.

Gumtooo thought that it was finally time to exercise its mind. It was time to reread some ancient books from the Great Crystal's catalog. Perhaps reading would strengthen its telepathic sending abilities.

Gumtooo chose to read two "newer" books—somehow entered into the Great Crystal's database long after the destruction: Plato's "Timaeus" and "Critias," written in the Fifth Century B.C. Gumtooo surmised that these were two of the last books ever written containing knowledge of the Ancients. Gumtooo wondered how those books got there. Apparently, there were some things of which Gumtooo had no knowledge...

Gumtooo read at the same pace a human reads. That's why it was so good at telepathy. It thought in the same mode as humans. And it was time to think that way again. No more shutting down for epochs just to exist. It was time to come fully alive.

Gumtooo wondered how many great books had been written in later years, and thus were not contained in the database. Perhaps if it became friends with these new people, they would help enter these new books into the library.

Gumtooo wondered if the ancients—who had to flee during the final destruction—really *did* construct those pyramids around the globe like they purported they would. Perhaps there were many new books in the databases of those pyramids, if they were ever built.

Gumtooo was coming alive.

5

Olias, Kara and Jon walked lazily up the beach path. Cicadas trumpeted in the surrounding scrub, proclaiming that the dog days of summer had begun. The rickety screen door squeaked on its hinge and slammed behind them as they entered the house. The trebly cicadas could still be heard through the windows and walls.

Jon sat at the kitchen table. "So, what next?"

Olias plopped down onto the floor—right in the middle of the room—with a sad look in his eyes. "It's back to work for the week..."

Kara playfully jumped into his lap and grabbed ahold of his chin, forcing his lips into a smile. "Look! He's happy! He's happy!"

This made Olias laugh. "Ha ha ha! Yeah, not really looking forward to sanding the hulls of boats while all this Black Island craziness is waiting for us."

"Luv, how do you think *I* feel?! I have to work *in a couple hours!*"

"Yeah, I hear you, luv."

Jon was quiet, wishing they could go to Black right away.

Kara stood. "What say we finish making our breakfast, which we shall now officially refer to as lunch?"

"Sounds good, luv."

Kara started clanging pots and pans as Olias remained on the floor. Jon got up and walked slowly to the porch, where he sat and stared off into the islands. Something was wrong, but he couldn't feel what.

What he didn't know was that there were eyes watching him. Hidden behind an old, forgotten well on Olias's property, ancient eyes hated him.

Kara called from the kitchen. "Jon?! How many eggs do you want?"

"Two. Thanks, Kara."

"Sure."

Olias got up and nuked some bacon in the microwave— they liked their bacon as crunchy as possible—and made toast. Together, they had lunch prepared in ten minutes. They walked it out to the porch and ate.

Edna Black watched from the shadows.

Kara got ready and drove to work. Olias and Jon spent the afternoon discussing all the Black Island possibilities. Jon left around six o'clock for his apartment. Olias spent the night on the sofa, reading and watching TV. When Kara got out of work, she drove home and went right to bed. All three were very tired and went to sleep early.

6

The thing that sometimes pretended to be Edna Black whisked to and fro in the underground tunnels beneath Mount Haven. The humans didn't know about this maze of catacombs beneath their feet.

A few times each year, she would take the form of a beautiful woman and roam Main Street, looking for victims. She would find the right man—someone kind. (She could assess the aura of any human to see the amount of kindness contained within, which she considered weakness.) The victim had to be married or at least have a steady girlfriend. She would flirt with him, in hopes of turning his aura darker. Sometimes this took weeks, sometimes minutes.

She would lure men away from their girlfriends or wives, then turn on them, saying that they were ugly and not man enough for her, feeding off their resulting insecurity and fear. Then she'd leave them.

It was a hobby.

7

The hot water long gone, Dan stood in the cold flow and scraped his body raw, fighting the creeping realization of who and what he was becoming. After another hour, he turned off the water and got out.

He couldn't stop thinking about Olias. Grammie wanted him to go on a mission and take from Olias. Take his very essence. Zap him of his happiness, peace and prosperity. And *grow* as a result. But, how? Dan thought maybe he should befriend Olias, pretend to be his buddy, then fuck him the fuck over. "I could steal his bitch and show her what a real man is," he thought while shaking.

He calmed down for Grammie's sake, and began to formulate a plan to become Olias's "friend." He was so clever, it had to work! Maybe he could just show up at Olias's door? No, that might be too obvious... He had to be invited. It had to make sense...

He didn't know anyone in Olias's circle, or that bitch's circle, or that other ass's. What was Olias into? Boating. They played that band Yes, but he hated that band. The music was too confusing.

"I guess I have to make contact with one of them somehow, and turn on the charm," he said out loud. "I'll go to the See Food when that bitch is working. That's a good place to start."

After applying half of a tube of zit cream to his boil, he dressed and drove to the See Food.

Because it was a Sunday night, the place was dead. Kara had already gone home. He walked up to the bar and sat on the center stool. Olias, the asshole friend and the bitch were nowhere to be seen. The only other people at the bar were a man and a woman. They looked like a summer couple, sitting and having dinner.

Since it was a slow night, Todd was managing *and* bartending. He finished washing a few glasses by hand, dried his hands with a bar towel, flung the towel over his shoulder and approached Dan. "What'll you have?"

"I'll have a Bud."

Todd reached into the cooler and grabbed one. "Glass?"

"No," he said condescendingly, and couldn't wait to deliver his big line, "It's already *in* a glass."

"Ha," Todd chuckled weakly. He'd heard that one a billion times. "I hope I don't have to talk to this dork," he thought as he started walking away.

"So..." Dan began.

Todd stopped in his tracks and walked back.

"Pretty slow tonight," Dan said with a forced smile.

"Yup. Sunday night."

"What type 'a people usually come in on nights like this?"

Todd thought this question odd. "Well, same as any night, really. Some locals, some tourists. A few dinners, a few drinks, we close early."

"Ahhh." Dan couldn't come up with anything else to keep the conversation going and sat silently looking at Todd in hopes *he* would.

Todd took the initiative. "I've seen you before. You live in town, right?"

"Yup. Lived in town now for about a year."

"Well then, I'm surprised you don't know what a Sunday night at the See Food Bar and Grill is like."

"Oh, ha. Yeah, I don't eat out much."

"I see. Well, if you want anything to eat, here's a menu." Todd grabbed a menu from the stack and placed it near him.

"Thanks."

"Sure." Todd pretended to be busy by moving something under the bar, then walked into the kitchen—always a welcome sanctuary at times like this.

Dan drank his beer. There was a sports game on TV—he didn't notice which sport. He looked around the restaurant, scanning everyone's face. He knew none of these people. He was wasting his time and money. And didn't he have to work in the morning? "Shit! I forgot about work." His boil pain flared. "Ow!"

He plopped three one-dollar bills on the bar, chugged the rest of his beer and walked back to his car. He got in and sat in the dark, watching the restaurant. After fifteen minutes, not one person had entered or left.

The boil under his navel was burning and smelling even worse. He figured it was time for another shower. There might even be a little warm water in the beginning.

He drove to his apartment and undressed. The acrid stench from the oozing boil burned his nostrils. He jumped in the shower and started scrubbing and scraping. "Fucking spoiled rich boy piece of shit—I'm taking everything that's yours, because I deserve it all, you fucking cock!" he barked loudly under the water.

He scraped his skin so hard that he bled. When he went to bed, he got under the covers and spotted the sheets red. His boil grew, producing sheets of viscous goo that soiled the air.

8

Bob sat at his desk in his apartment. He thought about how his wife had gotten fat after having their children. He hated that. "Fat chicks suck," he said aloud.

This whole Stacy thing was coming together. This had been the plan all along: get far away from the wife for over half the year and bag a hotter chick.

"So far, so good," he thought, and smiled.

CHAPTER 7:   Rejection

1

Olias gazed dreamily at the island cluster while hand-sanding the hull of an old wooden sailboat that looked like it was built in the 1400s. Jon was at the other end of the boatyard, applying bottom paint to a fairly new motorboat.

Old Man Cranchet hobbled up to Olias. "Good work, son!"

"Thanks, Mr. Cranchet."

"Hey, I um, just wanted to thank you."

"Thank me?"

"Yes, for convincing me to hang out with my oldest and best friends instead of worrying about finishing the Stewart boat this weekend. It was the best decision I've ever made, and the Stewarts didn't even care that their yacht wasn't ready yesterday!"

Olias tried hiding his surprise. "...You're welcome, Mr. Cranchet."

"It was so nice to reconnect with the old fellas! And we're going to get together a lot now. Next Saturday we're having a drink-'n-sleep-over, like we used to, back when we were young."

"Wow, Mr. Cranchet, that's really awesome."

"Great job on the hull!"

"Thanks."

Cranchet limped into the boathouse as Olias stared in the direction of Black Island, which was out of sight. He tried to send a thought to Black Island, or to whoever was sending the mental messages. He polished his thought and tried to send, "I don't know who or what you are, but thank you."

He waited. There was no response.

Jon finished applying the marine paint and got out from under the boat as Jimmy's friend Shep walked up. "Hey there."

"Hey Shep."

"So, what you doin' this weekend?"

"I think I'm going up to camp."

"With your buddy Olias?"

"I don't know. Why?"

"Well, I was thinkin' of havin' a party, just wonderin' what yooz two was doin' is all."

"Thanks Shep, if we aren't going, I'll let you know."

"Yup," he grunted while walking away.

Jon walked right to Olias. "I'm thinking Shep might have been on that boat that stirred up the storm off Black Island."

"Oh? Why?"

"He pretended to invite me to a party, but was clearly only looking for information about what you and I are doing next weekend."

"Oh yeah? Let's keep an eye on him."

"Totally."

"Who does he hang with?"

"Hmm... I think he hangs out with that big guy, what's-his-name, the guy with the wild face twitch, the guy who yells at his girlfriend in public, you know... what *is* that dork's name?"

"Oh, right. I can't remember his name either. Wait... *Jimmy.*"

"Right, Shep hangs out with Jimmy."

"Kara can keep an eye on them at the See Food. She'll hear every little thing."

Jon's eyes sparkled. "Yeah, Kara can be talking to a table—taking their order, and hear a conversation in full happening at the bar! Kara's amazing."

Olias was tickled when Jon fawned over Kara, but felt bad for him at the same time. He was so lonely. "Yes she is, my friend. Yes she is."

"Jon?!" It was Old Man Cranchet calling from inside the boatyard.

"Got to go. Keep your eye on Shep."

"You got it. See you after work."

"Yup." Jon hurried into the boathouse as Olias went back to staring at the islands. "Help keep us safe from those who would harm us, please," he tried to send.

2

The first sunlight to hit the contiguous United States every morning graces the Maine islands. In fact, in late June, the first light of day begins in the sky around three o'clock in the morning. But now it was August, with first light around five o'clock.

The See Food was a lunch-and-dinner-only establishment, and as a result, all the employees could sleep in every morning.

Kara slept through the first two hours of August daylight as usual. After waking up at seven o'clock, she showered and slowly got ready for work, then drove to the restaurant.

She walked to a computer and clocked in before starting a pot of coffee. It was going to be a long day. A double. She was about to be running around without a real break for the next thirteen hours.

Todd was the daytime manager. He was in the office making up the server schedule for the week after next. Kara joined him. "Hi, Todd."

"Hi, Kara. How are you today?"

"I'm well, thanks. How are you doing? Teaching Stacy the managerial ropes?"

"Not really. I never see her anymore with our opposite schedules. And we haven't had a sleepover at either of our apartments in a long time. She's always so tired after her shift. It really sucks. At least I've got the night off."

"That's nice. Stacy's managing tonight?"

"Yeah, and probably Bob will be here too, to stand out in the street and flag down potential customers."

"Ha ha. Oh that Bob."

"Oh that Bob indeed. You here for the duration?"

"Yup. Another double."

"I'm glad you're here today, Kara. It makes my job easier."

"Thanks Todd, you're sweet." She went and filled all the sugar-packet containers at the tables, then set about filling all the salt and pepper shakers.

A little later, Manuel entered and started stocking the bar. Kara walked over. "Hi Manuel, are you on a double too?"

"Hi, Kara. No. I'm only going to be working days this week, which kind of sucks, I need to make money."

"Why don't they schedule you at night? You're the best nighttime bartender we've ever had!"

"Todd said that Bob has hired a new bartender and wants whoever it is to learn in the thick of things, on the night shift."

"What?! That's odd... It must be someone with a lot of experience, if they can just come in and start bartending without being trained."

"I guess."

"Sorry, Manuel, I hope you get some night shifts next week. I saw Todd doing the schedule right now, in the office."

"Oh?"

Manuel walked to the office. "Hi, Todd."

Todd was stand-offish. "Oh, um, hi, Manuel."

"Would it be possible for me to get some night shifts next week? I really need the money for bills and school."

"Oh, man... um, Bob said he can't have you on night shifts anymore."

"What?! Why?!"

"I don't know. Something about the new person being able to stay longer in the season, so she gets the nighttime gig. Is it true, that you can only stay until the first week of September?"

"Yes. I have to go back to school."

"Well, you know the season lasts all the way until Columbus Day in October, right?"

"Yes, but Bob assured me..."

"Hey, I get it." Todd dropped his voice to a whisper. "Bob's not the most honorable man when it comes to his word."

"I see that. Thank you, Todd."

"Sorry, Manuel."

Manuel walked slowly back to the bar and started cutting limes.

Jimmy entered—even though they weren't open—and stomped to the bar. "Hey Chico, you seen my girlfriend, Elsa?"

"Who?"

"Forget it, Chico." Jimmy looked around the room and saw Kara folding napkins. "Hey, did you see Elsa this morning?"

"No. Is everything alright?"

Jimmy turned and started marching out of the restaurant while mumbling, "Yeah."

As he walked through the door, Kara whispered, "Asshole."

Manuel laughed. He was glad Kara was working the day shift. "What's wrong with that guy?" he asked.

"I don't know. But he sure has issues."

"I see that."

Bob, who always showed up in the daylight hours to work in the office, never appeared this day. He had demoted Manuel through Todd, and saw no need to see Manuel in person—he wasn't ready with enough lies to deal with Manuel's questioning and pleading. When he was ready, he'd show up. He was glad that no one knew the real reason he demoted Manuel: "Stacy ain't lookin' at him ever again."

Before noon, the summer lunch crowd started entering in droves. Kara and the rest of the servers were very busy and made good money, but not Manuel. It was lunch time—the bar was empty.

3

Jimmy had all but forgotten about breaking into Olias's house and downloading everything off his computer. Lenny had to work on the docks everyday anyway, and all Jimmy could do was think about Elsa. He called off work on the lobster boat, not even caring that the boat captain might end up permanently giving the job to someone else. "Fuck it," he thought, "Some bub'll hook me up with a job if I need one."

And he knew the truth. Elsa had gone to her mother's. He didn't know how he was going to visit her, because the *last* thing he wanted was to see that mother bitch again. *Ever.*

He decided to get in his truck and drive. He drove on the North Shore Road, which led to the South Shore Road, which eventually led to the Middle Road, which led back to the North Shore Road... Jimmy drove in circles around Mount Haven, wishing there was a bridge to the mainland. The ferry made three trips a day, but in the summer the waiting line for vehicles was sometimes twenty-four hours long.

"It's five o'clock somewhere." He pulled out a large flask of cheap whiskey and started downing shots as he drove increasingly fast. "Fucking bitches." He saw a female deer on the side of the road eating apple leaves, slowed down and drunkenly yelled to her, "They're all fucking bitches! Only good enough to fuck!" The deer darted into the woods.

He kept driving and drinking past dusk, thinking only of Elsa. Finally, he couldn't resist. He swerved into the Village—to the little road that went to Elsa's mother's.

He didn't want Elsa—or especially the bitch mother—to see his truck. He knew Elsa might even hear it and know it was his. She knew just how it growled. "It's a fuckin' *man's* truck," he often boasted.

He parked in the shadows a couple blocks away. Flask in hand, he walked down the dark street. One house down from Elsa's mother's, a lone street light shone into a tree and created a web of shadows on the ground. That's where he went.

He crouched down and got a good look at the house. Many of the windows were lit up, and he was pretty sure he knew which upstairs room was Elsa's. She had shown him a year before, but he'd just wanted to get the hell out of that mother-bitch's house. "It's *that* room on the side! Or, wait... maybe it's *that* room there..."

He had nowhere to go and nothing to do, so he stood in the shadow web and watched. And drank.

Half an hour later, the light in a different upstairs room came on, and he saw Elsa through the window. "It's *that* room!" He stared intently, breathing in little bursts, hoping she'd start taking her clothes off. She did not.

For the next hour, he crouched in the shadows of the big tree on the quiet street in the corner of the Village of Mount Haven and spied through the window, watching his former girlfriend walk to and fro. It looked like she was unpacking. Music started to thump and she danced around the room. "She's... happy. It's like she's... celebrating." That hurt.

But, she was in a good mood, and Jimmy drunkenly knew he could always convince her of things when she was in a good mood. He thought that if he could just get her attention, maybe she'd see him and change her mind. See that he cared enough to be outside her window, even at that bitch's house. He stood in the shadows another fifteen minutes while she danced, debating if he should approach her. She started dancing sexily, prompting an erection.

He took the last sip of whiskey from the flask. It was time. He placed the empty flask by the tree, walked to the road and picked up a rock.

He strode three-legged into the bright street light and right up to the house. He stood on the front lawn as she danced, waiting for the song to be over. It seemed to be some long mix, lasting over ten minutes. (He didn't know it, but his phone was ringing back in the truck. It was Bob Lianelli, calling about Olias's computer.)

When the song ended, he launched the rock at the window, hoping she'd hear it, come to the window, and see how much he still cared about her. It was a perfect throw, right at the window.

The window shattered!

Elsa screamed.

He froze.

She ran and hid behind the bed.

He heard her mother yell from downstairs, "Elsa?! Are you alright?!"

She called back, "Someone just threw a rock through my window!"

The outside flood lights blasted the front yard. Jimmy was in the spotlight for all to see. He started running for cover as Elsa's mother opened the front door and saw him. "You better run, Jimmy! I'm calling the police!"

Elsa yelled through the broken window, "It's Jimmy?!"

He saw that the mother was holding something—perhaps some type of weapon—as she watched him run into the web-shadows of the tree.

"You hear me, Jimmy?! You better get out of here right now!"

Neighborhood dogs started barking. He grabbed the flask, but then questioned whether he should be caught holding it. He threw the flask into some bushes, but it landed loudly on a rock, then rolled loudly down an asphalt storm drain. Ding! Ping! Rattle! Ping!

He was frozen with drunken confusion—if he left the shadows he'd be seen clearly. But they already knew it was him...

The mother moved closer. "Jimmy, you better get out of here *now!*"

He stood like a deer in headlights, helplessly frozen. Then he did what came naturally. He started screaming for Elsa. "Elllsaaaaaaa!!! *Ellllllsaaaaaaaaaaaaaaaaaa!!!*"

Elsa yelled back, "Fuck you, Jimmy! You stupid piece of shit! Get out of myyyy liiiiiife!!!"

He just wanted to be held by her.

Now Elsa was at the broken window and could see him. It was now or never. He pleaded, "But Elsaaaaaaa, I.......... *love* yoooooooou!!!"

"Fuck you, you insane piece of shit! Go marry Lenny! *GET! OUT! OF! MY! LIIIIIIIIIIFE!!!*"

Outdoor lights in the neighborhood started snapping on and more dogs were barking.

Elsa's mother wasn't going anywhere. In fact, she'd walked closer and no longer needed to yell. Jimmy thought the weapon in her hands was a rifle.

"You heard her, Jimmy, get out of here, forever."

"You'll regret this, you bitch!" He started running but tripped and toppled headfirst into a storm drain, slicing his face on shards of broken glass.

The mother ran closer, shaking a rolling pin. "Get up and keep running, you scum!"

He got up and kept running. Blood droplets fanned down his face as he reached the truck and jumped in. She ran to the road and stopped, waving the rolling pin in the air. Jimmy, still thinking it was a rifle, hoped she wouldn't shoot out his windshield. He gunned the engine, but uncharacteristically didn't screech the tires or peel out. He drove away slowly in defeat and embarrassment.

Elsa came out the front door as her mother walked back to the house. "Mom?! Is he gone?!"

"Yes, dear, he's gone. He drove off."

"Well, I guess you see why I had to get away."

"Oh Elsa, it's about time you did. He always treated you horribly."

Jimmy drove out of the Village, obeying the speed limit. Blood was dripping and coagulating on his face. He didn't notice.

He fought an urge to go see Lenny, but he'd have to explain what happened, and he wasn't ready to do that. So, he drove home.

He grabbed a glass, filled it with ice, grabbed his big bottle of cheap whiskey and poured the glass full. He sat at the kitchen table with the blood drying on his face and drank. He eventually blacked out, falling in a heap onto the kitchen floor.

He came closer to death that night than he ever knew.

4

Todd was doing the checkouts for those servers only scheduled on the day shift. Stacy was about to arrive to take over the managerial duties. He looked forward to seeing her. Kara was busy taking food orders, bussing tables, taking food to tables and printing computer checks.

Bob was nowhere to be found. He hadn't even returned a call from Todd about an urgent credit card issue.

Todd kept glancing at the door in anticipation of Stacy's arrival.

Soon, Stacy marched into the restaurant, all business. She moved a couple barstools into their proper positions, read a copy of the daily specials, then finally looked up at Todd. "Hey, how's it been today?"

"Pretty slow," he said with a weak smile.

She walked through the restaurant in a beeline for the office, where she fired up the computer and looked at her personal emails.

Todd finished with the final server and walked to the office. Stacy was reading an email from a high school friend and laughing about something he wrote as Todd entered. He walked up behind her and touched the top of her left shoulder. "Hi lover... how've you been?"

"Hey. Not bad. So, nothing to report today, everything running smooth?"

"...Um, sort of."

"Cool."

"I needed to get ahold of Bob, but he hasn't been answering his phone."

"Oh?"

"Yeah, there was a complaint from a customer about their check. It seems that shady older server Paul put a hidden twenty-percent tip on it."

"Oh wow. I'll tell him. Paul needs to be canned. What a creepy douche."

"Totally. So, you think Bob'll be in tonight?"

She hesitated, knowing in her gut that Bob wanted only to see her. "I... guess."

"Well good, as long as you two can handle it."

"Yes, we can."

He kissed her forehead while caressing her shoulders. "I miss you, babe."

"Todd, I'm not in the mood. Please stop."

"Sorry..."

"So, is there anything else I need to know about today's business transactions?"

"No babe, nothing."

"Okay then, you can go. I'll see you soon, Todd."

"….I…"

"Do you have all the checkouts?"

"Yes, they're right here." He handed them to her.

"Thank you. Now go. I have to finish my emails."

"K, bye." Todd walked slowly out of the office.

Stacy knew she was breaking his heart, but figured the quicker the better. It was time to move on. There was a Sugar Daddy now. Movin' on up. To the skyyyyyyyyy! "I'll finally get a piece of the piiiiiiiiiiie!!!"

5

Dan never got out of bed. Horrible images raped his mind as he lay in a state between sleep and whatever Grammie was doing.

The apartment smelled like rotting eggs, excrement and burning flesh. His boil was the size of a golf ball, pumping out huge gobs of putrid goo into the sheets.

In every dream, he saw the boil as a mouth full of sharp teeth, whispering his name while biting and laughing. He screamed as he woke. The stench in the room hit him and he threw up onto his pillow. He tried to get out of bed, but intense pain doubled him over and he fell face first into the vomit.

His eyes rolled up in their sockets.

"Dan?"

"Grammie?"

"Yes, my son. It is your dearest Grammie. *Do* come for a visit right away, please Dan? Do come! It smells like bread and brownies baking here, and I do so wish for some company."

"I'll be right there, Grammie! But what do I do about this boil-mouth?!"

"Just ignore it and come right over. I will heal it for you. We will get you all cleaned up, Dan, my grandson."

"Yes, Grammie!"

He stumbled out of bed and slipped in a puddle of viscous goo on the floor, hitting his head on the side of the door. Pain shot through every muscle in his body as he stood. The boil now felt like twenty bees stinging one spot. He tried ignoring it for Grammie. He threw on some clothes, jumped into his shoes and bolted for the car. He raced to Edna's.

"Slow down, Dan, we don't want people taking notice of you today."

"Yes, Grammie." He drove the exact speed limit to Edna's. Once there, he parked at the old shed and stumbled inside.

There she was, in the kitchen. "Do sit down, my grandson."

He sat on a kitchen chair as she gently lifted his shirt and studied the boil. "Well, Dan... it looks like part of you doesn't like me very much and needs some further convincing."

"Yes, Grammie."

Soothing orchestral music began floating from the living room. It was a song he once knew, a song from his earliest, happiest memories. His body relaxed.

"Lift your arms, Dan."

He lifted his arms like a toddler as she took off his shirt and removed the rest of his clothes.

He saw toys—toys he'd long forgotten. "Red truck!"

"Yes, my son... See the red truck."

"Mommy! Mommy!"

She slowly turned her face away from him. When she turned back around, she had a different face. And body. She was a young, gorgeous woman. "Dan? It's right here, Dan, right here."

She lifted her shirt to reveal ample breasts that smelled of baking bread and chocolate milk. "Oh do eat, Dan, it will make you grow up *strong.*"

He instinctually found a nipple and began to feed. He moaned in delight while suckling the sweet, sweet nipple.

"Yesssssssss, Dan... There you go, my son..."

As he suckled, he felt his insides aligning. He smelled bread, chocolate and cinnamon. His penis was hard. He drank deeply as Mommy's long blond hair spilled over him. She smelled of beach roses and salt air.

He came all over her.

"Yessssssssss, Dan... I will always be here for you, my son."

He gurgled and cooed.

She hand-washed his entire body and shampooed his hair, using the kitchen rinse-gun to wash everything off. "I have your room ready, son."

He wasn't listening. He was feeding and about to ejaculate on her again.

"Alright son, that's all you need."

He stopped and looked up at the now gorgeous young girl, and burped.

"There there, Dan..." She lifted him as though he was light as a pebble and placed him standing upright. "Now, come." She sauntered out of the kitchen and started climbing the staircase.

He clumsily followed, a smile pulling at his face.

Each step she took, she became older, and by the time she reached the top she appeared as the old woman. "This way, grandson."

Still naked, he walked to the top of the stairs where she stood waiting. She pointed to a door at the end of a long, narrow hallway. "There's your room, darling, please get some sleep."

"Yes, Grammie," he blurted in a daze and walked like a ghost to the end of the hallway.

He entered the room. The bed's clean covers were folded open where he needed to slip under them. He immersed himself into his cradle as the sweet music from his babyhood played through the floor boards from below. It all smelled so clean. He fell into the deepest sleep of his life. Then burped.

Edna watched, pleased. "You'll now be completely mine, you puny little thing."

In the flash of an eye, she rocketed out of the house in a black streak and flew down the well—there were soft yet discernible screams of human agony in her wake when she moved at such speeds.

6

Todd had originally thought he'd stay at the See Food after his shift, have a drink, maybe get some hang time with Stacy, watch some TV, talk with friends, whatever. But the way he felt now... He just wanted to cry.

All duties completed, he fought an urge to say bye to Stacy, who was still in the office as if waiting for him to leave. Part of him wanted to *not* say bye—to show her he can be a cold bitch too. But another part just wanted to hug her. Yet, another part wanted to storm into that office and rip her a new one, yelling at the top of his lungs and calling her a bitch.

Todd was a gentle man. A good man. He chose to walk by the office on his way out and float a "See ya" to Stacy, who returned it with a blunt "See ya" of her own. He walked to his car, got in, looked around, put his head on the steering wheel and cried.

Stacy emerged from the office and walked to the front of the restaurant, carrying the dinner-specials sheets for the bar and tables.

Kara had noticed Todd's mood and wanted to ask Stacy if she'd broken up with him, but didn't want to open that can of worms. Stacy was best kept at bay. Kara knew that if she had lied to Todd, she would lie to anyone, and Kara only wanted honest friends.

Stacy started looking at Kara while distributing the sheets. Kara smiled at her, hurriedly wiped down a table and went into the kitchen for a quick bite of anything to hold her over for another hour. She hoped the night would be slow. She didn't care if she made any money; she wanted an easy night with an early close. She grabbed a piece of table bread and buttered it, then walked back into the house.

Bob bounded in the door holding a bag of assorted "fun-size" mini chocolate bars. "Helllloooooo, all!"

The employees gave an overly happy "Hi!" But Kara remained silent, eating her bread.

Bob was in all his glory. "Who wants chocolate?!"

"Me! Me!" cried a few waitresses.

Stacy made sure to hang back. She didn't want anyone but Kara to know of her attraction to Bob. She knew the chocolates were for her. She waited until a few of the girls got their chocolate, and walked up to Bob with a curt and professional air, holding out her hand. "I'll have a dark chocolate bar, Bob."

"Aaaaaand a dark chocolate for Stacy!" Bob also knew not to let anyone see the growing feelings between them and emotionlessly plopped a couple dark-chocolate bars into her hand, quickly moving on to the next person. "Wendy? What's your preference?"

"Peanut bar!"

"Here ya go! Kara?!"

"Umm, I'll have the *Three Musketeers* bar, thanks Bob."

Bob played the role of Santa Claus all the way through the kitchen, making sure all his employees saw what a great guy he was. He retreated into his office and closed the door.

His phone rang. "Hello, See Food Restaurant Bar and Grill! Come see the exact kinda food you wanna see from the sea!!!"

"Hello Bob, it's Edna."

"Mrs. Black!"

"How is that special project going?"

"Well, I haven't heard from my guy yet, but he should be getting that information soon, I'm sure."

"Please tell him to hurry, Bob. I wouldn't want to have to go to someone else for this."

This stung him at a level he hadn't known existed. "Uh—of course you won't, ma'am! No, no, no! We'll get this done for you, I promise!"

"Oh Bob, you're such a dear, thank you so much, son."

"Thank *you* ma'am!" he said as she abruptly hung up. For twenty seconds, he sat staring straight ahead, his face shining with a crazy glow. Slowly, the glow dissipated into a scowl. "Fucking asshole Jimmy."

He dialed Jimmy's cell. This was right at the time when Jimmy was approaching Elsa's window from the shadows of the tree—his phone was sitting in the passenger seat of the truck.

"Fucking asshole!" hissed Bob as he slammed the phone down.

7

Seth was enjoying sleeping in his old bed lately, even though he shared an apartment in the Village with a friend from high school. He didn't mind hanging out and watching TV with his parents, either. They'd always been good to him, and now that he was grown up, none of those pesky problems with his combative youth gummed up the relationship. So together the three sat, watching the new Melissa Joan Hart and Joey Lawrence show, *Melissa and Joey.*

"I love Joey Lawrence!" his mother said.

"That Melissa girl ain't so bad," his father added.

"The teenage girl looks like the main actress on *Haven*," Seth observed.

They laughed along with the live studio audience.

During promos for other shows, such as *The Wizards of Waverly Place* and *The Suite Life On Deck* with Zack and Cody,

Seth's mom had an idea. "Seth, what do you think about us inviting Edna Black to dinner some night this week?"

"Sounds like a great idea!"

"I'd like to meet her as well," his dad added, "She sounds like quite a nice old lady."

"She is! I can call her and ask. What night do you want to have her over?"

"Give me a couple of days to prepare, so any night starting on Wednesday would be good."

"Okay." Seth whipped out his cell and dialed. After six or seven rings, he was about to give up.

Then she answered. "Hellooo?"

"Hi Mrs. Black, this is Seth!"

"Oh hello, son, how are you, my dear?"

"I'm great. I'm here with my parents. My mom was wondering if you'd like to come to dinner here on Wednesday or Thursday night?"

Without skipping a beat she replied, "But of course! I will see you Wednesday night. What time should I arrive?"

"Mom, what time should she arrive?"

"Tell her any time after six o'clock."

"She says anytime after six o'clock, Mrs. Black."

"Good! I'm going to be visiting friends nearby. I'll see you then."

"Great! Bye, Mrs. Black." Seth put his phone away. "How about that? It sounds like she's really looking forward to it."

"So nice to make an old woman happy," his father said, while watching a promo for *Hannah Montana*.

Seth's mom put hand to chin. "Hmm, so, what should I cook for the big dinner?"

Seth wanted to impress. "How about surf and turf?"

"Well, for the occasion, I think it's a grand idea," she agreed. "Lobster and steak it is!"

They went back to watching their show.

The thing that said she was Edna Black chuckled. All she wanted to do was serve a little annoyance and pain to these humans and ingest the resulting anger and fear. She knew how.

8

Monday night came to a close on Mount Haven. Kara's double wasn't too stressful, and she got home at a reasonable time, watched a little TV, talked with Olias on the phone for an hour, read some of a romance/mystery novel in bed and slid into a deep sleep. Olias's night was similar. Jon drank too much whiskey while watching TV in his apartment and threw up in the sink. It sobered him up enough to get a decent night's sleep.

Dan had gone to sleep in the afternoon in his new bedroom at Edna Black's, and was still asleep.

Seth and his parents moved on from watching ABC Family to the actual ABC—police procedural shows. Afterwards, he went to sleep in his childhood bed, which his mom had made sure was freshly laundered. He woke up around two o'clock in the morning and happily pigged out at the full fridge.

Todd tossed and turned all night, achieving only tiny pockets of disjointed sleep.

Stacy finished all the server checkouts and jumped on Facebook, hoping her goading of Bob to finally get on Facebook worked.

Bob went home and tried getting on Facebook, but couldn't figure out how, and spent the rest of the night coming up with a lie as to why he didn't.

Jimmy lay on his kitchen floor with blood all over his face, barely alive.

Lenny happily watched his little-boy shows.

Old Man Cranchet had dinner with one of his oldest friends and dreamt happy dreams for the third night in a row.

The thing that called itself Edna Black bandied to and fro in the catacombs beneath Mount Haven, never at rest, never at peace.

Gumtooo read book after book—ancient tome upon ancient tome. It knew the next attempt at telepathy with the new people would yield superior results. Its mind and spirit continued to grow.

And on the other side of the wall of black, a few more little lights snapped on in the inner chamber of the Great Crystal.

CHAPTER 8:   Home Sweet Home

1

Dan woke to find himself immersed in the fluffiest, driest, cleanest bed he had ever been in. It was daylight. A gentle ocean breeze wafted through an open window, breathing thin white curtains in and out. The only two sounds were the waves on the beach and the rustling of leaves in the trees. His eyes searched the pretty room for a clock or any timepiece, to no avail. All he knew was that the sun was high in the sky.

He didn't want to get out of this bed. He didn't want to think about anything. He wanted to lie in it forever, and fell back asleep.

He woke later, at night. Moonlight streamed through the pretty white curtains. Gentle waves lapped at the beach stones. A lone cricket chirped softly, its song blending with the wind and waves. He fell back asleep.

He woke. It was daylight again, another pristine summer day. He was about to fall back asleep, but something stopped him. A hole in his stomach. He was ravenous. He hadn't ever felt this hungry in his life—not even when he was living in the woods with no food.

He sat up, stretched and left his fluffy healing spot. He walked to the open bedroom door and peeked out. "Grammie?" Nothing.

He walked through the thin hallway and down the creaky staircase to the kitchen. There was a note on the table.

"Dan, I thought you might be hungry so I left you some sandwich fixings and bread in the fridge. I'm visiting friends and might be gone quite a while. Make yourself at home, son!"

He blasted into the fridge, grabbing all the fixings. He erected a large stacker and attacked it, eating almost without chewing—like a lizard swallowing a large bird egg. He constructed and ate a second. Then a third. He was thirsty. There were many options—juices, sodas, even beer. One container had a strip of tape with writing—"Edna's milk." He grabbed some lemonade, filled the big empty glass on the table and chugged.

Sated, he sat down at the kitchen table and belched the loudest burp his body had ever produced. He felt a pleasant equilibrium. He had never felt this good. "I should do something nice for Grammie." He cleaned the kitchen and walked outside to check the lawn. It was a hot, sunny day, but a cooling wind was coming right off the cold ocean. The lawn wasn't very overgrown—waiting a few more days to mow would be the norm—but a good mowing *would* improve it, and his heart was completely devoted to helping his Grammie; so he marched to the old shed, pulled out the ancient mower and mowed as immaculately as he could, making sure every little blade was manicured to perfection. He even did some by hand, with tiny scissors.

From inside the house, an old rotary-dial phone blared. He went in. The dusty phone sat on a rickety wooden table at the foot of the staircase. "Hello? Black residence!"

"Hello? Dan?"

"Seth! Hi, how are you?"

"Great. I just felt a real urge to call Mrs. Black just now. Just checking in."

"Well, Gra—Mrs. Black isn't here right now. I'm mowing the lawn. I moved in!"

"Wow, you live there now? Nice." Something inside Seth already knew this.

"Yeah man, this place kicks ass!"

"Hey, you know what? I need to go check on my apartment in the Village... What say I swing by?"

"Sounds good, my brotha-from-anotha-motha. See you soon!"

"K, see ya."

Dan returned to his individual-blades-of-grass care as Seth drove to the apartment he'd been neglecting. He parked and walked up the outside steps to the second floor loft. While unlocking the door, he looked down into the woods behind the backyard and saw an old well. "I've never noticed that before."

He put his hand on the doorknob and froze. His eyes rolled up in their sockets with a gurgle. He stayed frozen for a few seconds, then his eyes returned and his body relaxed.

He turned the knob and walked in. "Hello?!" His roommate was gone. He bolted out the door and down the steps, grabbed an empty trash bag from the car, ran back inside and started packing his things. He didn't think about why he was doing this.

126

He gently placed the full bag in his backseat and drove to Edna Black's.

He parked while Dan was mowing. "Hi, Seth!"

"Hi, Dan!" Seth took his bag into the house. Dan didn't think twice about this personal affront to his territory because it felt right.

Seth brought the bag into the living room and placed it on the sofa, then sat in a chair with a view of the Black Island picture. He stared at it, waiting.

Dan was busy tending to some weeds near the kitchen door and didn't notice Edna snake up from the well. She walked up behind him. He twirled. "Hi, Grammie!"

"Hello, son." She walked into the house as Dan started whistling while he worked.

Seth sat waiting. "Hello, Mrs. Black."

"Hello son, you may call me Nana."

"Yes, Nana!"

"Now let me show you to your room, son."

"Thank you, Nana!"

He followed her up the creaky stairs and through the narrow upper hall to the room across from Dan's, his face contorted in a gross smile.

She stood in the doorway smiling demurely. "There you go, son. You'll always be safe here."

"Thank you, Nana, for letting me come home."

"You're welcome, dear."

He sat on the bed, his eyes jumping like he was being shocked by a car battery, not noticing that the thing that called herself an old woman had rocketed back downstairs in the form of a black energy streak.

"Home sweet home!" he screamed.

2

Jimmy woke on his kitchen floor in a pool of puke, urine and diarrhea. Caked blood lay spider-webbed across his face. "Smells like Lenny's place," he thought.

He slowly got to his feet, teetered, and almost fell back down with a splash.

He shuffled toward the stairs, dripping a most heinous liquid onto the carpet. His head beat like a timpani drum in tandem with his heartbeat. He slowly climbed the stairs. The loud creaking ripped into his ears.

His heartbeat *was* his head... The blood in his veins seemed to be boiling. He got to the bathroom, turned on the shower and got under the water fully clothed. "Ahhhhhhh..." He slowly took off his clothes under the water.

He ached for Elsa.

Once clean, he got out of the shower and dried his body by aimlessly walking around the apartment naked. He'd stop and stand in spots, staring at nothing with cloudy eyes, deep in remorse.

The phone rang—Elsa?! "Hello?!" It was Lenny.

"Hey there, Jimmy, how you doin' today?"

"Pretty good," he lied. "Just woke up."

"Well, guess what? They gave me the day off!"

"Oh, wow." This news slowly seeped into him, as did the possibility of what they could do with their day.

"Yeah, Jimmy, we can break into Olias's house today and record what's on his computer with Bob Lianelli's device!"

"Okay, Lenny, I just woke up is all. Lemme get dressed and call you back."

"Okay, Jimmy."

Jimmy put on fresh clothes and set about the unpleasant task of cleaning the sections of floor he'd soiled. Afterwards, he called his buddy Shep at the boatyard.

"Yo Jimmy, what up?"

"Hey Shep. Was wonderin', is that faggot Olias and his fag friend workin' there today?"

"Yup, they are, Bub."

"Good. Call me if you lose sight of 'em."

"You got it, Bub."

Jimmy called Lenny. "Lenny, it's a go. We break in today."

"Good! When should I drive over and pick you up?"

Jimmy wondered if he was hungry and the pain inside him said he was not. "Anytime, Lenny. Let's get this job done so we can get paid by Lianelli."

"Be there in a few."

Jimmy continued to walk around the apartment in a daze, waiting for Lenny's knock. Soon Lenny was there, and they set off in Lenny's beat-up car for Olias's.

"So, how do we do this, Jimmy?"

Jimmy's head was still pounding, but he didn't want Lenny to know. "We park out in the street. You wait in the car as a lookout. I walk up to the house and ring the bell or knock on the door or whatever, acting like a guy goin' to visit him if anyone's lookin.' We make sure no one's lookin.' I then credit-card my way through his front door, go to his computer, download all the shit on there with this thing, then I get the fuck out of there and we drive to the See Food and give it to Lianelli and get our money."

"Sounds good, Jimmy." Lenny turned onto the smaller back road that led to Olias's.

Jimmy smirked, already feeling more himself. "We'll get all the dirt on this transplant fag. I wonder what shit this asshole is into."

"Probably doin' it with animals and shit!" said Lenny.

"Ha ha yeah! Park here."

Lenny parked. Jimmy dialed Shep.

"Hey Jimmy."

"Yo. You still lookin' at the transplant fags?"

"Yeah Bub."

Jimmy hung up. "Okay, I'm goin' in. Keep a look out for *anyone* Lenny, and call me right away if you see anything."

"You got it, Jimmy."

Jimmy walked up the road to Olias's as Lenny looked to and fro from the driver's seat. Jimmy saw no one and approached the house as though he was going to knock on the front door. He figured he'd try the door handle just in case the door was unlocked. *It was!* "Ha! What a dick!" he laughed as he entered the house, quickly shutting the door behind him.

He looked around and found the computer in the living room. Even a monkey could operate the jump-drive device Bob Lianelli had supplied, so Jimmy dumped all Olias's files onto it. "Fucking chump," he hissed. He removed the device and walked back to the car. "Let's get to the restaurant and give this to Lianelli."

"You got it, Jimmy."

It was a little past two o'clock in the afternoon—always a lull in the restaurant. Todd was tending bar, which meant he was watching TV. Kara had a couple low-maintenance four-tops.

Jimmy and Lenny sauntered in and sat at the bar. Jimmy always did the talking. "Hey there. Is Bob in?"

"What a couple of boring tools," Todd thought. "He's in the office."

"Well? C'mon! Get him. Now. Tell him Jimmy's here."

"Asshole," thought Todd. "Okay, hold on."

Todd walked to the office where Bob sat doing paperwork (illegally fudging the books by switching around money from three different accounts, after having used cash for certain expenses such as payroll). "Bob? That guy Jimmy and his buddy Lenny are here, and they want to see you."

"Tell them they can come back here. I'll see 'em in here."

This surprised Todd. "Um, alright…" He walked back to the bar. "Bob says to go see him in his office."

Jimmy and Lenny walked into the kitchen for the very first time. They didn't know which way to go. Jimmy walked up to Scott the cook, who had a couple burgers on the grill. "Hey, where the hell's the office?"

"It's right there," Scott replied, pointing and thinking what an ass this guy was.

"This way, Lenny."

"Yes, Jimmy."

Jimmy "rhinoed" through the kitchen, Lenny navigating his wake.

Bob looked up from the books. "Hey there, you two. Close the door behind you there, huh? Huh?!"

Jimmy and Lenny crammed into the tiny office. Lenny closed the door.

Bob put his ledger in a drawer. "You got the goods?"

"Yes we do, Bob. Here." Jimmy handed him the device.

"Good work, boys. When I confirm that all of Olias's info is on this thing, you get paid."

"But… can't we get paid now?"

"No. Now get out of here."

Jimmy and Lenny stayed.

Bob was annoyed. "C'mon, get out of here. People will get suspicious."

"Okay, but we need to get paid soon, Bob."

"Yeah-yeah, don't get your panties in a bunch."

Jimmy and Lenny left.

"Inbred hicks," Lianelli said under his breath.

The two walked through the kitchen and back to the bar.

Todd wondered why they had met with Bob in his office. "So, what can I get you guys?"

"I'll have a beer."

"Me too."

Todd grabbed them a couple Buds, popped the caps and placed them on the bar. "There you go. So, what business do you guys have with Bob?"

Jimmy looked down at the bar. "Oh, nothin'. He told us he might know a place we can rent, 'cuz we're startin' a business. A bait store."

"We're startin' a business?" Lenny blurted.

Jimmy was dumbfounded by Lenny's stupidity. "Yeah Lenny, I tol' you..."

"Oh... right. We're gonna make some serious coin."

Todd stared at them, amazed. "I'll keep my ears open too."

Jimmy ignored him.

Lenny thought he'd change the subject to smokescreen the situation and pointed at Todd. "Hey Jimmy, look at this guy, looks like he got some guns under that shirt there."

Jimmy looked at Todd's arms. "You the big man now?"

Todd hadn't thought he could get more amazed at these idiots, but he'd been wrong. "Um... no, no guns."

"Yeah, well, Jimmy here's got major guns, bigger than yours. Jimmy spars wit' a professional wrestler in Ellsworth and shit. Tell him, Jimmy."

"Yup, I do."

"Wow." Todd couldn't walk away fast enough. "That's great. Pretty cool there." He all but fled to the kitchen.

"What a fuckin' tool," Jimmy said.

As Jimmy and Lenny drank their beers, laughter erupted from the kitchen.

3

Olias was sanding the hull of an old skiff as Jon walked over. "Olias, have you noticed that Shep seems to be watching us?"

"No. I can't stop thinking about Black Island. What the hell *is* it all?!"

"I know... I mean, I don't know... but I'm telling you, something feels weird about Shep today. Whenever he looks over at me, it feels... weird."

"What's that about?"

Shep walked around the corner of the boathouse. "So, how yooz two doin' today?"

"Pretty good there, Shep," Jon returned.

"Good, good." He walked away.

"You see that little smile on his face?" asked Olias.

"Yup. It feels like he knows something we don't."

"Well, *let* him know whatever the hell he knows. I know for sure he doesn't know about the wall of black or the extreme powers at Black Island."

"Yeah, that dude can't see past his own wall of boring macho bullshit."

4

Jimmy and Lenny thought that the pursuit of getting under people's skin was clever. They would sit at the bar, waiting for their next victim. Eventually, some male tourist would come in for a cold one. They would try and see a physical flaw in him—baldness, girth, anything—then talk about that thing loudly. They were energy vampires. They loved sucking out the energy that was given to them by someone they made uncomfortable.

So, they stayed at the bar, hoping a victim would join them.

"Jimmy, what did you see on that Olias-fag's computer?"

"Not much. Some pictures, some writing, I don't know."

"Ha! What a sicko!"

5

An idea came to Seth. Was it his own? He didn't care. He got up from his new, clean bed and walked downstairs to the kitchen.

Dan was putting away all the sandwich fixings. "Hi bro. Want a sandwich?"

"No thanks, bro. But I just got a great idea about how to get into Olias's life, bro."

"Oh yeah? What is it, bro?"

"I know this guy named Greg Eating, who's really good at disabling people's boat motors. We get Greg to rig it so that Olias's boat engine dies on him when he's out on the water, and then you and I swoop in on my dad's boat and rescue him! Then, we're working on the inside, bro."

"Nice! That's a great idea, bro. When can you get this Eating dude to fuck up Olias's engine?"

"Well, Eating does what he does at night, and it works the next time the person uses the boat. It usually takes like half an hour after starting for the motor to fail."

"So, all we got to do is make sure we're out in your boat when Olias and his bitch and that dick are out in their boat. We watch 'em from a distance, then swoop in to save them, ha!"

"Yup. Ha."

"So, when do you think they'll go out in the boat next, bro?"

"Probably the weekend. Saturday'd be my guess, bro."

"Me too." Dan finished clearing the kitchen table and didn't notice he'd also wiped it down thoroughly with a moist rag. "So, how much do we pay this Greg Eating guy to fuck up Olias's motor?"

"Hmm, like, a hundred and twenty-five bucks or so."

"Shit, I'm tapped."

Edna walked in from outside. "Oh, my boys! I forgot to give you your allowance! Here you go!" She handed them each five one-hundred dollar bills.

Dan and Seth were wide-eyed with joy. "Thank you, Grammie!" "Thank you, Nana!"

"You're so welcome, boys, thank *you!*"

Dan was excited about their new plan. "Ma'am, we have a way to get closer to Olias and his evil friends!"

"That's good, boys. I have to go. See you soon. Get some sleep."

"Yes, ma'am!" they chimed in unison.

Edna walked quickly out the door.

"Seth, can you call this Greg guy and ask him to fuck with Olias's motor before Saturday? They might be planning on going to Black Island on Saturday."

"I'll call him right now, bro." Seth took out his cell, found Eating's number, and dialed. "Hi Greg, it's Seth."

"What the hell ya doin'?"

"Oh nothin', just hangin' with my bro, Dan. Hey, we got a job for ya if you're into it."

"Oh, yeah?"

"You know that transplant tool Olias, with his little speed boat?"

"Yeah, I've seen that fuckin' asshole around. Thinks he's the shit."

"Ha! Yup. Well, his motor needs a little work…"

"Ha ha ha okay, Seth. That'll be a hunnert bucks for that job."

"Already got it. Can you do it before Saturday?"

"Yup. Consider it done."

"Great. See ya soon, Greg."

"Yup."

Dan was listening intently. "So, it's on?"

"Yes it is, bro. Yes it is."

6

It was Thursday night, almost midnight. Olias sat on the sofa watching Letterman, his eyelids feeling heavy from a long day at the boatyard. The vapid talk from the boring actor promoting a cop procedural show wasn't helping him stay awake. After almost falling asleep twice, he decided it was time for bed.

He snapped off the set and walked slowly up the stairs. Once under the covers, he read a little Stephen King—his favorite—then turned off the light and fell fast asleep.

Meanwhile, about a mile off his beach in deep water, Greg Eating sat quietly in his boat, drifting slowly with the current, all lights and gear turned off. When he saw Olias's final house light go dark, he knew his wait was almost over. He pulled out a foot-long hoagie and devoured it. Eating liked his food.

About forty minutes later, with a hunk of salami in his beard, Eating revved the engine, took the RPM's down to the softest possible trolling speed and slowly made his way toward Olias's beach.

It took fifteen minutes to reach Ziggy at this slow putter. Greg was lucky that the waves hitting the beach were substantial enough to mask the motor sound at first, but soon he had to cut the engine. He used an oar to paddle up to Ziggy. He slowly maneuvered himself around to Ziggy's starboard side—to the gas tank—and unscrewed the cap. From his pocket, he produced a vial of tiny metal filings, which would go through the gas hose into the motor and cause extensive damage. He dropped the filings into the gas tank, screwed the top back on, and let the wind and current slowly take him away.

When he was out of earshot, he revved the engine and set off towards his mooring in the Village. He inhaled his second foot-long sub of the hour. Upon finishing, he fumbled in his jacket for his phone and dialed Seth with greasy fingers.

Dan and Seth were devouring dark hunks of uncooked flesh from a garbage bag in the fridge labeled "Edna's porcupine" when Seth's phone rang.

"Hello?"

"Yo Seth, it's done. That fag's motor is gonna bust next time he goes out."

"Ha haaa! Nice. Thanks, Greg. Where should I meet you with the hundred bucks?"

"How 'bout down at the docks tomorrow around sunset."

"Sounds good, see you then."

Dan was listening while chewing an obstinately sinewy hunk. "So, it's done?"

"Yeah my bro, it's done."

7

Kara was getting home from a hellish thirteen-hour double in which she had only one lone, fifteen-minute break from constant, stressful running to and fro. She fell onto the couch. She almost fell asleep, but there was something she wanted to do first, an idea that had been percolating. She called Todd.

"Hello?" Todd answered.

"Todd? You're awake?"

"Oh, hi Kara, yeah, I'm not sleeping well lately."

"Sorry to hear that. Hey, remember how you told me you were looking for some night shifts? Well, how about you take my Saturday night?"

At this point, Todd didn't know if he wanted to be around Stacy, things weren't going well. It was so uncomfortable... But, he couldn't stay away. He held out hope that their relationship would go back to normal. "Okay, Kara. That sounds good. And I'll see *you* in less than seven hours!"

"Don't remind me."

"Ha ha! Thanks Kara, see you in the morning."

"You mean later *this* morning. See you soon, and thank you."

Kara dialed Olias and got his voicemail. "Saturday to Black Island! It's on!"

8

Friday was a nice day on the islands—mid seventies, sunny, with a cooling ocean breeze. A classic Maine summer day.

Jimmy spent the day working on a friend's lobster boat. He saw Lenny working with bait on the docks.

Bob Lianelli sat in his Village apartment working on the restaurant books, waiting for the night shift to begin so he could see Stacy.

Kara and Todd busted their humps on the day shift. Kara was ecstatic that she had the night off to hang with Olias and the next day off for Black Island.

Todd was hopeful—he'd officially resolved to win Stacy back.

Olias and Jon worked at the boatyard, then, after some time alone, Jon drove to Olias's for a fun porch night of barbeque, wine, beer and Red Sox. Kara joined them around game time.

Old Man Cranchet spent the night hosting a sleepover of his oldest friends.

The thing that purported to be an elderly human female whipped around the dank catacombs beneath the island.

Gumtooo kept rereading the ancient tomes contained in the Great Crystal's library, feeling stronger and happier.

Dan and Seth spent the day cleaning already-clean sections of Edna's house. Dan drove Seth to Seth's parents' place, and Seth took the boat and its tender back to Edna's, where he anchored off her beach.

Near dusk, they drove to the Village docks and found Greg Eating standing by his boat, devouring a pizza—a large pie he'd folded over a few times for easy handling. They walked up to him and were overwhelmed by the stench. The aroma of fresh pizza mixed with Eating's body odor made Dan want to hurl.

Eating tucked the large pie under his armpit and put out his hand.

Seth tried not to breathe. "Here you go, Greg," he said while placing a hundred-dollar bill in Eating's dirty hand. "I'll let you know how it goes tomorrow."

"Yup. Okay then," Eating spat as he chewed, "yooz call me tomorrah."

"We will, thanks."

Dan and Seth briskly walked away until they were out of earshot. "Man, that dude *stinks*," Dan said.

"Yeah, wow... that's just unholy."

They went back to Edna's and set about re-cleaning the already-spotless kitchen.

CHAPTER 9:   Alliances

1

Olias, Kara and Jon had another fun night partying on the porch in the ocean air, even though the Red Sox didn't win. The hate-filled thing spied from the old well and felt their pain at the loss. It tasted scrumptious.

The next morning, Jon woke before Kara and Olias and drove home. After cleaning his apartment and going through some unopened mail, a photograph lying atop his dresser caught his eye. He picked it up and stared into it, reliving the frozen moment. It was the night the Red Sox won the World Series in 2007. He was partying with Olias, Kara and Kara's friends. In the picture were Olias, Kara, himself and Kara's best friend Tawny, celebrating just seconds after the final out. Jon stared at Tawny, as he was wont to do for years. So gorgeous...

He gently placed the photo back on the dresser, gathered all the rope he'd found and drove back to Olias's to find his friends doing just what he'd hoped—making breakfast.

"There you are!" exclaimed Kara, "How many eggs?"

"Two, thanks."

After breakfast, Jon showed Olias and Kara the rope he had brought.

"With all this rope, I could walk across half the island while you hold the other end!" Olias said.

"Yup, I made sure you can go as far into that freaky desert-ground black-universe as possible, to see what that humming thing is."

The day was half cloudy, the ocean calm. The Three Musketeers gathered all the boat gear. They made sandwiches and tucked them into a cooler with beverages. Olias rowed the supplies out to Ziggy, then rowed Kara and Jon out. They slipped the tender into the stern. Jon unhooked Ziggy from his mooring as Olias gunned the engine. They were off.

After navigating around the ledgy section, Olias pointed Ziggy towards High Island. Soon they entered deep water. Seagulls followed for awhile, wondering if there might be food in it for them. Jon thought one of the gulls had really black eyes, but didn't get a good look and forgot about it.

2

Hours earlier, Dan and Seth woke before daylight at the exact same time. They simultaneously stretched in their clean beds. They got up, turned on the lights, got dressed and met in the narrow upper hallway. Dan took the lead as they walked downstairs to the kitchen and made sandwiches.

They ate. A lot. And drank. A lot. Seth was overly partial to the beverage labeled "Edna's milk." They ate ravenously and barbarically, creating stains and spills all over the table and floor. They didn't clean up. They gathered boat gear and marched to the beach.

Edna was nowhere to be found. They didn't question this. If asked, "She's visiting friends," would have been their response.

The first hint of daylight was born in the east—joining the stars and planets in the sky—as the two faux brothers rowed to the boat. Soon they were off, in the direction of High Island.

3

Kara and Jon tied a few ropes together while Olias captained Ziggy towards High Island.

Suddenly, the boat engine roared loudly, emitting a clicking noise. "Shit!" yelled Olias. He took the motor down to a low rumble and tried speeding up again. This time, the clicks got even louder and the motor seized up.

Silence. They were dead in the water.

"What's wrong with it?!" wondered Jon.

"I don't know!"

They sat in silence as Olias turned the ignition key a few times to no avail. "Shit." He looked at Kara. "Pull out the radio, luv, it looks like we have to call for a tow."

"Dude... this majorly sucks," Jon said.

"Tell me about it, that engine ain't cheap."

Kara found the radio in the gear bag and handed it to Olias.

"Look!" said Jon, pointing at an approaching boat.

It was Seth and Dan.

Kara was hopeful. "Maybe they can tow us back."

Seth piloted his craft right off Ziggy's starboard bow, where Olias stood at the steering wheel. "Hi there! You guys alright?!"

"Our motor just conked out. We're dead in the water."

"We're heading back to Mount Haven, where were you guys going?"

"We were going to… High Island, for a hike up Duck Mountain."

"Would you like a tow back to Mount Haven?"

"We'd love one! Thanks. Your timing is amazing."

"Ha, cool. Throw me a rope."

Kara took one of their new ropes and tied it to Ziggy's bow, then threw the other end to Dan, who had been standing as still as a statue and smiling only with his mouth. "There you go," Dan finally spoke, catching the rope and tying it to the stern.

There was ample room for everyone in Seth's boat, so the Ziggy crew disembarked. Seth set course for Mount Haven.

"Thanks, guys," Olias said.

"No sweat," replied Seth, "glad to help out my fellow Mount Haven dwellers. I've seen you three around the island. Hi, I'm Seth."

Kara, who was born and raised on Mount Haven, had of course seen Seth before, but they were a decade apart in age. She didn't remember ever waiting on him at the restaurant. Her only memories of Seth were from childhood. "You went to high school like ten years before me, right? You're from the southern side of the island, and this is your parents' boat, right?"

"Right."

"Well hi, nice to finally meet you for real. I'm Kara." She held out her hand and they shook.

Olias was in a mood to turn a crappy situation into something better. "Hey, we're having a barbeque at my place tonight. Would you guys like to come? The alcohol and food are on me."

"Sounds great!" Dan said, the whole time remembering being hidden behind the tree and watching this hot bitch on the porch. "She thinks she's so much better than me. She'll learn," he thought as he smiled pleasantly at Olias and Jon, never looking at her.

Kara noticed, but chalked it up to shyness. She knew that because she was pretty, guys were often shy in front of her, so she dismissed Dan's behavior.

They all threw small talk into the mix, about the Village news—mainly how more dredging of the inner harbor was needed. Soon they approached Olias's beach. Olias moored Ziggy as Jon and Kara got hold of the tender and slid it into the water. Seth and Dan watched, motionless and emotionless.

"How's seven o'clock sound, guys?" asked Kara.

"Sounds great," replied Seth. "See you then."

Seth and Dan took off around the point as the musketeers rowed ashore. Olias rowed back for the gear after Jon and Kara were on land. They carried the tender above the high tide line and walked up to the house.

"Those guys seem cool," Jon said.

"They're alright, I guess," said Olias.

Kara thought about Dan not looking at her. "Hopefully, they'll be fun to hang with tonight."

4

Todd whistled while he worked. He was on a double, but that didn't bother him, because he'd finally be working with Stacy at night. She'd take over as manager, and he'd step into waiter shoes for the big Saturday night shift. He finally had a good reason to spend some time with her—he was doing Kara a favor, and everyone respected Kara. And everyone respected someone who did favors, right?

Kara hadn't told anyone she had given her shift to Todd. Her name was still on the schedule. Todd erased her name and wrote in his. Stacy would see this right away—the first thing she always did upon arriving for work was check who she was managing that night. And she'd be managing *him* that night. Ha! Todd whistled.

It was a busy Saturday lunch at the See Food, but things ran smoothly. Todd found that he was a little nervous—maybe a lot nervous. He had to show Stacy that he was the man for her. "At least there's no other guy in the picture," he thought. "She's still mine, and I'm keeping her!" A hopeful smile formed on his face as he gathered server checkouts for inspection. He looked at his watch. "She'll be here any minute now."

Stacy entered. His heart skipped. She had her fake Todd-greeting-smile down at this point. "Hi, Todd."

"Hi!" He let her walk into the kitchen and see for herself that he was working the floor. He heard her walk up to the schedule board and stop. He listened intently. He expected her to come back out in surprise—maybe even happy surprise—but he heard her footfalls escape farther back into the kitchen, to the office. This was another knife in his heart. "This isn't right," he thought.

Stacy sat in the office, worried. Her feelings for Bob had grown, and he'd be in soon. She knew she should have officially ended it with Todd. She was hoping her coldness was enough to turn him off—that he'd get the hint. He'd given her a lot of space lately, so she thought it was working and, because of the new schedule, she never had to see him anyway. But she should have expected this. She scolded herself for messing up.

Her eyes wandered across Bob's desk to a bright pink post-it note stuck to the far corner. It was Bob's handwriting—quickly written; his pen had pressed down onto the paper with authority to the point of punching through a few times. It simply said "Olias." The dot above the "i" was a hole. She sat and stared at it. She didn't know Bob even knew Olias. The only interaction she'd ever seen them have wasn't a proper two-way interaction—Olias and Jon racing by the See Food the other day and Bob cursing them out. "Maybe Olias applied for a job here?" she wondered aloud.

She returned to the matter at hand and, in a whisper, pretended to be talking to Todd. "But we haven't even been together for a year!" she pretended to plea. She pictured him being dumbfounded by this logic as she shook her head at him. After the little play in her mind was over, she continued to shake her head at him.

Todd fought the urge to go into the office, but figured the level-headed thing to do was be nonchalant, so he went about his management closing tasks, waiting for her to appear.

She emerged ten minutes later, her fake smile glaring. Another knife. While placing newly printed dinner-specials sheets on the bar and tables, she passed him and said, "So, is Kara alright?"

"Yes. She had plans, and wanted someone to come through for her."

"That was nice of you." She walked away, continuing to place sheets on tables. The route she took through the tables was now slowly bringing her back to him. He stood his ground, waiting.

He was staring at her. She pretended not to know. He stood right in her way, getting between her and the next table on her mission.

"Todd!" she said with a forced playful lilt.

"I think we should talk in the office."

She knew this was coming, and knew the smart thing to do was deal with it. It was time. "Okay, Todd."

They walked to the office and closed the door. She sat at the desk, not looking at him. "So, what's up?"

"What's up?! Seriously?! *What's up?!!* You basically break up with me without breaking up with me, and you want to know what the fuck's up?!" he accused, his voice getting louder.

"Shhhhhh! Don't let anyone hear you! I don't want anyone in the restaurant gossiping about us! Look, Todd... I'm sorry. I haven't known how to tell you... I feel that we need some time apart."

"But why? What did I do?!"

"Nothing, Todd, nothing..." She fought an urge to hurt him—to fabricate something about his personality that would hurt him for the rest of time—but just barely chose not to.

"Nothing?! Then I don't get it. Things were so great between us, Stace..."

"I just don't want to be with anyone right now," she lied. "I need time to be alone. To find myself, you know? Maybe, in the future..." She coldly calculated that it was always good to keep her options open. Hell, maybe Todd would make a lot of money some day. "Todd, who knows what the future will hold?"

"So we're broken up, just like that?!"

"Yes, Todd."

She stood to hug him, but he left before she could. He walked briskly to his car, where he bent down behind the dashboard and bawled.

After five minutes his crying tapered off to a few guttural gulps and sniffs. He blew his nose, dried his eyes, got out of the car and walked back into the restaurant, ready to work this damn shift and hey, maybe even flirt with some girls in front of her, dammit.

Stacy, on the other hand, felt relief. Relief because it was finally over. She almost did a fist pump. But that would be garish and insensitive... Todd didn't deserve that. "He really *is* a good guy," she thought. Fond memories of her past year with him started falling through her mind as she sat at Bob's desk. Todd listening to her all night and consoling her when her grandmother died... She really did like Todd. Her eyes got a little wet, but she quickly dried them and started thinking about Bob's masculine strength, maturity, confidence and money. Those traits in a man are very intoxicating to a girl who grew up dirt poor with flaky hippie parents. "Bob's a *real* man," she thought.

5

Olias was cleaning the barbeque grill, sitting in the grass next to the tree that Dan had clutched and clawed. He saw the marks on the tree and figured they must have been from a rutting deer.

Kara returned from the island store with goodies for the party. "Hi, luv!"

"Hi, luv!" He watched her golden mane float in the breeze as she walked the groceries inside and thought, "I'm going to marry that girl."

She got set up in the kitchen and started preparing food for grilling. Jon arrived with a couple cases of beer and a couple bottles of wine. Olias had music wafting out of the living room as they each set about their separate tasks. Kara sat down at the drums and played to a few songs, even though she was the keyboardist in their burgeoning band.

By six-thirty, they were all congregated on the porch, having their first drink of the night. Olias lit the charcoal. "Our lives aren't the worst, are they?"

"No, luv, not the worst," she said, smiling.

"But with all this Black Island stuff, we haven't practiced as a band in weeks."

"It can wait, luv. Things to do, things to do."

Jon squinted. "So, their names are Seth and Dan... Seth is a born-and-bred islander and Dan is from away. Does anyone know where Dan's from?"

Kara and Olias shook their heads. "We'll find out soon enough," she said.

Soon, Seth and Dan arrived in Dan's car. Empty-handed, they knocked on the kitchen door. Olias greeted them and guided them through the house and out to the porch.

"Help yourselves to some beer or wine, guys," offered Kara. Olias loved when it felt like they were already married.

Dan and Seth each grabbed a beer and stood around the flaming grill. Kara decided to talk to Dan, in hopes he'd finally look her in the eyes. "So, Dan... where are you from?"

He didn't look at her. He stared into the fire with a robotic smile. "I'm from Florida originally, where my parents died when I was young."

"Oh, that sucks," Jon said.

"Yes. And I slowly made my way north to the islands of Maine, and here I am."

"Well, I sure know what it's like to want to move to the islands of Maine," said Olias. "I grew up in Concord, Massachusetts, but my family always summered on Mount Haven, and I couldn't *wait* to get here every summer. When I was a kid, at the end of the summer, when we had to take the ferry off the island and drive home, I always cried. So now, I don't have to leave."

"But he still cries," ribbed Jon.

Seth turned to Kara. "Kara, did you go stir crazy growing up on the island when you were young?"

"Oh my *God* yes! There's something about being young and trapped on a small island while the rest of the world is out there... *Everywhere* else in the country—and world—seems more exotic and more cultural. But after traveling the country, I feel differently. There's a reason that we islanders always want to return to Mount Haven to raise our children. To raise them in a place where you don't have to lock your doors. There's a reason that rich people—who only get two or three weeks off from work a year—wind up in our backyards. This place is *special.*"

Olias couldn't believe how strongly he wanted Kara at that moment. "How 'bout the rest of ya go home now so's we can make a baby right here on the floor," he thought as a little smile flew across his face.

It was Jon's turn. "For me, I had a similar experience to Olias's, where I visited Mount Haven as a kid and fell in love with it."

Kara and Olias threw some burgers, dogs and a large tuna steak on the grill. Everyone seemed to have a pleasant time. Dan was stand-offish, but the musketeers equated that with his rough childhood. At one point, he had to use the bathroom. Jon showed him where it was.

Olias's bathroom had old calendars on the wall from previous years, and there was writing on them—a journal of events that transpired each day of his life. Dan saw this and felt the need to steal one of the months of the calendar. He needed to feel clever. He needed to feel special. Somewhere, he felt

Grammie's goading. So, he ripped out the September from the 2005 calendar and crumpled it into his pocket. "That asshole Olias! I could beat the *fuck* out of that stuck-up spoiled rich boy! Fucking thinks he's better than everyone! I seen what a fucking dick he really is, and I'm gonna fuck him up!"

He patted down the calendar page in his pocket so it didn't bulge and walked back to the porch. For the rest of the night, that important, intimate item of Olias's, stolen and in his pocket, gave him confidence.

6

While Todd was in the kitchen getting a food order ready for a table and Stacy was fixing a computer mistake by a waitress, Bob sauntered in. Stacy didn't see him—her rear end faced him as she stood at the computer. "Tonight, the flirting gets me that bitch's ass," he thought, and crept quietly toward her, stopping when they were almost touching. She was deep in thought over the computer issue, oblivious.

Just then, Todd walked out of the kitchen holding three full entrée plates of steaming food.

Bob gently—and sexily—put his hands on Stacy's shoulders. Todd saw.

Stacy was surprised, turned around and sexily hugged Bob, burying her head in his neck.

Todd walked headfirst into a customer. All the plates went flying—splattering hot food on the customers, Todd, and a table of four elderly diners.

The plates exploded onto the floor. There were a few screams.

Bob and Stacy whipped around to see Todd standing in the rubble, staring back at them.

Bob was surprised to see Todd. "Todd! Buddy!" half-yelled Bob as he walked over. "Accidents happen, everybody! Accidents happen!"

Todd addressed everyone covered with hot food. "I... am... so... *sorry...*"

Bob snorted. "Todd, buddy, go get cleaned up. I'll take over out here, big guy."

Todd was humiliated. "Yes, yes, okay..." He went into the kitchen.

Stacy grabbed some towels and handed them to the customers covered in food.

Bob took a towel and started cleaning food off the table hit hardest. "Please, everyone, we're so sorry. All your food and drink is on us tonight! Even though, it's on *you* at the moment! Ha ha ha!!!"

Waiters and waitresses ran over with bar towels and paper towels and helped Bob and Stacy with the clean up.

"Please accept a voucher for a free dinner on a different night as well! So sorry, so sorry, everyone. Stacy, get them their vouchers."

"Yes, Bob," she said while jumping to the register. She pulled out a pack and started handing them out.

The patrons were sufficiently appeased and made light of the bad situation to show they were good sports.

Bob took Stacy aside. "What's Todd doing here?!"

"Kara asked him to work for her tonight."

Bob didn't want to say anything against Kara, because he knew it would make him look bad. And truth be told, he was a little scared of her. "Oh... okay, thanks, Stacy. Hey, I love your shirt tonight."

"Thanks, Bob..." she said, batting her eyes. "I have to go finish fixing a check."

"Alright," he said softly, while placing his hand gently on her shoulder.

She put her hand on his shoulder, and for a few fleeting seconds, they stared at each other like there was no one else in the room. They both knew their first kiss was coming.

She walked back to the computer, making sure to give him a good look at her ass.

He smiled, then stomped into the kitchen. "Scott, where's Todd?"

"He's in the back, by the dishwasher."

Bob marched to the back, where he found Todd scrubbing away at red sauce stains on his shirt. "Todd, buddy... you got to get your fucking shit *together* boy, otherwise this won't work out!"

Todd, completely dominated and humiliated, looked down. "Yes, Bob."

"Why don't you go home. You aren't going to get those red stains out of that shirt, you need to buy another shirt. We have enough wait staff here tonight to cover your ass. I need you

as a manager, not a waiter. Now get going. I'll see you soon."
Bob aggressively thrust open the back door and gestured for
Todd to walk through. Even though Todd's jacket was in the
office with his cell phone in one of the pockets, he slumped
through the door—stepping down the two steps that placed him
in the back alley—and turned towards Bob, who now towered
over him.

"Clean up your act, buddy." Bob slammed the door.

Todd was frozen, facing the door with sauce all over his
shirt, a squiggle of pasta in his hair and his pants stained with a
creamy cheese sauce. It was a lot quieter outside. A distant dog's
bark echoed through the alley.

7

Things were winding down on Olias's porch. Everyone was
sitting, stuffed with tasty food, as soft, mellow tunes drifted out
of the living room. Dan was pleased that they didn't play any of
that Yes music.

Seth stood. "Well guys, I'm pretty beat. Thanks for the
awesome grub."

"Thanks for coming," Olias said, standing. Everyone stood.

"Would you like to go out in my dad's boat with us
sometime? We can go to High Island for that hike up Duck
Mountain that you guys wanted to do."

Olias smiled. "That sounds great. I'll call you, Seth."

Seth and Dan walked through the house to their car. They
drove away as Olias, Kara and Jon waved from the kitchen door.

"That Dan dude is a little weird, huh?" Jon asked.

"Yes. There's something creepy about him," Kara replied.

They walked back to the porch. "So, when are we going to
Black Island?" Jon asked. "I mean, how quickly can we get the
motor fixed?"

Olias leaned on the railing and looked out over the dark
ocean. "I'll call someone tomorrow who can look at it and assess
the situation."

"I'm going to bed," said Kara, yawning, and walked up the
steps to Olias's bedroom. She didn't recognize it, but Dan's
creepy, evil thoughts—at her expense—had sucked energy from
her. She took off her shirt, jeans and socks, and fell onto the
bed. She was asleep in seconds.

"Olias, I'm hittin' the sofa," Jon said with half-closed eyes as he walked into the living room and plopped down. He didn't turn on the TV as he usually did and was instantly snoring.

Olias grabbed a few items off the porch and put them in the fridge, then followed Kara to bed and fell asleep right away.

Meanwhile, Dan and Seth drove in silence to their new home and set about cleaning Edna's kitchen for hours. Neither said a word. After cleaning the kitchen twice, they silently walked up the rickety staircase to the narrow hallway.

At the exact same time, without looking at each other, they said, "G'night." They had no dreams.

8

Old Man Cranchet got out of bed in the middle of the night, put his clothes on and marched to the garage. He took a small tarp off an old boat engine that had been sitting in the same spot for years—he'd been meaning to fix the ol' gal, but work at the boatyard was always trumping the project.

He slid his tool case off an upper shelf, removed the cover from the motor and began unscrewing things. He never set up a work light, even though the light from the lone garage bulb was so weak it was akin to a candle. There were more shadows than light cast across the old, oily garage as he diligently found what parts needed replacing. He had those parts at the boatyard. He got in his truck and drove there, found them and drove back to his garage, where he proceeded to fix the motor. He didn't need to test it. It would work. It would now run better than it ever had.

Once finished, he put his tools away and walked back to bed. He took off his clothes and got under the covers. But he didn't return to sleep.

He had never woken up.

CHAPTER 10:   Questions and Answers

1

Elsa's moving out had made it rough on Jimmy in more than one way. They had shared all the expenses. Now that she was gone, he had no spending money and the bills were piling up. He didn't even have enough for rent. He needed that damn Bob Lianelli cash. He could always ask Lenny for a loan, but that wouldn't feel right. It would be like the school bully asking for his victim's help. "Lenny needs *me*. I don't need *him*."

After fighting the urge for an hour, he called Lianelli.

Bob was in his apartment watching ESPN. He was a Yankees fan, and needed to find out if they won the previous night. His cell phone rang. He saw it was Jimmy. "Fucking asshole hick," he hissed as he flipped open the phone. "What."

"Oh, um, hey, Bob... it's Jimmy..."

"Whadaya want."

"Well, I've got a money situation here, where, I need some money, and I was wonderin' when you're gonna pay me and Lenny."

"I don't fuckin' know. Whenever the guy I gave the device to calls me back and tells me what's on Olias's computer, that's when I'll pay ya."

"But hey, Bob, I really need that money. Do you know when the guy is gonna call you back?"

"No." ESPN was showing commercials, so Bob stayed on the phone.

"Can you, um, call *him?*"

Bob was annoyed, but knew he might need these two lug nuts for another job—Mrs. Black had said she'd probably need more help. "Look, you did me a good turn there, Jimmy, so look, I'll call the guy. I'll call you back soon."

"Thanks, Bob!"

Bob threw the phone to the other side of the couch as the baseball scores started coming in. "Stupid hick."

The Yankees won. "They're gonna gut-kick those wuss-ass Red Sox again this year," he said out loud. He burped and a little hot bile bubbled up into his throat. His face soured as he swallowed it.

Jimmy tried to have faith that his rent wouldn't be late. He sat back in his kitchen chair in an attempt to relax, but images of Elsa kept invading his mind. How they'd made sweet love... "And them meals she'd make," he said in a daze, an erection blooming. He was rock hard in seconds and felt an urge to yell "Elsaaaaa!!!" to help relieve this need, but the neighbors would hear, and they'd already heard enough yelling. He almost went upstairs and screamed into his pillow, but instead turned his thoughts back to getting the money. His erection softened as he nervously tapped his foot. His facial twitch went into overdrive, spreading into his entire body.

Bob dialed his computer guy. "If only I knew what the fuck I was doing with computers, I wouldn't need this guy," he thought.

"Yeah?"

"Hey there, Dicky. It's Bob. I need that computer info on that sicko."

"Oh yeah, I got that done for yez, Bob. It's all on a disk. Ya just load the disk into yez computah, and ya can see everything what's on the jamoke's computah. I gotz it all set up for yez." Dicky couldn't believe how computer illiterate Bob was—because Dicky was practically computer-illiterate himself.

"Oh yeah? That's great! Thanks Dicky. Why don't you come in to the See Food today for a free steak lunch, on me, huh?"

"Sounds good, Bob. See yez soon."

"See ya." Bob dialed Jimmy.

"Hello, Bob?!"

"Hey there, buddy. Yup, he's bringing it by the See Food today, so I'll pay you this afternoon. Come in anytime after three o'clock."

"Thanks, Bob! See you then!"

"Go get 'em!"

2

Lenny sat in his smelly chair, watching a rerun of an old *Home Improvement* episode. There was that particular young boy with feathered hair on the show... Lenny couldn't get enough of that boy. Lenny wished that kid never grew up. He wished all the little feathery-haired Leif Garrett/Justin Beiber-types never grew up. Lenny liked 'em just the way they were. Liked 'em just fine is all.

There was a knock on the door. Startled, he froze. *No one knocked on Lenny's door at eleven o'clock on a Sunday morning, not even Jimmy!* He knew that Jimmy and Elsa always spent Sunday mornings together...

Another knock! Lenny quietly got up and crept stealthily to the door. He could see the shadow of the person hitting the blinds. The person looked short. He figured what the hell, and opened the door.

A ten-year-old-ish blond boy with exquisitely feathered hair stood at the door. Lenny's tongue curled back into his throat. He choked a little, recovered and said, "Hi, can I help you?" He coughed as the boy started speaking.

"Yes. Hello, my name is Lars Vorhees, and I am selling hoagies for the elementary-school band. Would you like to purchase a hoagie? Your fine purchase will help our band buy much-needed sheet music for our big winter concert." It was obvious Lars had rehearsed his speech.

Lenny was floored. He never had one of these pretty little boys standing before him in the flesh. "Um, yeah, sure, I'll help out..."

Just then, Jimmy walked up behind Lars! "Hey Lenny, we got to talk." He walked right past Lenny and into the apartment.

Lenny was in shock, unprepared for this onslaught of events. He stood in the doorway, looking back and forth between the kid and Jimmy. He addressed the kid. "So, you mean, you got hoagies with you right now?"

"No, we will make and deliver them next Sunday."

Jimmy shoved his head into the doorway between them. "Look, he don't want no lame kiddie hoagies! Go away, kid! I got to talk to him!" Jimmy shoved his face into Lars's face and yelled, "Goooo awaaayyyy!!!"

Lars was petrified and his legs took flight. He disappeared around the corner of the building. Jimmy laughed.

"Hey, what are you doin', Jimmy?!!! I wanted one 'a them hoagies!!!"

"Look, I'll buy you a fucking hoagie, dude, with the money we're gonna get from Lianelli! I just talked to him." Jimmy thought he'd see happy surprise in Lenny's face, but all he saw was... anger?

Lenny was pissed. "Look, Jim, I was about to buy a hoagie from that guy and you made him run away!"

"Dude, what the fuck?! Who cares?! Dude, I'll buy you a fucking hoagie. Lianelli's gonna pay us *today.*"

Lenny was unresponsive, still standing in the doorway, looking in the direction Lars had run. He had a hard-on.

"Lenny, dude, what the fuck's your problem?" Jimmy was starting to get angry.

"Sorry, Jimmy, I was just hungry, is all."

"Lenny, he didn't have any hoagies *with* him!"

"Oh, right, got it, Jimmy. So, when today are we going to get paid?"

"Anytime after three o'clock. Lianelli said to come in to the restaurant then."

"Are we going to get any more jobs from him?"

"I think we might. Maybe he's gonna wanna fuck with Olias's friends and shit too, I don't know."

"That's good, Jimmy."

Jimmy noticed the *Home Improvement* repeat on TV. "I remember this one! This is where the three sons go on a camping trip with their dad."

"Yeah, ha ha. Good stuff."

Jimmy wanted to tell Lenny that Elsa had moved out, but didn't know how. "Elsa hates this show." Jimmy walked to the kitchen, grabbed a plastic lawn chair and plopped it in front of the TV. Lenny sat in his chair. They watched the rest of the show. Jimmy tried not to inhale too deeply. "Elsa never wants nuttin' to do with this show. She also hates *Rambo,* football, *The Three Stooges, Smallville, Predator vs. Alien,* wrestling, and the band Rush."

"Is that why you ain't with her this morning?"

"Um, somethin' like that."

3

Jon woke on Olias's sofa and saw that the sun was already well up in the sky, the dew of early morning a memory. He walked into the kitchen and replenished his overly-dehydrated body with much-needed water. While chugging, he saw Olias's answering machine blinking. He looked at the caller ID. Dan had left a message. Jon almost played it, but didn't want to wake Kara or Olias, so he set about quietly starting a pot of coffee.

He grabbed an empty garbage bag and walked to the porch. It had gotten windy, and the lighter garbage was being tossed around. He started cleaning up as the gulls, cormorants and fish hawks socialized loudly over the water. "Man, we sure left this place a mess."

The surf hitting Olias's beach was much larger and louder than usual.

Jon was still hungover. The sound of the waves began lulling him; he fell into a porch chair and sat glassy-eyed, facing the island cluster. He was asleep in seconds, dreaming of a huge chandelier.

Twenty minutes later, he woke to a rustling inside the house. He was still holding the garbage bag. He got out of the chair and continued cleaning up.

Kara came out holding a full mug of steaming coffee. "Coffee's ready, Jon! Thanks for making it."

"Welcome." It looked to Jon like she was ready to go out on the town, but she had literally gotten out of bed only minutes before. Her golden hair fell over her shoulders in big curls. "I need a girlfriend," he thought. "I need a girlfriend like Kara."

She sat and stared out across the bay. There were little white explosions hitting the distant islands. "Wow, it's really rough."

Jon continued picking up garbage as Olias joined them. "Morning. Damn, it's rough! This surf is from an approaching hurricane, Hurricane David, I think."

"I bet some of the island teenagers'll be surfing at Crabtree Point today," Kara said.

Jon's bag was full. "Olias, did you see the message blinking from Dan?"

"What? He called already?"

"Let's listen!" Kara said. They went to the kitchen and she pushed the button.

"Hi Olias, it's Dan. Thank you for a fun night. Seth and I had a fun night. It was fun to have such a night. Let's have more fun times. We can go on a hike at High Island, if you want. I bet that would be fun. Give me a call."

The musketeers looked at each other. Jon spoke first. "Sounds... *fun!*" They laughed.

Olias asked, "What time did he call?"

John checked. "Holy crap, he called at four-seventeen in the morning!"

"What?!"

"Maybe he has a sleep disorder," Kara said, refreshing her coffee and walking back to the porch. The guys followed.

Ziggy, moored front and center, was bobbing up and down. "Ziggy's having fun," she smiled. "So, should we go boating and hiking with them? Dan is creepy, but Seth's okay."

Olias put hand to chin. "I don't know... not really feelin' it. But there's at least one thing I do know. We need to get Ziggy's motor fixed. But, I have to wait 'til Monday morning at the boatyard, where there are a few guys I can ask. Maybe I'll even ask Old Man Cranchet how best to go about fixing it."

Suddenly, a voice spoke through an odd part of their minds, clear as a bell, *"Come back to Black Island."*

Even before the sentence was over, the musketeers whipped around to face each other. "Oh. My. God." uttered Kara.

They stood in silence as the waves boomed.

A voice had again swept through a new section of their brains—a section previously dormant. But this time it was stronger. Their minds felt stretched. An odd tingling sensation remained, winding and meandering through unknown corridors in their thoughts and emotions. Reality itself seemed to expand. They each collapsed into a chair as if physically winded.

Jon spoke first. "I guess we need to get that motor fixed quickly!"

4

Todd showed up for work on Sunday morning determined to exhibit a polished and professional detachment while doing his job to the utmost. He'd already decided that when Stacy came in for the night shift, he would give her an even colder "hello" than she'd been giving him. Very logical. He'd wear the same emotionless smile that she'd been sporting. He woke up especially early—after only three hours of disjointed sleep in which he kept seeing Stacy and Bob hugging—and practiced this cold-yet-professional smile in the bathroom mirror. However, he wasn't able to perfect it... There was always a smidgen of underlying emotion, a trace of hidden passion trying to burst out.

But, *he* thought he had it down. "That'll teach her." He was ready for a *very* professional work day.

As he printed out the lunch specials in the office, one thing dominated his mind: the sexual touching of Stacy and Bob. That image was boring a deeper and deeper hole in his heart. It kept involuntarily looping. And it answered questions...

He practiced his new professional "detachment-smile" while the image burned. After awhile, he thought he was getting rather adept at picturing Stacy sexually touching that fat asshole while wearing the cold smile.

It was a busy Sunday lunch. The clock seemed to tick louder and louder as Stacy's arrival approached.

A few regulars who always ate lunch at the bar gave him some minor grief about the previous night's spilled plates, but it was just in fun. Yet it hurt. His new smile was road-tested. The regulars saw that he was feeling very insecure about the dropped plates—or about something—and stopped ribbing him, prompting him to believe his new smile was *golden.* Oh boy, was he ready for her!

He finished the final server checkout and was peering through the big glass windows of the restaurant, waiting.

Here she came! He would show her. Show her he didn't care at all. Ever since he woke prematurely in the middle of the night and couldn't get back to sleep, he'd been living a slowly rising crescendo *for just this moment.* Here came the pinnacle of the last thirteen hours: It was time to show her how much he didn't care!

She entered. He was pretending to count the checkouts as she passed him. He looked up at her as she walked by. It was smile-time—but wait, she was walking right *up* to him...

She put her hand on his shoulder in a consoling, motherly gesture. "Hey... how *are* you today? That must have really sucked, dropping those dinners onto people and then Bob booting you out the back. I found your jacket and cell phone in the office. Did you see where I left them for you?"

"...Yeah, thank you..." He was *not* ready for this.

Then she hugged him. "Oh Todd, I hope you're okay."

His eyes started tearing up. She didn't want anyone to see, kept one arm wrapped around him and quickly got him on the move. They entered the bathroom together.

"Stacy... why?! *Why?* Do you like Bob? How can you like *Bob?!*"

"I guess I kind of like him, but I just need to be alone, Todd. I need to find myself," she lied (she'd been practicing on the drive over).

"But, isn't he married?!"

"He told me he's in the middle of a messy divorce, and she's a major bitch."

"He has kids, right?!"

"Yes. But I'm not thinking about any of that. I don't even care."

"Are we really over, Stace?"

"Yes, Todd, I'm sorry." She hugged him, and his crying started to get loud as she caressed the back of his head. "You'll find someone else, Todd, there are many girls out there who'd be very lucky to even just go on a date with you."

He let the crying out in belching, gulping sobs.

Minutes later, he was wiping his eyes as she continued to hold him. "Thanks, Stace..." He left her embrace, grabbed a few paper towels and patted his soaked face. "There hasn't been better than you."

"There will be Todd, there will be."

They hugged one more time—the crying tried to erupt again, but he held his ground. "Thank you Stace, I knew you couldn't just end it coldly," he sniffed.

"Of course not. Now come on, lemme see a smile."

The smallest peep of a genuine smile formed on Todd's face.

5

Jimmy had more time now that he was single. That was why he was still slumped in a plastic chair at Lenny's, hours later, watching a *Home Improvement* marathon. "Lenny, do you have any other shows on tape?"

"Um, maybe, I don't know."

"Why do you got all these *Home Improvement* episodes?"

"...It's a good show, is all."

"That's true, it is." The stink was slowly seeping into his marrow. "Hey, what say we go for a 'get-stoned-a-thon' drive, dude?"

"Sounds good."

Lenny snapped off the set and they made their way to Jimmy's truck. They motored out of town and wound up on the Middle Road, roaring past a few small vegetable and cow farms and the island's one large fresh pond. While ignoring the passing scenery, they toked their bowl clean.

"Ahhhhh, that's the shit," exhaled Jimmy. "Hey, you think that douche-bag faggot Chico will be working at the See Food tonight?"

"I bet he will, ha ha."

"Well let's fuckin' *fuck* with him bro."

"Ha ha yeah, let—"

A female deer ran onto the road—right into the speeding truck. It rolled upward over the grill and smashed the windshield. Sharp glass flew into Jimmy's face and hair. He instinctively kicked down hard on the brakes and the deer flew off the hood to the left. The truck screeched to a halt as the deer flopped dead onto the road.

"Fuuuuuuck!" yelled Lenny.

They sat in shock as the truck's engine continued growling.

"Dude, your face," Lenny whispered.

Jimmy looked in the rear view mirror and saw cuts all over his face, blood starting to trickle down.

Lenny only had glass in his hair. He shook it out. "An' you already had cuts on yer face before!"

"Shut up, Lenny! Gotta check the truck," he said in a daze. He shut off the engine, got out, stepped over the dead deer's right hind leg and got a look at the front of his truck. "Shiiiiiit…"

The grill was broken, the hood was dented, the left headlight was shattered and the windshield was smashed.

Lenny got out to look. "Holy shit! Dude, that was fuckin' intense!"

"My fuckin' truck…"

"Who wants venison for dinner, dude?!" Lenny joked as he walked up to the dead deer and poked it with his right foot. "Venison kabobs, bro! Ha! Ha!"

Jimmy wasn't laughing. He was staring at his broken truck, defeated. First Elsa leaving, now this. What next? "Shut up, Lenny."

They stood in silence. The only sound was a light breeze through the tall, thin spruce trees.

"At least we're gettin' our money from Lianelli today," Lenny said.

Jimmy didn't respond, he just stared at the truck.

"Should we move the deer outta the road, Jimmy?"

"Yeah, I guess. You take the back legs, I'll take the front legs. Let's drag it to the side of the road." Jimmy grabbed the front hooves as Lenny grabbed the hind hooves. Gravel from the road got in the dead deer's mouth and eyes as they dragged it to the foot of the woods. "Okay, that's good."

"So what now, Jimmy?"

"Let's get the rest of the windshield glass off."

They worked for a good ten minutes removing the sharp shards. Jimmy cut his finger.

"Hey Jimmy, what do you want to do now?"

"I don't know... Let's go to my place and drink, then go to the See Food at three o'clock."

"But, what about Elsa?"

"Oh, she's at... her mother's house."

"Sounds good, Jimmy."

Jimmy extracted the last remaining shard from the windshield rim and threw it into the woods.

"What about all the glass in the street, Jimmy?"

"Fuck it. Let some other asshole deal with it."

Jimmy roared the truck to life and they crunched over some glass. The amount of wind flying in their faces forced him to drive slowly.

"I see why they call it a windshield!" Lenny yelled over the sound of the engine.

They passed a car full of summer tourists who slowed down to get a look at the mangled truck.

"Fuck you, assholes!!!" Jimmy yelled.

They looked away.

Soon they were driving down Jimmy's street in the Village. He parked the spectacle right in front of the apartment as neighbors peeked through closed curtains. Jimmy and his sidekick walked inside.

Jimmy snapped on the set and found an episode of *Step By Step*. They plopped down in front of Suzanne Somers and Patrick Duffy.

"I think that father dude was Manimal," Lenny said.

"Yup."

"Wow, look at the way they put the ocean next to that amusement park! That looks really fake!"

"Yup."

"Your truck is fucked, dude."

"Yup."

6

Olias, Kara and Jon sat in silence, mulling over the odd voice that had opened pathways in their brains.

"How quick can we get Ziggy's motor fixed?" asked Jon.

The kitchen phone rang. Kara ran and answered it. "Hello?"

"Kara, this is Cranchet. I have the motor. Bring the boat to the boatyard today. I will put the new motor on it."

"...What?"

Olias called from the porch, "Kara, who is it?"

"Hold on! Um, Mr. Cranchet? How did you know that we needed a motor?"

"We are monitoring your events. Bring the boat to us at the boatyard. The motor must be attached before the storm hits. Phone call over."

"*Who* are you? Who is *we?!* Why is all this happening?!"

Whatever was inside Old Man Cranchet had already hung up.

"Hello?! Hello?!" Kara ran to the porch. "It was Old Man Cranchet—but I think it was someone else speaking through him! He or it or whoever said that *they* have a motor for Ziggy, and we need to bring Ziggy to the boatyard today!"

"Oh my God!" Olias yelled. "*They?!*"

"He said '*we* are monitoring your events,' and 'bring the boat to *us*'!"

They had a moment of silence, taking this in.

A strong gust of wind swept across the porch, prompting Kara to tie her hair into a ponytail. "And, he said there's a storm coming."

"Hurricane David," Olias said.

"How do we get Ziggy to the boatyard?" Jon wondered.

"Well, I'd rather not ask Seth to tow him... Kara, do you know anyone with a trailer?"

"Of course. Many people. Hmm, let's see… Tawny has one sitting in her parents' driveway. It would fit Ziggy. I'm sure they'll let us borrow it." She got her cell and dialed her best friend. Jon's eyes glazed over. Tawny…

"Hi Tawns, can we borrow the trailer in your parents' driveway today?"

"Sure, Kay-Kay. Go over and get it anytime, I'll tell my parents you're coming. I'm on my way to work. So what's up?"

"Olias's boat conked out, and we need to bring it to the boatyard."

"Oh. Tell Olias and Jon I say hi!"

"I will Tawns, thanks." Kara put her cell down and sat. "She says hi, and that we can go over anytime and get the trailer."

"Nice," said Olias. "I'm glad I still have the trailer hitch on my car." He stood. "So luv, did Cranchet sound different in any way?"

"No, he sounded like the gruff Old Man Cranchet, but maybe a little more formal. A little more stiff."

"That's the way he was when his eyes rolled up into his head," Jon said.

While the musketeers spoke, an odd breeze fanned the underside of the leaves in the front yard, changing the color of the trees to a lighter green. The breeze smelled of copper and dust. No one noticed.

7

Five minutes after Todd left the See Food to go home and squirt out a few final sobs, Bob Lianelli bounded through the front door holding a box. With an authoritative air, he boomed, "Stacy! Come into my office!"

She was surprised. "Um, yes Bob."

He beelined through the kitchen to the office, sat in his chair and placed the box on the desk. When Stacy entered, he yelled for all to hear, "Close the door!"

She was wide-eyed, but knew he must be working a scam on everyone. His eyes weren't angry at all—he wasn't a very good actor.

"Yes, sir!" She closed the door.

"Please sit down, Stacy." She sat, looking into his eyes with a growing smile.

He lifted the box a few inches off the desk. "For you, Girlie…"

Her eyes lit up as she took it. She opened the top to see a bouquet of red roses. "Oh, Bob! They're beautiful!"

He came around the desk and they hugged, her face nestled in his neck. They slowly came out of the hug and their eyes met.

Stacy and Bob kissed.

8

In the driveway of Tawny's parents' house, Jon and Olias were hitching the trailer to the back of Olias's car in the growing wind. Kara was indoors talking to Tawny's parents—she knew them very well, having largely grown up in their house. She brought them outside to say hi.

"Thank you so much for letting us borrow your trailer!" Olias said loudly over the swirl.

"Of course, Olias! Are you taking your boat out of the water because of the hurricane?"

"Oh, Hurricane David. We've been a little out of the loop. Is it coming near us?"

"You haven't heard the big news?"

"No, we've been… busy."

"It's coming right *for* us! The Weather Channel just said that Hurricane David is on a direct path to mid-coast Maine! One-hundred mile-per-hour winds! Keep your boat out of the water!"

"We're bringing it to the boatyard to get a new motor installed."

"Great! Keep it out of the ocean until the storm's over."

"I guess we will. Thank you."

After Jon checked to see if the trailer's tail lights were hooked to the car, the three musketeers said goodbye and drove back to Olias's.

Olias drove down the side of his property and backed the trailer into the wavy Atlantic. "We're really lucky it's high tide. We couldn't do this in any other tide," he said.

"Is it really luck?" Kara wondered to herself.

Jon rowed the tender through choppy surf to Ziggy, tied a rope to his eye, unhooked him from the mooring and rowed back.

The musketeers pulled Ziggy onto the trailer and drove to the boatyard.

"I wonder if this thing will still be inside Cranchet," Olias said. "Maybe we'll be able to ask him or them or her or it what the hell's going on!"

Kara was looking at the darkening sky from the passenger seat. "So, what do we ask?"

"Who are you?" Jon offered.

Olias nodded. "Definitely. Who are you, and how are you connected to Black Island, and why do you want us to go to Black Island? What do you want from us? Are you an alien?"

"Do you really think they're aliens, luv?"

"Who knows, luv. Who knows."

"Maybe they're from the future," added Jon.

Soon they pulled into the boatyard.

"Look!" Kara said, pointing.

Old Man Cranchet was standing outside one of the buildings. Olias drove slowly up to him and stopped the car. "I guess we get out and talk to him now?" he asked.

They opened their doors and started to get out, but Cranchet held up his palm in a "stop" gesture. They got back in and he motioned for Olias to follow him.

Cranchet walked around the main building, Olias driving slowly behind. Cranchet pointed to an open door.

"He's not using his cane!" Jon exclaimed.

Olias drove inside the building and saw where the new motor was waiting. He backed Ziggy up to it. Cranchet motioned for Olias to turn off the car. Olias obliged, then announced, "It's show time."

Olias, Kara and Jon stared at him while slowly getting out. He started removing the old motor. They approached him as he worked.

"Hello," Olias started.

"Hello."

"We know you aren't really Mr. Cranchet. So, who are you?"

"I am what is left of the ancient ones."

"You're from Black Island?"

"Yes, and I must go back as quickly as possible. The power reserves are very low." He started to move at an impossibly fast speed as the musketeers backed away in awe, hearts racing.

"Who were the ancient ones?!" Kara asked.

"We were the Rescue Souls. We came to this reality long ago." His mouth moved normally, while his body became a blur.

"Who were you here to rescue?"

"The Hybrids."

"Who were the Hybrids?"

"They were the ones who... ate the apple."

"You mean, like, Adam and Eve?"

"Yes." He had the old motor off and was already fastening the repaired motor to Ziggy's stern. His body started moving even faster, but his head—and especially mouth—stayed stable.

Olias and Jon lost themselves in shock. Kara kept her wits and continued. "What is behind the wall of black?"

"The Great Crystal."

"Can we see it?"

"You must go inside the Inner Chamber."

"What do we do when we get there?"

"You must activate the Sun Collectors," he said while jumping into Ziggy and finishing the electrical work underneath the dashboard. The musketeers had to walk around the trailer to see him.

"How will we know how to do that?!"

"Look for the Sun symbol on the wall, Aing." This froze Kara, as she vividly remembered her dream.

"You must put Ziggy into the water as soon as possible due to the tides. He'll be safe at his mooring in the high surf thanks to the device I am installing. We've made sure the storm will begin to dissipate well before its time. You must leave early on the morning after the high surf. We have made that morning's weather for you. It will be dead low tide. Thus, Ziggy must be put into the water immediately." He finished installing the motor and set about flushing out the gas and removing the rest of the dangerous metal filings with a small filter. He put the now-clean gas into the tank.

He rocketed to a cabinet at the far end of the large room, grabbed an odd-looking device and ran back to the boat. He quickly installed it under Ziggy's floor.

"What's that?" asked Olias.

"It is a modified roll-control device, which will keep Ziggy safe in the high surf. I've given it its own power source."

Jon needed to ask a billion questions. "Will our lives be changed by any of this?"

"Yes."

"How?"

"That is up to you."

"Will we have special powers?!"

"No, but the Great Crystal does."

"Will we be able to control the weather?"

"Yes."

"Will we be able to make people talk and say things we want them to say?"

"Yes, but it is not suggested. Power corrupts."

"Were we chosen to do this?"

"Yes."

"Who chose us?"

"You were chosen by the ancient Rescue Souls."

"But... why us?"

"Because you are good people. You are just. Olias, Kara and Jon... your first instinct is to be honest and to help others. There are other reasons, but these two are the most important."

"So, will our lives be *really* changed by this?!"

"That is up to you."

"Will we have to keep our jobs to make money?"

"No."

Cranchet finished putting the floor back into place in a few whirling seconds and walked quickly to a waiting chair. He sat and his eyes rolled up into their sockets. He shook, then his body relaxed and he closed his eyes.

The musketeers slowly approached him. "Mr. Cranchet? Are you okay?" Kara asked.

Cranchet opened his eyes and saw Olias, Kara and Jon standing in front of him, staring. He coughed. "What's... going on?"

"Oh, hi, Mr. Cranchet. You came in early and must have fallen asleep in your chair," Olias said.

"I what?! Shit. I must have had too much to drink last night. Ha! But, what another fun night I had with my oldest friends! You know, kids, we all hung out when we were your age and always had such good times... Never take your friendships for granted!"

"We won't, sir, thank you," Kara said.

Cranchet saw his motor on Olias's boat. "Good, I see the motor's fastened to your boat. Let me know how she runs!"

"Sure, Mr. Cranchet."

"Alright, kids, I gotta close up shop here. I'm cooking dinner for seven people tonight!"

"Okay sir, and thank you!" Olias said.

"Don't mention it!"

The musketeers got into the car and drove out of the building. The wind had picked up and garbage was being tossed around the lot.

Cranchet hobbled with his cane over to the side of the big doorway, looking more in pain than ever. He hit the big bay-door mechanism and the door slowly closed.

The threesome waved goodbye and drove to the South Shore Road.

Cranchet slowly limped his way back to the chair and sat. He was in a lot of pain, and felt as if he was about to die.

He was.

"I'll see you soon, Loretta," he said to the heavens.

Kara was the first to speak as they drove. "So, we have to restart some ancient technology inside the wall of black called the 'Sun Collectors'!"

"Pretty intense," Olias said dreamily.

"What was that about Adam and Eve?" asked Jon, "I was too busy watching him go insanely fast!"

"Well," said Kara, "it seems there were beings called Hybrids that came here long ago who ate some apple—or probably that's just a metaphor—and then Rescue Souls came to save them or something, and it was way back then that they built this Black Island Great Crystal machine, which we are supposed to bring back to life!"

They sat in awe, trying to take this in. Jon looked out the window and then up into the sky. "Oh, is that all?!"

Kara smiled. "I think the most incredible thing is that they chose *us.*"

CHAPTER 11:   Love Is in the Air

1

Jimmy and Lenny were now watching an old *Family Matters*, and even though it was one of Jimmy's all-time favorite shows, he wasn't enjoying it. Too many worries. Lenny was laughing every time the canned laughter sounded, but not Jimmy. He didn't want to show up at the See Food in his mangled truck. "Lenny, it's time I drive you home and we get your car, come back here so's I can park my truck, and then drive to the See Food in your car."

"But why dri—, oh, got it, Jimmy. You ain't want no one askin' no questions about your truck and like that, huh?"

"Somethin' like that." Jimmy stood while clicking off the set. He went briskly out the door, Lenny dutifully following. They walked into a gusty wind. "Storm's a-comin'," Jimmy said in his wisest-sounding voice.

There were some neighborhood kids surrounding the truck and whispering. They saw Jimmy and scattered. Lenny looked at him to see what he was going to do. Jimmy just ignored them. So, Lenny ignored them too. Not one of them had sexy feathered hair anyway. They got into the truck and Jimmy drove away slowly.

"Jimmy, why is Elsa at her mother's for so long?"

Jimmy was ready for this. "Her mother is sick and she's taking care of her."

"Hey Jimmy, remember that time when that guy at the bar showed Elsa a poem he wrote about the islands or whatever, and you fucking freaked on him? Ha!"

"Yup."

"Fuckin' funny shit. You were all 'I do the readin'!,' and took the poem and wouldn't let Elsa read it! Ha ha ha!"

"Yup."

"You were all, 'My woman only reads what I *allow* her to read and shit!"

"Yup."

"You kept it in your truck so she couldn't read it!"

"Yup."

"You're the *man* Jimmy, the *man!*"

"...Yup."

They changed vehicles and drove to the See Food. The restaurant was a little over half full. They entered, looked around for Lianelli, and finally saw him sitting at a slightly hidden four-top table talking to a guy in a three-piece suit. The guy had black, shiny, slick-backed hair—each mini crevasse made by his plastic comb's teeth frozen by product.

They approached the table. "Hey there, Bob," Jimmy said out of the side of his mouth.

"Heyyyyyy there fellas, take a seat, take a seat. This is my buddy, Dicky."

After introductions, Dicky and Bob resumed their conversation as Jimmy and Lenny sat in awkward silence.

"So, Dicky, you say I just take this here CD and put it in my computer, and I'll see everything that's on Olias's computer?"

"That's kinda right, Bob. Yeh can see all his poisenal files. I did all da woik for yez. Yeh just put that disk into yeh computah's disk drive. Do you know howda do dat?"

"Umm, yeh, I think so..."

Dicky rolled his eyes. "If yooz have a problem wit' it, gimme a call. Okay, I'm outta here. I got me a meet-'n-greet I gotta get to and like dat." He stood up to leave. "Nice meetin' yez."

Jimmy was so in his own head that he didn't respond. It was Lenny who spoke for them—a rare occurrence. "Yeh, nice meetin' yooz, is all."

Bob reached into his briefcase and took out an envelope that clearly looked bloated with cash and handed it to Dicky. "Thanks for your help, Dicky."

Dicky talked out of the side of his mouth. "Yup. T'anks. You got it. See yez." He shuffled out of the restaurant, shiny black shoes clicking on linoleum.

"He iooks like a pretty together guy," Jimmy said.

Dicky click-clacked to his car through the swirling wind, got in, checked himself in the rear-view mirror to make sure his hair was still slicked-back with hardened product, took out a cigarette and lit it while glancing over at the See Food and saying, "Computah jamoke." He inhaled the smoke deeply, started the car and drove off into the approaching storm.

"Alright, fellas, let's go to my office and make sure all of Olias's shit is on here." They followed Bob through the kitchen to the office, went in and closed the door. "Okay, so, I'm supposed to put this CD into something..."

Lenny pointed at the disk drive. "There, Mr. Lianelli."

"Huh?"

"Look." Lenny hit the button that opened the disk drive. Bob jumped. "Oh! I didn't know that was in there!"

Jimmy and Lenny shared a smirk. "Okay, put the disk in there," Jimmy said.

Bob inserted the disk upside down and hit the close button. A warning beep sounded and it re-opened. "The disk is bad! He fuckin' ripped me off! No money for either 'a you!"

"Bob, wait." Jimmy took out the disk and put it in the right way. The computer knowingly whirred and began loading.

"Oh, so, it's workin' now, huh?"

"Yes, Bob."

Soon a file popped up saying "computer."

"Click on that, Bob."

"Huh?!"

"Here." Jimmy clicked on the file, and Olias's personal desktop came into full view. "See, Bob? There's everything on Olias's computer for you to look at. We got the job done. You got the cash?"

"...Okay, job well done, boys." Bob reached into his briefcase and pulled out a thick wad of weathered hundreds and crumpled twenties.

Jimmy and Lenny looked at the huge wad in awe. Bob loved that. He doled out grubby bills to each henchman. "There you go, boys. I might have more work for you in the near future."

"Thanks, Bob!" Lenny said.

"You guys go have a drink on me at the bar, huh?"

"Go, Bob!" championed Jimmy, thrilled that he was going to get a free drink on top of this.

Bob stood and directed them to open the door and exit the office, which they happily did. "Alright you two, have a drink on me!" yelled Bob for all the kitchen workers to hear. "Everybody loves me," he thought to himself as a few kitchen workers smiled mechanically at him.

Jimmy and Lenny walked through the bustling kitchen to the bar and sat.

The new bartender replacing Manuel was a short, highly flustered young girl named Tammy. "Just call me Tamz! Call me

Tamz!" she'd implore everyone in a forced, nervously cute voice. Currently, she was trying to figure out how to make a margarita. She had a long bar spoon in one hand, and the bartender's guide book in the other. She was reading intently, one of her feet rapidly tapping on the floor.

Rob the waiter stood at the end of the bar waiting for the margarita so he could bring it to his 4-top table, where the customer was getting testy due to how long he'd already waited for earlier drinks. "Everything okay, Tammy?" asked Rob.

"Just call me Tamz! Call me Tamz!" she responded while studying the recipe.

"I wish Manuel was here," Rob uttered under his breath.

Jimmy started to feel good. "So, um, *Tamz,* a little service here, huh?"

"Oh! Oh! What can I get *you?!*" she said, looking him up and down.

He had to think about this for a second. The drink was free, so should he just get a beer like always? Shouldn't he get something expensive and exotic? "I'll have a beer."

"Me too," Lenny followed.

"I know how to make that!" Tammy chirped. She ran to the beer cooler and extracted two Buds, popped the caps and placed them in front of Jimmy and Lenny.

"And these beers are on the house, a gift from Bob Lianelli, there, um, *Tamz.*"

"Oh! Okay!"

"So, where ya from, girlie?"

"My family just moved here from Deer Isle!" she said while looking back down at the book. She searched the bottles behind her for the Triple Sec, which was in the speed rack in front of her.

Rob saw that Stacy was busy fixing a check for irate customers, and he'd had enough. He marched behind the bar. "Here's how you make a margarita," he scolded.

Tammy watched as Rob took a metal shaker, filled it with ice, took the Triple Sec and the cheap tequila from the speed rack and poured them simultaneously, took a wedge of lime and squeezed in some juice, took the soda gun and squirted in a dash of lemon sour mix, put the shaker's top on and placed it on the bar. He immediately found the glass-rim salter, took a margarita glass off the ceiling rack and rimmed it with a fresh lime, salted it, shook the shaker, poured the contents into the glass and threw in a straw and a lime wedge.

"There. 'Ja get that?!"

Tammy had stared at the process like a deer in headlights.

Rob took the drink and quickly served it. The thirsty customer who watched him make it was overly happy and placed a twenty in his hand. "Well done!"

"So, *Tamz*, didja learn how to make that drink there?" asked Jimmy.

"You have to shake it! Have to shake it! Shake your booooty! Shake your boooooty!"

Jimmy and Lenny stared at her, dumbfounded.

2

With Ziggy in tow, Olias, Kara and Jon drove up the South Shore Road to the dirt road that led to Olias's, thunder and lightning exploding from above.

A large, fallen branch lay in the middle of the road. Jon and Olias jumped out and wrestled it to the side. They got back in the car and continued.

"I think the tide might still be high enough to get him in the water right here," Olias said, pulling into his side yard. He turned the trailer around and began backing the boat up to the ocean.

"What happens when the tide goes out a little more?" asked Jon.

"I think it already has," Olias said. "Once past high tide, the gradient of the beach isn't conducive for using the trailer—half the car would have to be in the water just to get the boat off the trailer. If that happens, the ocean's going to take my car!"

They pulled to the water's edge and got out in the gale-force wind.

"The ocean's gone down—we have to do this right away!" yelled Olias over the pounding waves. "Jon! Drive Ziggy into the water as far as you can! I'll try pulling him off the trailer from behind! Don't let the ocean take my car!"

Olias took off his pants and walked into the cold water. Jon brought Olias's car to the water's edge—the back wheels were more than half-submerged in the angry surf. Ziggy and the trailer were in barely enough water to get the task done.

Kara took off her jeans and threw them up the beach. A gust of wind lifted them and they flew into the beach pea plants. "You aren't doing this alone, luv!"

Olias and Kara stood in the wavy surf, unhooking bungees and clamps. They pulled Ziggy backwards. Soon he came off the trailer and floated free in the rough ocean. He bobbed up and down, but the roll device Cranchet installed kept him fairly steady.

"Wow! Look how Ziggy's not fully affected by the waves!" yelled Olias.

There was a little rip current pulling Ziggy away from the shore. If the musketeers hadn't have been so busy, they might of noticed that the whole area smelled of copper and dust. If it wasn't for that rip current, Ziggy would have been quickly beached and the waves would have bashed him against the larger rocks, pounding sections of his fiberglass hull to shards.

Jon drove the trailer out of the water. Kara and Olias jumped into Ziggy. Olias put the "new" motor down and stuck the key in the ignition. It started right up with a roar.

"Woooo hoooooo!" Kara cheered over the wind.

They puttered out to the mooring, pitching and bobbing. Olias cut the motor. Kara snared the mooring line and secured Ziggy. Jon was already in the tender, rowing out to get them.

Even though the high surf bounced them up and down, they were seasoned boaters and got into the tender without incident.

Kara, in her panties, sat in the bow. That was easy on Jon, who was rowing, thus facing the stern. Olias got in the stern.

As they rowed around Ziggy's bow, Kara said, "Ziggy looks happy—I think he's smiling!"

Then the rain began.

3
Bob Lianelli sat in his office looking through everything on Olias's computer. He saw nothing that could incriminate Olias. In emails to friends, Olias sometimes mocked liars, calling them out for not being men. That pissed Bob off. "Does he fucking think he's Jesus fucking Christ?!"

He searched, but couldn't find any porn in Olias's Internet history. "Sicko," he spat.

He picked up the phone and dialed Edna Black. She answered right away. "Hello?"

"Hi, Mrs. Black, it's Bob."

"Oh helloooooo, son!"

Little fuzzies shot through his lower intestinal tract. He couldn't believe how much he loved this old woman. "I have all the computer info on Olias, Mrs. Black. I'm looking at it right here."

"Oh good, son. Is there anything about boating and going to islands?"

"Yes. He has a diary kind of thing called 'Ship's Log,' which looks like a journal of his boating trips. The last entry is from a few weeks ago."

The thing that sounded like an old human knew that Olias hadn't been to Black Island at that point. She correctly assumed that there was no mention of Black Island in the journal. If Black Island *had* been mentioned, Lianelli would be out cold on the floor of his office. "Oh well, thank you, Bob, for your diligence. Can you print out a copy of that Ship's Log for me?"

"Umm, I think I can do that, ma'am," he floundered.

"Thank you, Bob. If you come across anything else, please let me know."

"Yes, ma'am. And why don't you come on down to the See Food for a free dinner? We'll treat ya right! Why don't ya see what kinda food ya wanna see from the sea?!"

"Thank you, son, perhaps sometime I will. Goodbye."

"...Goodbye."

She curtly hung up. That hurt. Bob felt like a failure for his beloved grandmamma.

4

The end of the stored power inside the Great Crystal was nigh.

Old Man Cranchet sat alone in a cold metal chair in the darkened boathouse, his eyes rolled up into their sockets. Strong gusts pushed and pulled at the outside of the building.

The overuse of Cranchet's body by the Great Crystal's demands had left him very drained.

Cranchet was dying in the cold metal chair.

A strong odor of copper and dust grew in the room, and then the room lit up—bright light coming from no specific source.

His body began to heal. The congestive heart failure that had been about to kill him, the incipient cancer that would have grown fairly rapidly and the crippling joint and muscle ailments were being eliminated. Even his cholesterol problem.

With the final expenditure of power contained within the Great Crystal, Cranchet was rewarded for his service with at least twenty years added to his life.

This was the last breath from the Great Crystal, the last decision implemented by what was left of the Rescue Souls, who were now only a computer memory.

It was over. The room went dark. The aroma of copper and dust was gone.

On Black Island, the lights in the inner chamber went out. The book Gumtooo was reading disappeared. "Gumtooo reports no more power."

Cranchet's eyes returned to normal. As warm memories of helping Olias with the motor floated around his mind, he sat upright. His thoughts cleared. "I fell asleep in this horrible chair? This is going to hurt."

He looked around for his cane, and saw it on the other side of the room, propped against a door. "Damn. I don't remember putting it way over there. What the hell was I thinking? This isn't going to feel pleasant."

He stood up and began to hobble—but there was no pain! He could walk normally! He walked right to the cane.

"Wooooo hooooooo!!!"

He couldn't figure out the source of this miracle, and paced around the boathouse with vigor, pondering it. He ran in circles, then back to the cane, picked it up and pointed it straight up. "I guess someone up there likes me!" he yelled as the storm pounded the outside of the boathouse. "Look at me, Loretta!!!"

And then he danced. Old Man Cranchet could once cut a mean rug, and now he could again. He danced around the boathouse while singing.

He all but skipped to his car—completely ignoring the storm—and drove home.

Ravenous, he devoured a huge bowl of pasta while preparing a meal for his close friends. It was to be a fun night. He'd play a joke on them: he'd hobble with his cane until everyone arrived, then yell "Catch!" and throw the cane to someone, then start running in a tight circle around them! After that, he'd blast some music and start dancing! "What the hell is everyone going to think about this?!" he wondered with the happiness of a child. "I wish Loretta was still alive to see this!" he said out loud.

He walked to his big bay window and looked up into the flashing lightning.

"Did *you* do this, Loretta?!"

He waited for a response, but there was only the wind. He thought of her, and the good times they'd had. He cried. "I really miss you, Loretta."

His emotions were whirring. He jumped up and down, dried his eyes and laughed.

"Look at me, Loretta!" He ran vigorously in place. "I feel so *alive!"*

5

Jimmy and Lenny chugged their free beers. "Hey there, *Tamz*, another round over here!" Jimmy demanded.

"Oh! Ha ha! Right away! I can make that! Ha ha ha!" She grabbed two beers from the cooler.

"So, *Tamz*, when did you move to Mount Haven?" Jimmy asked.

"Only a few weeks ago! I can't believe I got a job already! Everyone said I wouldn't be able to find work! Ha ha ha!"

Lenny stared at her with growing hatred. This annoying bitch needed to go. Where was Manuel and Manuel's rock hard abs and fluffy feathered hair? This bitch was so fucking annoying. Stubby little fake bitch.

Jimmy thought that if he slammed another few beers, this bitch might look "do-able."

"Hey, Lenny, watch this." Jimmy chugged his beer in one huge gulp.

"Ha! Good one, Jimmy!"

Tammy couldn't believe how fast the beer went into the big strapping man. "Wow! You're good at that!"

"Yup. Now, let's have another over here," Jimmy ordered.

"Right away!" She ran and got the next beer. "Here you go!"

"Thanks there, little lady. So, if I wanted a margarita right now, could you make one for me?"

Tammy's eyes showed fear. Jimmy and Lenny loved that. It felt like food. And they were always hungry.

"Um, sure, let me just get that book—"

"Oh, don't worry about it, little lady, I'm just messin' with ya, ha ha."

"Oh yoooooooooou! Ha ha ha!" Tammy went and got the book anyway, and plopped it down on the bar between her and Jimmy. "So, what other drinks can we make?!"

Lenny tried remembering what all the "rich fucks" drink. "Martini. Let's see you make a martini."

"Oh! Ha ha ha!" She started looking for the "M's" while reciting the alphabet song under her breath. She flipped through the pages around the beginning of the book, then around the end, as Jimmy and Lenny looked at each other and chuckled. Eventually, she found them. "The 'M's'!" she triumphed. "Okay, let's see... here it is! Martini!"

"Why don't you make one 'a them," suggested Lenny, with no intention of buying or drinking it.

"Okay!" She read that there were only two ingredients, and this time had the wherewithal to look in the speed rack first, finding them both—gin and vermouth.

Stacy looked over to see the new bartender mixing a drink and figured everything was fine, but wished Manuel was working instead. It was always more exciting when Manuel was behind the bar. But this is what Sugar Daddy wanted, and Sugar Daddy was king.

Tammy took a water glass and poured gin into it, then poured in an equal amount of vermouth, filling the glass. "Martini! Martini!"

"I think it goes in a different glass," Lenny said, chuckling.

"Oh! Oh! A martini glass, right?!"

"Sounds about right," Jimmy said.

She looked around for the martini glasses, and eventually found them at the other end of the bar, took one and walked back. She poured the contents of the water glass into the martini glass, only to find that not even half of it fit. A third of the drink spilled onto the floor. "Oh! I guess I made it too big!"

"Guess you did, little lady."

"Oh! Ha ha ha!"

Jimmy had already imbibed his next beer. "Well whattaya know. My bottle's empty over here."

"Oh!" While running to the cooler, she slipped on the martini-puddle, but recovered with the agility of a cat. She snagged Jimmy another. "Here you go!"

"Thank you, little lady. Nice move there."

"Oh! Thank you! Grr, I'm a cat! Grr, I'm a cat!"

Lenny squinted. "Jeez Jimmy, you're really downin' them beers there."

"Yup."

Tammy looked to see if Stacy was watching, saw that she was occupied at the computer, and dumped what was left in the water glass down the bar sink. "So, who's drinking this martini?!"

Lenny smiled. "I don't want it. Jimmy?"

"Naw, not me."

"But... I made it! I made the martini like you asked!"

"We just wanted you to get some practice, little lady. Don't worry, it'll be in your tip."

"Oh! Thank you!"

"Now dump it and get rid 'a the glass there, so's no one sees."

"Okay!" She made sure Stacy was still occupied and no servers were watching, and dumped the rest down the drain.

Jimmy was drunk, and Tammy was starting to look acceptable. "Hey there, Tamzh, watch thish." He chugged. "Another, little lady."

"Oh! Oh!" She ran and grabbed another. "Here!"

Lenny's face contorted. "So, Jimmy, is Elsa gonna be gone tonight?"

"Oh... I think."

"Oh." Lenny was appeased.

"Who's Elsa?!" asked Tammy.

Lenny started to respond as Jimmy thrust an arm over his face. "She's jusht some girl that'sh all into me, right Lenny?"

Lenny smiled. "Ha, yup, just some girl. All the girls like Jimmy, ain't that so, Jimmy?"

"Yup."

"Jimmy here spars with a professional wrestler in Ellsworth."

"Oh! You must be so stroooonggggg!"

"Yup, little lady."

Lenny was itching to get back to his Zack and Cody. "I'm gettin' tired, Jimmy."

Jimmy knew he couldn't have sex with Tammy tonight, unless he stayed at the bar until her shift was over, and that was probably hours away. But, his intoxication experiment had been a success—she looked "do-able."

"Yeah, Lenny, I guessh you can drive me home." Jimmy reached into his pants pocket, pulled out a crumpled twenty dollar bill and held it up.

"Here, Tamzh." She extended her hand and he placed the twenty in it with a sexy tickle on her thumb.

"Oh! Thank you! Tee heeeeee!"

"Don' mention it, li'l lerdy."

6

Stacy solved the computer problems and began printing out a remedied check for waiting patrons. She finally looked up and saw Jimmy and Lenny leaving the restaurant into a strong wind. Tammy was behind the bar, watching TV—one of the shopping channels. Most customers had left early due to the storm; only two tables remained occupied, and they already had their checks. It was time to visit Bob in the office. A little sexy grin lit across her face as she almost skipped through the kitchen to his door and knocked.

"Yeah?"

"Bob, it's me."

"C'mon in!"

She quickly opened and closed the door while playfully slipping inside. "Hiya Mr. Mannnn!"

They hugged.

"Heyyyy Girlie…"

They kissed their second kiss.

"Oh, Bob…"

"Hey Girlie, I got you another present."

"Oh!"

From under his desk he produced a tiny wrapped box crowned with a fancy purple bow.

"Oh, Bob!" She quickly opened it to find a pretty gold necklace. "It's beautiful! Oh Bob!" They hugged.

"One more little gift there, Girlie," he said smarmily while producing a small, expensively wrapped box.

A brief thought slipped through the cracks of her psyche and was forgotten: "Money is true love!"

She opened the second present. Inside the box was a golden key. "Bob? What's this?"

"It's the key to my apartment, Girlie. You're invited anytime."

"Oh, Bob!"

They hugged again, this time with their bodies in full frontal touch. Stacy felt Bob's hard penis press against her stomach. It felt right. "Bob..."

"Heh heh."

7

Jimmy got a final drunken look at Tamz as he and Lenny walked out of the See Food into the storm. The rain had strengthened into a pounding downpour.

Lenny never had a reason to lock his car—locks weren't used much on the island. So, after walking across the street, Jimmy beat Lenny to the car and hunkered into the passenger seat. Lenny got in and drove slowly through the storm. "Jimmy, you got any doob?"

"No, I don'. Hey, that Tamzh chick getsh better lookin' after shlammin' a few, huh? She looked fuck'ble at th' end," he slurred.

"Sure Jimmy, ha ha."

"I could be slammin' into *her!*"

"Ha ha, good one Jimmy."

The alcohol was still hitting him. "Yeah, I should bring her back to th' 'partment *tonight!*"

"But, when's Elsa gettin' back from her mom's?"

"Oh... hey... been meanin' to tell ya, Lenny... Elsha and me, we broke up."

"What?!"

"Yup. The bitch was givin' me conshtant shit an' yellin' an' shit, and I tol' her *get out!*"

"When was that, Jimmy?! When was that?!"

"A... few daysh ago."

"Why didn't you tell me, Jimmy?"

"I, didn' wanna."

"What?"

"Let her shtay at her fuckin' asshole mother'sh, they're both fuckin' shtupid asshole bitches!"

Lenny saw the sadness in Jimmy's heart. "Maybe you should get back with her, you seemed to like her a lot sometimes."

"That bitch ain't comin' back."

"But Jimmy, pump some iron in front of her, show her who the big man is! She'll come around, I thi—"

"SHUT UUUUUP YOU FUCKIN' ASSHOLE!!!"

Lenny froze. He wasn't taking this conversation any further.

"Lenny, jusht drive me home."

Lenny drove to Jimmy's truck, and they stared at it. The driving rain was thoroughly soaking the seats.

"I'll deal with this shit after th' shtorm," he said while getting out. "Talk ya shoon."

"See ya, Jimmy." Lenny went home and fantasized about Lars Vorhees and his hoagies.

8

Seth's mom paced her kitchen, intermittently looking out at the dark, rough ocean. Lightning transformed the world into daylight for a second at a time, before returning it to black.

Where was Seth?! He blew off dinner with Edna Black, and so did she! Neither of them even called! He wasn't answering his phone and the old woman wasn't answering hers!

She went back to cutting leftover steak for yet another steak sandwich dinner, but again she wasn't hungry.

"If he hadn't left that message saying he was alright and that he'd call back to explain, the mainland police would be here in force," she thought to herself for the umpteenth time.

Seth's dad entered the kitchen. "Steak sandwiches for dinner again, I take it?"

"Of course dear, what do you think?"

"I think we should go knock on his apartment door again, like tomorrow, and ream him the damn out!"

"I know, dear, I know."

"So, what's on TV tonight?"

CHAPTER 12:   Secrets

1

$\mathbf{D}$an's rent payment was two weeks late. The landlord, Ol' Tommy Mulligan, knocked on Dan's apartment door for the third day in a row and again there was no answer. Dan wasn't answering his phone, either. "Damn asshole," muttered Mulligan, standing at the door as the wind raged. He figured he'd find the kid home on a Sunday night during a storm, but no.

As the rain pummeled the back of his neck, Mulligan figured what the hell, pulled out the key and turned the lock.

The horrific stench hit him. It smelled like rotting death.

He expected to find a body. He stiffened with fear.

"...Hellllo?!"

He lifted his shirt over his nose and crept forward. The odor was coming from the bedroom. A cold sweat swiftly coated his body. "Helllllll...o?"

He approached the room, his legs becoming rubbery. The door was wide open. His knees almost buckled as he entered.

There was blood and what looked like feces everywhere. The shirt he was breathing through wasn't much help. He thought he was going to retch and held his breath.

"Whatever happened, happened in the bed," he surmised. He made sure there was no body and ran back outside into the swirling storm, gulping the first few breaths.

He almost dialed the mainland police in Rockport, but on second thought decided otherwise. There was no body. Yet. Until there was, the island could handle this problem. "No law past the breakwater," he said aloud as a nearby tree branch bent and snapped.

He spent the next hour on the phone, calling Mount Haven Village residents. He learned from Dan's employer that Dan had been fired days ago for abandoning his job. He thought of one more place he could call. The See Food.

Todd was nearing the end of his shift. "Hello? See Food Bar and Grill, Todd speaking, how may I help you?"

"Hello, this is Thomas Mulligan. I rent some apartments on Calderwood Street, and one of my residents has gone missing. His name is Dan Smith. Do you know him?"

"Not by name, sorry. What does he look like?"

"He's young, thin, about five foot six, short brown hair."

"Sorry, that's not enough to go on. Do you have a picture of the guy?"

"...No, I don't."

"Well, if I hear of anyone named Dan Smith who abandoned his apartment, I'll let you know, Mr. Mulligan." Todd's promises were sincere.

"Alright, thank you." Mulligan put his phone away. "What a crappy day," he thought. "At least tonight'll be fun." He looked forward to the night ahead with his oldest pal Burt Cranchet and his other childhood friends, hurricane be damned.

2

Dan and Seth sat on Edna's sofa in a daze, legs and arms touching, staring into a roaring fire, not noticing that they didn't have to feed new wood into the fireplace. Outside, the gale's surf pounded the beach.

Their eyes closed simultaneously and they began dreaming the same dream. They saw sweet Edna Black, holding court from a huge altar, speaking to billions of enraptured people spread across the Earth. The people held up cupped, praying hands. Some seemed to have cupped, praying claws. Some had talons.

They saw floating ships and crystalline light flying through the sky. They saw themselves suckling at Edna's teat, their bodies growing. They saw Edna holding a cooing baby in her arms, kissing it, the baby screaming—its body on fire. They saw another convulsing infant pop in a bloom of fire. They saw people engulfed in dark flames.

They saw children lying in gutters and ditches with huge boils on their stomachs. The boils had screaming mouths.

They saw how wise and happy Grammie/Nana was.

They saw millions of people dying in agony, their bodies exploding outward in beautiful red-rose-colored flowery arrays.

And the whole time, Dan and Seth were standing at Grammie/Nana's side. They were powerful. Their lives had meaning. They were more important than they'd ever thought possible.

On the sofa, asleep in front of the crackling fire, Dan and Seth symbiotically smiled and farted.

3

Not long after Bob gave Stacy the necklace and the key, they closed the restaurant early and went back to his apartment. They had sex as the storm wrapped around the eaves.

Bob thought it was wild sex. And, he thought they did it twice, but the second time was just wishful thinking.

Stacy wasn't thinking about it directly—she needed to retain some denial when it came to being sexual with Bob—but she had not enjoyed it. Bob was as good in bed as he was at music—his performance was erratic, devoid of rhythm and finesse. She had only felt like a Bob Receptacle. She didn't come close to an orgasm, and she was a girl who came to a full orgasm more often than not. But, it was only their first time, and he was Mr. Man Sugar Daddy after all, so it didn't matter. "It's only sex, really. Bob offers me so much more," she justified while falling asleep beside him.

At some point during the night, the power went out across the island.

Stacy woke in the morning to see the storm blowing. She looked over at Bob and saw him sleeping deeply. She got out of bed stealthily, but didn't have to move around the room quietly due to the loud wind whistling at the windows and Bob's snoring. She dressed and found a rain jacket.

She braved the storm, walking to her apartment down Main Street. "This hurricane isn't as bad as they said it was going to be," she thought.

A couple hours later, Bob woke in the empty bed. He sat up, stretched and said, "And I don't have to hear her yappin' in the mornin'!" He got dressed while whistling. Suddenly, the power came on. "Nice!"

All his bitches were in a row. "Well, the two of them." He started some coffee brewing and sauntered into the living room. He plopped onto the sofa, clicked on the TV and watched ESPN. He was content. It was all coming together. Stacy had stayed the night and now had a toothbrush in the bathroom. Next step, more of her clothes needed to find their way into the apartment. He pictured her clothes sexily strewn about, especially in the bedroom. He liked that image. And, most importantly, she needed to find her bitch-ass in his bed every night.

However, the California bitch needed tending to. This would be easy. "Like lying to a baby," he thought. He dialed her number.

"Bob! Hi! I was just thinking about you! I love you, Bob!"

"Hey, wassup. So, it looks like I ain't gonna make it home this week, I gotta reschedule the trip, got problems here."

"Oh, Bob... maybe we *should* visit Maine. The kids have to be back in school in a few weeks, so it should be soon!"

"No, too busy here. Got problems with the staff. People are quitting prematurely before the end of the season. I was washing dishes last night!" (This was only partly a lie—Bob had washed one dish to show a new dishwasher how to work the machine.)

"But, Bob, you promised me I'd get to see you!"

"Yeah, sorry there. Look, I'll call you tomorrow if I hire more people, okay?"

She was silent. Bob knew this was a warning sign. "Look, baaaaabe, I miss you—I do—I love you, too."

"...Oh Bob, then please make this work? Please?!"

"You got it! I'll call ya tomorrow! Go get 'em!"

"Oh Bob, ha ha. Alright, talk to you tomorrow."

Bob snapped his phone closed while she was saying "tomorrow" and threw it to the other side of the sofa. The California bitch was growing an attitude and might need damage control. He put his feet up on the coffee table and exhaled, fantasizing about Stacy's body. "That bitch got herself one hell of an ass," he said out loud.

His phone rang. He rolled to the other side of the sofa and let out a little snort as he grabbed it. It was Stacy. "Heyyyyyy, Girlie!"

"Hi, Mr. Mannnnnn!"

"So whattaya doin'? Why aren't ya here right now with me?! Huh? Huh?!"

"Ha ha Bob, you're so funny! I'll be there soon. I was wondering, is there any room in one of your closets for some of my clothes?"

"Is there *room?!!* I've been cleanin' the closets out for ya!"

"Thank you! Hee hee!"

"Am I gonna see ya before your shift tonight, Girlie?"

"Yes, Bob," she said playfully, "I'll be there soon."

"Girlie, see ya soon!" He jumped off the sofa and did a little dance.

4

Kara didn't want to work in the restaurant business. The stress level was too high. Like so many, she fantasized about winning the lottery. But with that fantasy, came no meaning for her life, and she always felt her life needed *purpose.*

And what a joy that Cranchet—or whoever that was—said they wouldn't need their jobs anymore. There was a huge new chapter of her life unfolding, and it had *meaning.*

But on Monday morning when the power returned, she called Todd to ask if the See Food was opening for lunch. She knew that if she quit abruptly, it would make his day hellish. In the restaurant business, blowing off work is not an option unless you can get someone to cover your shift. If not, you directly hurt your fellow employees and friends. Kara knew she'd be quitting, but would not quit without warning. She didn't have it in her to do something that insensitive. "Hi Todd, so, are we opening?"

"Yes we are, Kara. You'll probably make good money today, too."

At this point, that was something she still needed. "Great, see you soon. And Todd, I'm telling you first. I'll be leaving the See Food."

"What?! Kara, that really sucks. Why? Did you find a better job?"

"I think so..."

"Well, I'm sure you'll always be welcomed back!"

"Thanks Todd, you're sweet. See you soon."

"See ya."

Kara threw on her nylon windbreaker and walked to work through the "hurricane," which had only amounted to a gale thanks to the Great Crystal.

She always worked a double on Mondays. This particular Monday was a busy day-shift for her because the See Food was slammed due to the storm—many on the island hadn't gotten their power back and craved a hot meal. She was running from table to table and making great tips. Meanwhile, Manuel was tending a mostly-empty bar.

Near the end of the day, Kara's tables were emptying and she finally had a chance to breathe. She needed a couple sodas for a table, and Manuel poured them for her—he'd been pouring sodas all day. He had them sitting at the end of the bar for pickup while he leaned against the wall, depressed.

"Thanks, Manuel," she said.

"You got it, Kara."

Kara brought the sodas to her table and walked back. "How are you doing, Manuel?"

"I'm really worried about not having enough money for rent and utilities on the island. I took this job because Bob begged me. He promised I'd have the night shift until the first week of September, so I crunched those numbers, and it worked out. So, I stayed on Mount Haven and took the job."

"I'm really glad you did. You're by far the best bartender we've ever had in this little town."

"Thank you, Kara, you're always so nice. And I'm glad I took the job. The islands of Maine are beautiful, as are the pretty summer girls. And I have already purchased all my textbooks for the coming semester."

"Is there any possibility of you getting more night shifts? The word around here is that Tammy doesn't know anything. I hear she can't even make a rum and coke!"

"Ha, yes, I heard that too. But Bob is pretty adamant about this. I can only beg so many times." Manuel took his voice down to a whisper. "I'm done begging a man whose words have no honor."

Kara whispered, "They certainly don't. I hope things go well for you, Manuel."

"Thank you, you're a good friend."

Kara wished Olias was here to help—he was great at consoling others. "You should come party with Olias, Jon and me some night."

"That would be great! Thanks."

"Welcome."

Bob bounded into the restaurant. "Hiya there Kara. Hiya Manuel," he blurted while walking briskly by them toward the office.

"Hi Bob," they said with strained smiles. He was gone as soon as he'd appeared.

"What a dick," Kara said softly.

"Totally."

Todd was in the office checking his emails as Bob burst in, startling him. "Hey there buddy, you can go. I got the shift until Stacy arrives."

"...Okay, Bob, um, thanks, see you."

"Yup yup."

Todd left as Bob put the Olias disk into the computer and studied everything on it one more time. "Sicko," he muttered.

Stacy entered the restaurant. While she was at the computer clocking in, Manuel walked over. "Stacy, you weren't home this morning! I walked by your apartment on the way to work to give you your CD back." He handed her a CD she had lent him. "Don't worry, it didn't get wet."

"Thanks, Manuel. Um, yes, I went for a walk this morning."

"Oh," he said while walking back behind the bar.

Kara approached Stacy. "Stacy, I'm going to grab something to eat while I have time, I'll be in the kitchen if you need me."

"Okay, Kara." Stacy went and looked at the schedule to see who was working that night as Kara made herself a sandwich and walked to the far back of the kitchen to enjoy it.

Two waitresses working the night shift entered—Romona and Ellie. Romona had her ritual flirt with Manuel. "Hiiiiiii Manuel..."

"Hi, Romona."

Stacy wanted to go into the office and see Bob, but he had said not to. "I don't want these idiots around here knowing our business," he'd said after they had sex in the early afternoon. So, she started talking with Ellie and Romona, gossiping about island events.

Bob finished looking at everything he stole from Olias's computer and decided to walk into the house and be social with his waitstaff. He exited the office and strode through the kitchen. The bitch and her ass were his! "Mission accomplished. Wave the fucking flag and salute," he thought while smiling at employees.

He walked out in the middle of Stacy, Ellie and Romona's conversation. They didn't see him. They were facing Manuel, who was bending over, looking into the beer cooler and jotting items down on a pad. He figured he'd take inventory for Tammy, who was late.

The girls were giggling while speaking in hushed tones. "My God, Manuel, take it off, take it alllll off!" Ellie said.

"Oh my God, yes!" Romona agreed.

"That level of hot shouldn't be legal," added Stacy.

Bob was floored. An angry glower flooded his reddening face. He retreated back into the kitchen without being seen and stormed to the office, where he sat at his desk, trying to maintain a level of composure, but his eyes were burning with jealousy. He waited until it wouldn't look weird to leave his office again, and stormed through the kitchen to the house. "Manuel, buddy! Come see me in my office when you get a sec, huh?!"

Manuel peered up from the cooler as the girls broke apart and started filling salt and pepper shakers.

"Yes, Bob," Manuel said.

Bob blasted through the kitchen to his desk, where he sat and stared angrily at the wall, getting ready for his act. The curtain was about to rise and he was going over his lines.

Manuel came to the door and knocked, hopeful that Bob was going to give him some night shifts due to how bad a bartender Tammy was.

"C'mon in," Bob said.

Manuel sat. "What's up, Bob?"

"Look, buddy, I'm gonna have to let you go. I'm losin' money with this restaurant, and this time 'a year I gotta slash the payroll and only keep the workers who stay until the end of October."

The rest of the air left Manuel's sails. "But, Bob, I really need the money... I'm behind on rent... Is there anything you can do? I'll work any shift you want. I'll be a waiter, a busser, anything," he pleaded. "A dishwashing shift. Anything."

"Sorry there, buddy. It's just business. You're going off to school anyway, right?"

"Yes, but—"

"Ha ha well great! You're gonna do great! Go get 'em!"

Manuel worried about his rent and bills. He sat in a broody silence, looking at the floor.

Bob was already sick of it. "Okay, buddy, I got some important paperwork I gotta do. Thanks for your help this summer, buddy! You can go! Go get 'em!"

Manuel stood, defeated. "Thanks, Bob..." He couldn't believe this was happening. He walked through the restaurant and out the front door. No one saw him leave. He walked all the way to his apartment far down Main Street, never looking back.

5

Stacy called Tammy to find out where she was, got an answering service, but didn't leave a message. She walked behind the bar, picked up the remote and turned to the Weather Channel. What was once Hurricane David was now a light rain.

Tammy scurried in, frazzled.

Stacy was changing channels. "Hi, Tammy."

"Hi! Hi! Sorry I'm late! I took a cat nap and woke up late! Purrrr! Purrrrr! Cat nap!"

Stacy wondered why she was so odd. It wasn't good for business. But, Bob had told everyone to treat Tammy nicely as she learned the job. "That's okay, Tammy, it happens to all of us sometimes."

"Call me Tamz! Call me Tamz!" She ran to the computer and clocked in.

Stacy hadn't gotten her "bye" from Manuel, and wondered if he was still around. "Did you see Manuel out there, Tammy— um, Tamz?"

"No! No! No! I didn't see him!"

Stacy was confused. She took the pile of freshly printed dinner specials and started placing them on empty tables. Romona had a four-top of elderly early-bird patrons and needed four martinis. She typed the order into the computer and "martini – 4" came through the little bar printer. Tammy had gotten sidetracked by a commercial for girls' running shoes. "I want those shoes!" she proclaimed loudly to no one. She didn't notice the bar order.

Romona stood at the end of the bar, waiting for her drinks. "Tammy? I put an order through."

"Oh! Oh! Right away!" She ripped the tiny slip out of the printer and put it up to her face. "Four martinis! Four martinis! Coming right up!" She all but lunged for the bar book, having forgotten the ingredients. Romona stared, dumbfounded.

6

Lenny woke early Monday morning to find the power out and his cupboards bare. He decided to go to the market in hopes it was open. He threw on some smelly clothes, jumped in his car and drove there. It was open.

While filling his cart with Natural Ice beer and Ramen Noodles, he bumped into Elsa in aisle two. "Hey there, Elsa."

"Oh, hi, Lenny."

"So, you and Jimmy are broke up, huh?"

"Yes, Lenny." She just wanted to get away from him.

"He's bein' stubborn. I tol' him he should get back with you, but he said he don' wanna."

"Oh? Because Lenny, *I* broke up with *him.*"

"Wha-?"

"Don't listen to a bullshitting word that asshole says, Lenny. He came to my mother's house and threw a rock through my bedroom window and screamed that he loved me and wanted me back. I said no fucking way."

"Wha—?!"

"Yup. So when you see him next—and I know you will, sooner rather than later—tell him I still say *no fucking way.*"

"Oh, okay, I will, Elsa, I will."

"Goodbye, Lenny." She walked away rapidly, grabbed a few essentials, and got into the checkout line.

Lenny was surprised how much Jimmy had lied about the breakup, but then thought about it. "I guess Jimmy don' wanna look like the loser... But damn, Jimmy *is* the loser!"

7

Stacy woke up on Monday morning in Bob's big bed. Bob was already up, drinking coffee and working on the restaurant books. "Half these inbred idiots don't even know that they're not gettin' Social Security," he chuckled to himself.

Stacy came up behind him and gave him a warm hug.

"Heyyy there, Girlie. Sleep well?"

"Yes! I'd like to sleep that well every night."

"Well hey, Girlieeeee, I think it's time you moved in permanently."

"But, Bob! My lease isn't up for another seven months!"

"Oh yeah? Look babe, I'll make some calls. We'll get you outta that lease toute frikkin' suite. That way, you don't have to pay rent any more!"

"Really, Bob?! Oh!" She squeezed him with the biggest bear hug she could muster. She couldn't believe how confident and powerful he was. She didn't know if she was falling in love, but she sure liked the benefits. This guy wasn't Todd... Todd was just a boy. This guy was a *man*. "A man's man," she thought.

Later that morning, Bob called the owner of Stacy's apartment and convinced him to let her out of the lease as a favor. Business owners on the island had a special way of bartering and interacting. It took all of a two-minute phone call, during which the weather was mentioned twice.

Stacy was elated and spent the morning packing her things and driving them to Bob's while he did his paperwork.

In a few hours, Stacy was almost completely moved in. She still had a few odds and ends left at her place, but she knew she had a couple days to move them. He had arranged that. "My Bob!" She was in the kitchen whistling happily and removing clean silverware from the dishwasher. Bob entered, wearing a pre-packaged expression that was meant to denote concern mixed with wisdom. "Now Stace, I've been really thinking about this, and, we can't tell anyone that you're living here yet. It will be the talk of the town."

"What?! But Bob, I'm proud to be your girl!"

"I know, Girlie, but, you know how rumors go on this island. And, my divorce isn't final just yet."

"Bob, you said you were 'basically' divorced!"

"I am, I am, just a couple little loose ends to tie up is all. Now calm *down* there little lady, don't be so selfish. Have patience. With the money you save on not having to pay rent, you'll be able to buy a new car!"

"Really? Yeah, I guess that's true! But we can't keep something so obvious a secret for long!"

"I know, Girlie, but, just for awhile? For me?"

"Okay, I'll keep us a secret, Bob. For you."

8

Olias ate the last of the toast he'd made and sipped coffee alone at his kitchen table.

He wondered what would happen at the boatyard with Old Man Cranchet. There was no way Olias would just quit on the nice old man without warning. Neither would Jon, he knew. And did "Cranchet" have more messages for them?

It was almost the end of August, which meant autumn on the islands would now begin. It would still be mostly summer for another month, but the advent of the Dead Season would make itself known with scattered chilly nights. And where would he, Kara and Jon be in a month? What were their lives going to be like?

He picked up Jon and they drove to the boatyard. Shep, Jeffy and the rest of the guys were already there, strewn about the yard, focused on their different tasks.

Olias and Jon walked all over the grounds looking for Old Man Cranchet, but couldn't find him.

"I'll call him," Olias said.

"Hello?"

"Hi Mr. Cranchet, it's Olias. I forgot what my job is for today."

"Olias?! Are you playing a joke on me?!"

"Um, well ha ha... What do *you* think?"

"I think you're quite the comedian. Now you and Jon enjoy your new lives, and thank you for the work you've done for me. You guys are hard workers. And thanks for the two-week notice. That was respectful."

"Sure..."

"You gotta see me dance sometime!"

"Okay... Sounds fun?"

"This storm's fizzled and the ocean will calm overnight, so go get ready, and I'll see you around the island, kiddo!"

"Thanks, Mr. Cranchet."

Jon heard the conversation. "Wow. That was easy."

"I guess we should go get our gear packed and ready!"

Olias dropped Jon off at his apartment and drove home. They each enjoyed a mellow morning and afternoon in a way they never would again. This chapter in their lives was waning quicker than the hurricane.

Around six o'clock, the ocean was still rough and the waves loud as Olias went to his computer and looked at the satellite radar of the dead storm, his interest solely in the morning marine forecast. He needed to know when the high surf was going to diminish.

The forecast was positive. Sunny and calm by morning. He called Kara, who was just getting home.

"'Ello, luv!" she said in a butchered, "Dick-Van-Dyke" style Cockney accent.

"'Ello, me luv!," Olias mirrored. "It looks like we are a go for the morning!"

"Wow... This is all a dream..."

"I know..."

"Are we going to bring our camping gear?"

"I don't see how it could hurt. I say we bring as many supplies as we can fit in Ziggy."

"Yes. And, let me guess, you're looking at the weather forecast as we speak."

"Did I mention how much I love you?"

"And I you, my lover boy."

"So, want to hang tonight?"

"Sure, just give me some time to shower and bring clothes for tomorrow."

"K."

Kara started going through her closet as she spoke. "I take it it'll be nice weather?"

"Yes, as far as the sun shining in the sky is concerned. But it's still a little too early to get an accurate marine forecast. I hope the ocean's not too rough. Huge rollers could send us into the cold-ass ocean. Ziggy's a trooper, but he's small."

"I know. But I trust your touch at the helm. Remember that time off Moose Island, trying to get home in that crazy huge surf after dark in November?"

"Don't remind me."

"Well, you got us out of that alive, luv."

"Just barely."

CHAPTER 13: Horizons

1

Overnight, the clouds blew away and the wind ceased. The air dried like a desert. A brilliant star field burned across the sky. It was a new moon—the only light was from the stars and planets. The ocean calmed so completely that there were no waves. Not even a ripple. The islands—barely framed by starlight—appeared to be surrounded by dark glass. The ocean was as calm as a puddle on a lazy summer morning. It was a very rare occurrence, if it had ever happened before. Not a sound on the island cluster. Not a puff of breeze. Nature herself seemed in prayer.

2

Edna felt the drop in power at Black Island, and knew there was a possible opening for her to finally set foot on that once-desert peak. It wouldn't be her first time. She had been there during the First Destruction of Atlantis (which, for all intents and purposes, she had caused).

Inside her ocean cottage it was black as pitch. The lack of wind and waves produced complete silence.

Dan and Seth slept soundly in their immaculate cribs as she floated slowly up the staircase.

She first wafted into Seth's room, and looked through him—saw his skeletal structure, every skin blemish, every little thing wrong. She probed his brain for anything that might not take direct orders. She didn't want one of these puny humans to suddenly contract a mind of its own at a critical juncture on Black Island. She needed extensions of herself—puppets. After doing a full diagnostic on his body and brain, she found him acceptable for service.

She floated into Dan's room and scanned him. There was still some residue from that rebellious boil, but she decided that he was also ready. Her milk had seen to that.

While moving in pure silence down the staircase, she inserted into Seth's mind a command to get his parents' boat.

Knowing Olias and his friends had fixed their boat, she had to know when they were going to Black Island. They might have secrets as to how to access the Great Crystal. She would have to observe them on the island, then swoop in and claim the power that should have been her destiny. Once in control of the Great Crystal, she would reign on earth. She would again create abominations—half human, half animal: hybrids. The perfect slaves. All of humanity would bow with cupped hands—or whatever appendages they'd have—to her, and would again call her by her proper name, *Lillith.*

3

Seth shot up in bed at two o'clock in the morning. He dressed, ran to his car and drove to his parents' place. All their lights were out. He stealthily parked away from the house and snuck through the front yard to the ocean. He quietly brought the tender to the water and rowed out to the boat. He unhooked the mooring line and waited for the wind and current to carry him out of earshot. But there was no wind or current... He waited over a half hour, but was still right at the mooring. If he started the motor, they'd hear it.

The black-eyed gull sat on the boat's roof. Seth stared into it. He pulled the keys out of his pocket and started the engines.

The light in his parents' bedroom snapped on.

He slammed her to full speed and loudly set off down the coast.

His father came running out of the house—wearing only underwear—and onto the dock, watching the boat's lights come on as it motored away. "What the damn! Seth?!!"

Seth piloted the boat to Edna's beach, where he anchored and rowed to shore in the tender. He creaked loudly up the old staircase and went back to bed, but didn't return to sleep.

He had never woken up.

4

Gumtooo expected the reincarnated Rescue Souls to arrive in the morning, and was ready to talk them through the process of going behind the wall of black and reaching the Inner Chamber of the Great Crystal. Gumtooo didn't know that the dark thing—Lillith—would also be arriving.

5

The first light of dawn broke over the ocean to the east, and the new day began. Olias, Kara and Jon were still fast asleep, garnering much-needed rest.

Meanwhile, Dan and Seth opened their eyes simultaneously and sat up. From the kitchen they heard Grammie/Nana call to them, "Boys! Breakfast! Come and get it!"

They jumped out of bed, met in the hallway and ran down the steps to the kitchen, where they ravenously devoured everything in sight.

Once they were full, Grammie/Nana called to them from the sofa in the living room, "Boooooooys! Come get your life milk!" They stood with contorted smiles and walked into the living room.

The crone sat in the middle of the sofa. She patted the left side and the right side as she said, "Dan, you come to Grammie here, and Seth, you come to Nana here." They did as she said.

Lillith exposed her breasts. With each hand, she touched Dan's and Seth's heads gently around their ears, and brought their mouths to her nipples.

"Feed, my children, *feed.*"

Dan and Seth suckled the rotten goo from Lillith's breasts—that in their minds was the whitest, cleanest milk imaginable—but in reality was venomous bile formed from epochs of hate. They gurgled and cooed.

Lillith stared straight ahead as they suckled, smiling one of her rare, genuine smiles.

6

Kara was the first of the musketeers to open her eyes. She looked at Olias, who was sleeping soundly. "I'm going to marry him," she thought. She watched him sleep for a few minutes.

He opened his eyes. "Morning, luv."

"Morning."

They kissed and held each other. "I can't believe this day has finally arrived," he said.

"I wonder how our lives are going to change."

They heard a clang in the kitchen, and knew Jon was making coffee. "I love how he does that," she said.

"Me too." He paused. "I've been thinking about his loneliness. He likes Tawny, you know."

"Oh, I know. I saw it right away. He always sneaks looks at her. And she sneaks looks at him."

"Do you think he's capable of too much angry drunken behavior for her?"

"It's possible. But if anyone could straighten him out, it's Tawny."

"We have more pressing and immediate things to consider, but…"

"I'm on it, luv. I've been on it. Let me work at my own speed with this."

"Hey, you're the master."

"You got that right!"

They kissed, got out of bed and dressed. Jon already had the kitchen smelling like fresh coffee and sweet cinnamon raisin toast. "Morning!" he said happily.

Kara hugged him while saying, "It means a lot to us that you always have the coffee ready, Jon. What will we do without you?"

"Without me? I'm not going anywhere!"

"Well, you never know whose kitchen you'll be making coffee in, when, you know…"

"What? Oh…" Jon's face reddened.

They had a filling breakfast as the sun—which would play an integral role in their lives this day—crossed over the horizon and splashed glorious light over the ocean. Sharp sparkles lit the island cluster. The salty air was warm and dry. Today was the day. Today was the day for which Olias, Kara and Jon were born.

7

Stacy woke up in Bob's bed and looked at him. He was still sleeping, his face contorted. She fought distaste, and focused on his power and money. She turned over and tried getting back to sleep, but couldn't.

She saw that his phone was blinking—he'd gotten an early call. "His ringer must be turned off so it wouldn't wake us. That was nice of him," she thought.

Bob snorted and turned over. His eyes opened.

"Morning, Mr. Mannnnn."

"Hey there."

"Looks like you got an early phone call."

He looked at the phone and knew that it could have been from his wife. "Eh, it's probably nothing."

She jumped out of bed playfully. "Let's see who it is!"

"No! Come back to bed Girlie! I got somethin' for ya..."

"Oh, Bob!" she sang, jumping on top of him. "Hee heeeeee!"

"Hey there, there's my Girlie."

They started kissing. Bob was already ready. She wrestled off her panties and he got his business done quickly.

She wanted to snuggle, but he jumped out of bed and looked at the phone. It *was* his wife. He hit delete on the machine. "Whoops! Damn! I hit delete instead of play! Shit!" he said, looking down and shaking his head.

"Did you at least see who it was?"

"No."

"Well, if it's important, they'll call back."

"Yup."

She got out of bed and went into the bathroom as he plotted. He had to get alone at some point to call her back. The bitch shouldn't be calling at such an early hour. "Stupid bitch," he thought. "She probably called drunk, late at night, crying and shit."

Soon, they were having breakfast. Bob's head was leaned down into his plate as he loudly chewed and slurped.

"He eats like a pig," she thought, and tried thinking of something else.

He finally looked up from his plate—chewing loudly—and smiled at her. There was egg on his chin. She looked away.

"So, Girlie, I gotta meet with some people at Town Hall today about expanding our restaurant."

"Really?! That's great!"

"Yup. Bigger is better! Up and up! Go get 'em!"

"Oh, Bob! You mean, for next summer?"

"That's right, little girlie. Next summer," he said as he slurped more eggs. "I'm gonna have to go over to Town Hall a lot in the next few weeks, and I'll need you to hold down the fort while I'm gone."

"Of course I will, Mr. Mannnnnn."

He belched. "Say, you know what? I think it's time you learned how to help me with the restaurant books."

"Oh, Bob!"

"Yup. Look, come here." He stood, shoveled more egg into his mouth and walked to his desk. She obediently followed. He pointed to a stack of payroll information as he chewed. "This is what the See Food has paid out, and I just need ya to enter these numbers here, into my personal business ledger here, see?" (He really liked the idea of someone else's handwriting in the books.)

"I can do that!" she said, kissing him on the neck.

"Great! You spend the morning doing that, Girlie, and I'll go down to Town Hall. Finally, I have a partner! We're quite a team!"

"Oh, Bob!" She squeezed him tight.

"Heh Heh."

8

While Olias, Kara and Jon were enjoying their breakfast, Lillith was using Seth's body to row her and Dan's body out to the boat. She knew she had to get to Black Island first, and hide behind it.

Dan and Seth were past the point of actually speaking— they were complete automatons now, extensions of her.

In silence, the three jumped from the tender into the main boat and got underway. She had Seth's hands power up the motors and point the boat toward High Island.

Dan wasn't needed until they were actually setting foot on Black Island, so she had him facing a wall, for one reason: to degrade him. That rebellious boil had angered her. Halfway through the voyage, she had him poke his finger deep into his left ear, gouging the lining of the ear canal. Blood started to flow out as she made him smile at the wall. She was about to have him sing happily while doing the same to his right ear, but she got bored. And she wanted those ears to work.

The dark three motored to High Island and began a slow, wide arc to the other side of Black. She was worried about another storm chasing her away, and proceeded cautiously.

CHAPTER 14:   Race

1

Olias, Kara and Jon carried gear to the beach and boarded Ziggy. The tension was thick—conversation was minimal, just a few "Yups" and "You-got-its."

Due to the amount of gear, the tender wouldn't fit in Ziggy, so they attached it with long tow ropes and got underway.

"Let's see what the Cranchet motor's got!" Olias said.

He pushed down on the stick. There was an electric *snap* as they blasted forward. Jon fell back off his seat onto a rolled-up tent. Kara grabbed ahold of a rail on the dashboard to keep from careening backwards.

Olias brought the speed back down. "That was pretty stupid of me. Sorry."

"Yes, luv, it was. The tender looks unharmed, at least."

They approached large and wild High Island—its two mountains looming. After navigating around it, Black came into view.

"Our futures await," they each thought at the same moment. They were quiet as it got closer.

They reached it. Olias brought the motor down to trolling speed.

"The ropes are still there!" Jon said.

Soon, Jon climbed onto the bow as Olias positioned him at the ropes. Jon took hold of the strongest one and tied Ziggy to Black Island.

At that moment, a boat appeared from the other side of the island!

"That's Seth's boat!" Jon said.

"Shit," muttered Olias while looking at Kara, who mirrored his expression. "This does *not* feel right."

Lillith had Seth bring the boat to Ziggy's starboard side. She spoke through Seth's mouth, trying to act as much like him as she could. "Hey, you guys!"

The musketeers were in shock. "Hey, there, Seth..." Olias said. He felt like he was being violated. He looked in Seth's boat and saw Dan and an old lady. It looked harmless... Dan was standing stiff as a board with a big smile on his face. The old lady sitting next to him was smiling.

"Looks like you got your boat fixed," Lillith/Seth said.

Kara's eyes were on fire as she tried staring into the souls on that boat. Doing so left her confused. It looked harmless...

Jon had an idea. "So, Seth: *ARE YOU GOING TO BLACK ISLAND?*"

"I don't know."

Jon looked at Dan. "Dan, you feel like climbin' those ropes *ONTO BLACK ISLAND?*"

"Sure! Hi guys!"

The musketeers silently raised their hands and waved back. Kara peeped out a "Hey."

Lillith stood and limped to the side of the boat. "Hello, kids! I'm Edna from the Village. If you want to go have fun on this island, I will stay here in the boat and read. At my age, I'm not going to go climbing ropes over jagged cliffs just to do a little island exploring! Ha ha ha."

They stiffly returned her laugh.

"Can we tie up to your boat?" asked Seth.

"Um, sure..." Olias said, hesitantly.

As Seth replied with "Cool," Dan was already throwing a rope to Jon, who barely got his arms up in time to catch it. He reluctantly wove it around a starboard cleat. Kara put out a few fenders.

Lillith smiled with as much fake warmth as she could, but they felt it as creepy. None of this made any sense. This was bad, this was very, very bad...

"So, who's goin' up that rope first?" Seth asked cheerily.

"Me," replied Kara. She threw on her backpack and went right to the bow, jumped to the rope and climbed up. Olias grabbed his pack and followed. Jon hung back. "You guys go next," he said.

"Alright!" said Dan and Seth in unison, making the musketeers' skin crawl.

Seth pulled the boat right against Ziggy, climbed onto Ziggy's bow, grabbed the rope and climbed up. Dan was right behind him.

Jon addressed the old woman. "Will you be okay out here, ma'am?"

"Yes, dear, yes! I absolutely adore reading on a boat in the summer!"

"Okay, sound the foghorn if there's a problem."

"Yes of course, dear. You kids have fun!"

For a split second, Jon thought he saw a bright purple thing floating next to her, but let it go and climbed onto the island.

Olias and Kara were starting to walk toward the field of unseen beasts. Dan and Seth followed at their heels.

"We need to separate ourselves from them somehow," Jon thought as he jogged to catch up. "So, where should we go?" he asked.

Olias knew what Jon was thinking. "Hmmm, I say we climb up to that cool rocky peak over there. It looks like there's a great view of Penobscot Bay from the top."

Jon nodded. "Yeah! Sounds great! C'mon, Seth and Dan!"

Lillith knew that the Great Crystal was on the other peak. "Cool!" said Seth.

They all started climbing. Olias and Kara hung back a little, slowly losing ground to them. When Jon, Dan and Seth were out of sight, Olias and Kara stopped.

"C'mon!" Kara said. They started running down the rocky hill. They reached the bottom and ran as fast as they could toward the Field of Unseen Beasts.

Meanwhile, Lillith didn't know if she could physically go up onto the island or not. Did the ancient "Rescue Souls" (she detested that arrogant moniker) have a trap set for her? She had felt an energy surge in the Great Crystal right before it went dormant, and assumed it had been used for a trap. A trap set only for her. She decided to let Seth and Dan be her eyes, ears, legs, arms and mouths. She felt she could accomplish all her goals with their bodies. It was pretty obvious, however, that Olias and that pretty little thing had run off towards the Great Crystal, so it was time to act.

Just as Jon, Dan and Seth were reaching the top, Dan took off down the hill, running at a dangerous speed.

Jon whirled. "Hey! Where the hell are you going?!!"

"He probably just has to pee or something," Seth said.

Jon was unsure how to deal with this problem. "Um, I think he's in trouble!" He took off after Dan. Seth followed.

2

Olias and Kara entered the field, running full-speed. The tall weeds and fronds were hard to avoid. Kara tripped over a thick lump of vegetation and went sprawling into a huge blade of grass.

"Kara! Are you okay?!" He helped her up.

"I'm fine, let's move!"

They continued sprinting, making sure their shadows stayed in the same place on the ground so that they were heading for the rocky hill that led to the baobab.

They heard no animal snorts or grunts. "No animals!" huffed Kara.

"I know! Maybe we should have been *running* through this field from the start!"

After a few minutes, they saw the forest high above the weeds, and came to the rocky hill. They started climbing as fast as they could.

3

Dan was entering the field. A guttural *snort* sounded to his right. "You don't scare me, you puny nothings."

Jon wasn't far behind, with Seth at his heels. They entered the field. Jon's anger was building. "What the hell do you want with Black Island?!"

"That which you want, puny human."

That did it. Jon stopped running and put out his leg, tripping Seth. Seth tumbled into a sharp branch, gashing his forehead.

Jon's anger was never greater. He started kicking Seth in the stomach, arms and legs.

Dan stopped pursuing Olias and Kara, turned around and ran right for Jon. He arrived as Jon was kicking Seth's stomach.

Dan tackled Jon to the ground and punched his head and face. Jon evaded as many hits as he could.

Seth got up and joined in the beating.

Battered, Jon collapsed.

4

Bob didn't need to go to Town Hall, he just needed to be alone to call his wife.

Stacy sat at his desk, looking over the task she'd been given. "I think this will be very easy, Bob!" she announced.

"There you go, Girlie. I'm off to talk to the chairman of the town council and the mayor and whoever the hell else will do what I need 'em to do for me! See ya!" he said as he stepped out.

"Oh, Bob!" She ran to the door, grabbed his left hand, pulled him back inside, and started planting a garden of kisses from his cheek to his neck.

"Ha ha, Girlie, come on! I gotta do this, huh?! Huh?!"

"Hee hee heeee! Oh alright, Mr. Mannnnnnnnnn!"

She let him go and watched him walk briskly down Main Street before getting back to her assigned task.

Once far enough away, he ducked into an alley and called his wife.

"Bob! There you are! Didn't you get my message?"

"Oh, that was you? Sorry babe, I accidentally erased the message on my machine this morning when I was wakin' up. So, what's the problem now?"

"Well, Bob... I need you to come pick me up!"

He froze. "What? Driving to California takes awhile there, babe..."

"I'm not *in* California, Bob. I'm in Bangor, Maine. At the airport."

Bob knew there was too much lag time in his response while he quickly thought, "Maybe she ain't as dumb as I thought." He recovered. "Oh! Wow! Really?! Are you lyin' to me?! Huh?! Huh?!"

She indeed noticed the lag. "No, silly! My mother gave me the money for the flight and is looking after the kids. She said it's her early birthday gift for me! Isn't that wonderful?!"

"Oh boy, yeah it is, ha ha! But you know, I'm busy like I told ya..."

"I know you're busy, Bob, but can you come get me? I've never seen our Maine restaurant! I'm so excited!"

Bob was scrambling, pushed to his bullshitting limits. "Well, you know I'm on an *island*, right?"

"What does that mean, Bob?"

"It means I gotta take my car over on the ferry to drive anywhere!"

"So, take your car over and come get me. I haaaaaaave something for you, lover..."

"Ha ha! That's so great! Look, it ain't that easy to get a car over this time 'a year. I don't know what to do."

"Bob, I'm here. I guess I can take a cab to Rockland. Isn't that where the ferry takes off from, Bob?"

Bob was starting to panic. This wasn't good. She'd done her homework. Was she even testing him? "Um, the ferry takes off from Rock*port*, hon."

"Ohhh, I see. Right, yes, I see it on a map here at the airport. So, what should we do about this, Bob? I'm here. In Maine."

Nothing had ever rocked Bob's lying ability this much. "Okay then, take a cab to Rockport. You can then be a ferry walk-on for the last trip today. I'll meet you at the ferry terminal on Mount Haven."

"Oh! Well then I *can* get to the island today! Ha ha, see you soon, Bob!"

"Ha ha haaa! See you, hon!" he replied, his heart dropping into his stomach.

He shoved his phone into his pants pocket, shaking and breathing heavily. What to do?!

This was going to be rough. Bob's bitches weren't in a row after all...

5

Dan and Seth left Jon unconscious in the field and set off in a sprint toward the high forest.

Aggressive growls and snorts sounded around them. Then they saw the animals—a squadron of huge badgers, closing.

Two badgers raced in from behind, gunning for the lag runner—Seth. They each took a chunk out of the back of his upper legs. Blood splayed.

Seth didn't scream or even acknowledge the injuries— Lillith didn't feel the pain.

The badgers lunged again and gouged into the flesh above his hips, tearing out flesh.

Seth whipped around and took each badger by an ear, flipping them over—their ears half-ripping at the base.

The badgers squealed and went sprawling into each other as Lillith's two bodies ran onward, escaping the rest of the pack. Lillith was able to cauterize the wounds on Seth.

They reached the base of the rocky hill. An army of mice flooded out of holes as Dan and Seth ran onto their bodies, squishing them and losing footing.

There were so many flowing mice that some spots were a foot deep with them. They bit into Dan's and Seth's legs and started climbing up their bodies. Lillith's puppets stumbled and fell, bashing their heads on rock.

They got up and ran back down the hill around the surging mice, reaching a clear section where they could start climbing all over again.

As they climbed, there were a few remaining mice on them, under their clothes. One was under Dan's shirt—it focused on his nipple and bit it off, then began boring a hole into his breast. Lillith ignored it.

6

Olias and Kara reached the baobab and continued running. The trees got thicker as they went, and soon they were half-crawling in parts.

A voice invaded their minds. *"Finally. You are here. Come this way."*

As the words shot through new parts of their brain, they felt a fainting feeling reminiscent of the original Black Island blackouts, but not enough to deter them.

Somehow, they knew what "this way" meant, and arced a little to the left.

As they approached Gumtooo, they knew *it* was the voice they had been hearing. They reached the little clearing in the bramble.

They stood before Gumtooo.

"Hello, Olias. Hello, Kara. I am Gumtooo. I will talk you through the process of activating the Sun Collectors."

"Do you know that there are people following us?!"

"Who are they?"

"People who somehow got invited to set foot on the island!"

"They didn't come with you?"

"No," Olias said. "They arrived right at the same time we did. They left an old woman sitting in the boat. Jon is trying to distract them, but they could be on our heels for all we know!"

"This is bad. Without power from the Great Crystal I cannot function adequately. You must hurry through the Black Barrier and start the Sun Collectors. It is the only way. Can you talk to me without using sound?"

"How do we do that?" asked Kara.

"Feel where my words go into your mind, and use that part to push your words back to me."

Olias and Kara felt the new area in their minds. Kara was the first to do it. "Can you hear this?!"

"Yes!" Olias yelled.

"Yes. Now go, quickly."

Olias and Kara continued toward the wall of black, now with guidance from Gumtooo. Olias tried to own this new part of his mind. It felt like a bubble of warm air in his head. He shut his mouth. "Can anyone hear me?" he asked.

"Yes, luv."

"Yes."

Olias noticed that they were going a different way. "Gumtooo, you are bringing us in a different direction than we've gone before."

"You are being brought to the best entry spot. You should see the old granite monument slabs soon."

They crawled around two spruce trunks and saw granite slabs lying on the forest floor, a larger slab resting across them.

"Oh my God, this is the monument from my dream," Kara said out loud.

"What?!" Olias asked.

"I dreamt that I was a child and this was all a desert peak. I... was a young boy, and I think you, Olias, were my younger brother..."

"Yes, it makes sense that your spirits were here before, probably before the First Destruction. Now hurry, please."

7

Dan and Seth reached the baobab and ran into the forest. They were highly agile and moved fast through the thickening trees—Lillith wasn't concerned about branches hitting their faces or arms. She only made sure that nothing pierced their eyes, because she needed to see.

As they raced at an inhuman speed, sharp branches knifed into their faces, hands and arms, drawing blood.

They weren't heading in the direction of Gumtooo, but were moving with increasing speed towards the wall of black.

8

On all fours, Olias and Kara reached the wall. Olias pulled a rope from his pack and handed one end to Kara. "Put this through your belt loops and tie it—I'll do the same. It's best if we're tied together in there."

They tied themselves together and stood up into some branches.

"Ready, luv?" he asked.

"Ready."

They walked through the wall into blackness. There was no more thicket. There was space to move.

"Oh wow!" exclaimed Kara. "This is unreal!"

"Tell me about it. C'mon."

They started walking. The silence was a vacuum.

"It sure is *still* in here," she said, kicking up a mote of dust from the ancient surface.

"Let's stop," Olias said. They stopped. Olias turned around, dropped to his knees and shone the flashlight on their footprints. He tried to discern whether they were in a straight line. He couldn't tell. "This could be like boating in the fog; you think you're going straight, but often you're going in a long circle... I can't tell. We'll just have to go on faith, luv."

"Yes, luv." Kara held out her hand as Olias was reaching for hers. They locked hands and marched with faith into pure blackness.

Meanwhile, Dan and Seth were scurrying on all fours like lizards through the thick branches. They reached the wall. Without hesitation, they crawled through, stood up and started running.

Lillith remembered this terrain.

CHAPTER 15:   The Sun Collectors

1

How could Bob keep his bitches in a row without telling Stacy that his wife was coming? He thought maybe he could put the wife up at a local inn, but that wouldn't keep her away from the restaurant... And it wouldn't keep her away from wanting to see his apartment... This was bad. Very bad. No, he had to tell her. He had to think fast.

"I'll tell her the wife gave me an ultimatum: either I get back together with her, or she'll file for divorce and take everything! Including our restaurant!"

He didn't like how shaky that was. He preferred his lie web securely spun. This flimsy one could spin out of control.

He dialed his wife.

"Yes, Bob?"

"Hey babe, I'm gettin' us a suite at the local inn! A romantic suite! Can't wait to see you!"

"Oh Bob, I love you."

"Love you too—gotta go. See you soon!" He called the local inn.

"Hello, Seacoast Manor."

"Hey there, this is Bob Lianelli, owner of the See Food."

"Hello, Mr. Lianelli. How may we help you?"

"I need a real romantic room for the week, you got somethin' like that?"

"Yes we do, but our suite is only available for the next 3 nights."

"You got any other rooms? Huh?!"

"Sorry Mr. Lianneli, we are fully booked."

"Okay then, I'll take it. You wanna do this now with my credit card, or what?"

"No need, sir. We can do that when you check in."

"Okay," Bob said while shoving the phone into his pocket. He walked back to the apartment.

Stacy was still sitting at the desk, entering data into the fudged books.

Bob put on his gravest, most serious expression. It was time for the curtain to rise.

"Hi, Mr. Mannnnnn!" she flirted as he entered. "That didn't take long!" Then she saw his expression. "What's wrong?!"

"I didn't make it to Town Hall, Girlie. Got a call from the wife. And this ain't good..."

Fear shot through her. "What?! What's the problem, Bob?"

"She's here, in Maine, and coming to the island today to give me an ultimatum: either I get back together with her, or she divorces me and takes everything I own, including *our* restaurant."

Stacy was stunned. "...Well, you aren't getting back together with her, right?!"

"Of course not! I love *you* Stacy, *you!*"

This barely appeased her stretched emotions. "What are you going to do?"

"I'll convince her that we need to get a normal divorce. She needs to know that she can't blackmail me. I'll remind her of the love we once shared. And I'll tell her that we must move on, now that the love is gone, and get that divorce. A fair, 'everyone's-happy' divorce. I'll put her up at the inn and treat her nice and try to get her to be civil and nice in return."

"Oh Bob, she doesn't deserve you."

"Tell me about it..."

2

Kara and Olias walked forward in the black. "Hold on, stop," Olias said. They stopped.

"What is it, luv?"

"The humming sound is gone..."

"I guess it needs *us* to turn it back on. Come on," she said, pulling his arm. "Let's just keep walking until we bump into the thing."

They continued at a faster clip, holding their hands straight out so they didn't walk into a wall.

They heard running footsteps approaching from the left.

"Oh my God, Olias! That's more than one person running!"

"Shhhh! Be still!"

Dan and Seth came within ten feet of them while running past, unseen in the murk.

"C'mon," whispered Olias. They followed the sound of the running as quickly and quietly as they could.

The footfalls stopped. Olias and Kara stopped short—she almost fell as he caught her. They listened. Nothing.

After what seemed like hours—but was only minutes—they heard a sound.

"What is that?" she asked.

"It sounds like... stone sliding over stone?"

"Let's go!" she insisted, pulling him. They set off in the direction of the sound.

Their outstretched hands hit a stone wall. "Whoa!" they quietly blurted in union.

Kara said, "We need Gumtooo's help." She felt the new part of her mind. "Hello, Gumtooo?"

"Hello." Clear as a bell.

"Which way do we go?"

"The Stone Door has opened. Did you open it?"

"No, it was the others."

"Oh my... Can you go in the direction you heard it?"

"Yes, over to the left somewhere."

"Find the opened door, go through it and to the left."

Olias could hear Kara and Gumtooo speaking. He used the expanded part of his mind to join them. "Hello, Gumtooo. Kara, let's hurry but be quiet."

They took off to the left, touching the smooth stone wall as they went.

The wall stopped. Empty space. "This must be the door!" Kara sent.

They hesitated. She went through, pulling Olias with her.

"Stop! Look for a little green light on the wall to the left."

"I see it!" sent Kara.

"Push it."

She pushed it and small lights lit up on the walls and ceiling.

They saw that they were in a hallway carved inside pure rock, with perfectly smooth walls, a shiny stone floor and an arced ceiling.

"You are almost at the Inner Chamber. Continue."

They jogged forward as quietly as they could.

3

Lillith didn't know that she could have rocketed to the door of the Inner Chamber this whole time. She didn't think the remnants of the Rescue Souls would be so "unwise" to have used their last bit of energy on something as meaningless as healing an old man, so she presumed there was still energy for defenses. For a trap. But she was wrong. She was fooled—her distrusting nature used against her by the ancients.

So, she waited in the boat while working her puppets up to the door of the Inner Chamber. Dan and Seth came to the closed door and stopped. The hallway lights came on—she knew Olias and Kara had entered the building.

She didn't know how to open the door. She used their eyes to look everywhere for a button.

Kara and Olias came around a bend in the hallway and saw Dan and Seth at the large closed door. They stopped and watched Dan and Seth looking all over the walls, floor and ceiling.

Kara tried sending a question to Gumtooo just as Dan and Seth looked up and saw them.

Dan and Seth froze, and at the exact same time put up their hands and waved, yelling in unison, "Hey there!"

Olias instinctively waved. "Hi guys!"

Just Dan was used to speak. "So, are you guys here for some fun exploring too?"

Kara and Olias discovered that the new part of their brains was diminished when they had to speak to others the conventional way—especially *these* others—and lost contact with Gumtooo.

4

Bob needed Stacy to return to her busy-work so he could start collecting her belongings. "Hey Babe, we really need that paperwork done. I'll tend to this divorce. With you doing that, at least we know the restaurant's safe."

"Okay, Bob." She got back to work as he ripped the covers and sheets off the bed and threw them into the washing machine.

Meanwhile, Babs Lianelli stood at the foot of Mother Atlantic, staring out over the ocean, waiting for the ferry to come around the bend and drop off its contingent of cars from Mount Haven. She'd already purchased a one-way ticket to the island as a "walk on."

She knew something was up. Bob had been too distant lately and almost never said he loved her anymore, and when he did, it sounded like a lie. Not that he'd ever said he loved her much to begin with... But, he seemed to want to escape every call she'd made in the past six months. She wanted to see why. She wanted to catch him red-handed. Who was *she?* What might *she* look like? What fucking *bitch* stole Bob? She'd see signs of it for sure.

"I'll smell the bitch on him," she said out loud as the ferry came around the bend.

Bob was scrambling. Bitch Number Two had to get all her shit out of his apartment so Bitch Number One didn't see it. That meant everything—all her clothes, unpacked boxes, toothbrush, everything. Or, was there another way? Maybe some story?

He knew Bitch Number One was already boarding the ferry. He didn't have time to spin lies.

This wasn't good—Bitch Number Two had nowhere to go. Her former apartment was already occupied. "Maybe I should've put Bitch Number Two up in the hotel," he thought. "And what the fuck with Bitch Number One?! Why is she showing up unannounced? This is bad, this is very very bad... She'll take the two kids and my California property and then take everything else she can get, leaving me with next to nothing! That fucking bitch!!!"

He was shaking.

Babs watched as the ferry employee directed the cars off the ferry, up the ramp and onto the mainland. Cars once caged by water on the island of Mount Haven were now free—free to drive to California, Mexico or Alaska.

After the boat was emptied, the walk-ons began trekking aboard. She grabbed her things and marched down the ramp onto the ferry. She found a seat in the starboard bus-like cabin, plopped her belongings on the floor and stared out the window as the cars were directed into their spots.

"You can't hide anymore, Bob," she said under her breath. "You lying, honorless, pathetic shell of a man."

Bob approached Stacy, who was working at the desk. "Hey, Stace... I think we need to make it look like you don't live here."

She was stunned, her emotions re-bludgeoned. "But, Bob, you said..."

Bob started yelling. "Look!!! Maybe I was a tad overzealous here, okay?! O-fucking-*kay?!!*"

Tears welled up in her eyes. She put the pen down. "So, what are you saying, Bob? I have to move out?"

"Look, don't you have some friend you can stay with for a couple days while the bitch is here?"

"You asked me to move in with you, Bob."

"Look, Girlie, I love ya, I do, but I don't wanna lose everything to this bitch! Please, work with me, don't be so selfish!"

Stacy looked down and said, "So, she'll take the restaurant away from us?"

"Yes! Yes!!! That's what I've been saying! She'll take *our* restaurant! Now come on, help me get all your shit out 'a here and into the car!"

"Alright..."

Now unencumbered, he ran to the bathroom and started hastily removing her belongings and throwing them into an empty paper shopping bag.

She started to cry as she neatly folded her clothes and gently placed them in her suitcase.

He bounded into the room. "Ya know, Girlie... maybe someday that restaurant could be mine and *yours,* huh?!"

This was hope enough for her. "Oh, Bob..." She walked to him and rested her head on his shoulder as he hurriedly threw her shoes into a dusty bucket.

5

Olias and Kara were facing Dan and Seth across the long expanse of rock hallway. Olias took Kara's hand and said, "Hey, you guys explore there! We'll explore over here! We'll be back soon to see if you've found anything!" He led her around the bend and out of sight.

She nodded and whispered, "Good idea, luv. It's time to regroup."

"It is. But I can't seem to access Gumtooo."

"Me either. With them here it makes it hard. If you look out for them while I try, I might be able to."

"Okay." He stood watch as she felt for the new part of her mind. "Gumtooo?"

"*Hello. You must go into the Inner Chamber and activate the systems. Olias must sit in the chair as you power the Sun Collectors. Hurry.*"

"But there are two guys standing right at the door, blocking our way! They don't seem to know how to open the door, and we don't know what they'll do to us if we open it—I think they'll try to hurt us!"

"*This is bad.*"

Olias tried to send words, but couldn't. "Luv, ask Gumtooo how to open the door, so we know."

"Gumtooo, how do we open the door?"

"*Walk to the center of the door and expose your open palm to it.*"

"That's simple enough. Maybe I can distract them? Maybe, flirt with them?"

Olias frowned. "I don't know, luv... that puts you in danger," he whispered.

"Well, what else can we do? Just wait for them to leave?!"

All three were stumped.

Olias found the sweet spot and sent, "Gumtooo, do you know where Jon is? Is he alright?"

"*I do not know. Until you get the Sun Collectors activated, my abilities are all but nonexistent. I am trying to locate him. He might be unconscious. Or worse.*"

Meanwhile, Lillith had her four puppet hands feel every inch of the hallway close to the door. She felt nothing that might open it. She was starting to get angry. Maybe those two puny things knew something she didn't. But they walked off in the wrong direction... Dan and Seth started walking in that direction.

Kara whispered, "I hear them coming!"

"Follow my lead, luv."

"Okay."

Dan and Seth walked up. Kara and Olias were startled to see all the scrapes, cuts and open wounds covering their bodies. Seth was caked with dried blood. And neither of them seemed to notice...

"Are you guys okay?" Kara asked.

"Yes, of course," replied Seth.

Olias stepped in front of Kara. "Are you sure? It looks like you got really scraped up!"

Dan spoke. "Just havin' fun. Say, do you guys have any idea how to get through that big door back there?"

"No," Olias said. "But we saw some ancient map on Old Man Cranchet's wall back on Mount Haven, which showed some secret passage to something called the 'New Inner Chamber' or something, which we think is in *this* direction," he said, pointing down the hall. "Something about a red button on the wall, I think. The whole thing sounded so stupid, I wasn't really listening. But this place really exists! It was a red button on some wall, right Kara?"

"I think it was a red button, yes, something about an Inner Chamber and a red button. Maybe you guys can help us find it?"

Olias smiled. "*We* should find it! Let's go, Kara! Why don't you guys go back to that door and try to open it? We'll be back." Olias took Kara's hand and pulled her briskly down the hall.

Lillith had Dan and Seth run past them.

"Hey! Wait for us!" Olias yelled.

They ran behind Dan and Seth.

"Hey, slow down! Wait for us!" yelled Kara.

They waited until Dan and Seth were out of sight, then turned and sprinted for the door to the Inner Chamber.

Lillith saw that Olias and Kara had stopped following, and sent Dan in pursuit, while looking for the purported red button through Seth.

Olias and Kara ran to the Inner Chamber and stopped. They put out their hands, palms facing the door.

A low, guttural *hum* ignited under their feet as the door let out an electric *crack* that felt like a pierce into their bones.

The door began to rise, its top disappearing into the rock ceiling. An aroma of copper and dust filled the hallway.

"Quick!" Olias tucked and rolled into the Inner Chamber as the door was opening, Kara right behind him.

They found themselves in a softly lit, huge circular stone room, with a main console in the center.

Kara faced her palm to the door, but it kept rising. "Olias, how do we close the door behind us?!"

"I don't know!" Olias tried sending the question to Gumtooo, but couldn't.

Dan was rounding the bend, running fast.

Kara sent, "Gumtooo, how do we close the door?! They're coming!!!"

"Quickly, put your palms to the door and clench your fists."

They did. The huge door stopped before reaching the top, and started to descend much faster.

Dan dove into the closing doorway. Lillith got only one of his arms into the Inner Chamber before there was a loud *crunch* as a section of Dan's arm—from wrist to elbow—was flattened.

The hand on the inside of the door was almost fully severed—only a few thin strings of bloody flesh kept it attached. Kara screamed.

The hand stayed animated, shaking, trying to extricate itself. The fingers started clawing away at what remained of the flattened wrist. The hand ripped itself off the arm and scurried away like a spider under the main console.

Kara screamed and ran to Olias, hugging him tightly. "It ran under there somewhere!"

Lillith—to some degree—was in the room. But she was blind. All she had to work with was the brief visual she'd gotten from Dan's eyes before the door closed.

Seth ran to the door and stood outside, motionless and ready.

6

Jon was at peace. He was surrounded by bright light and saw clouds floating above him. He heard a voice. *"Jon?"*

"Hello?" He didn't notice he was speaking with his mind.

"Jon. How are you?"

"I'm fine. Is this... Heaven? Are you... God?"

"I am Gumtooo, Jon. The voice that you, Olias and Kara have heard in your mind. You are on Black Island. Have you been injured?"

Jon faded in and out of consciousness. He felt a tickling sensation on his arm, then his leg, then all over his body. He laughed giddily.

"Jon, please, your friends need you. Are you injured?"

He opened his eyes. He was lying on his back in the tall weeds of the weird field, staring at the sky. Surrounding him were many sea otters, licking gently at his body. He smiled at them and said, "Hey you guys! Ha ha! Stop it! Ha! Ahhhhhhhhh, there's the spot..."

"Jon, Olias and Kara are in the Inner Chamber, but they are in trouble. Can you help?"

Jon started coming back to reality—which was a daunting task, seeing as this didn't feel like reality—there really *were* sea otters licking him.

As he started moving his body to try and get up, the otters quietly departed into the weeds. "Hey, you don't have to leave!" he said with sadness, still not realizing he was speaking with his mind.

"Jon, can you get to the Black Barrier from there?"

"I'm speaking with my mind!"

"Yes, Jon, you are very good at it. Now, can you get to the Barrier?"

"You are who? Gumtooo?"

"Yes, I am Gumtooo, the plant-like being you encountered twice so far."

"Holy crap—you're the purple mushroom?!"

"Not the best description of me, but it will do. Jon, your friends are in trouble. Can you get to the Black Barrier?"

"The wall of black? I... think so." He got up slowly. His head was pounding, his body aching. Blood was running down his legs, dripping and seeping into his socks. He looked down at his feet and saw they were soaked red. "It's like the World Champion 2004 Red Sox! Go Curt Schilling!" he yelled as he took off, limping toward the rocky hill.

7

Bob was throwing Stacy's things in boxes. "Hurry up! Hurry up!" he implored.

"When will she arrive, Bob?"

"In like a half hour! She's on the fucking ferry already! You got a place you can stay? Huh?! Huh?!"

She started tearing up. "Bob... I... this isn't right..."

He hugged her as she started crying. "Look, Girlie, don't be selfish now, okay? I get rid 'a her, and we can be together forever, okay? Now, lemme see a little smile there, Girlie. Can ya do that for me?"

She didn't smile, but she stopped crying, got out of his grip and dried her eyes. "Whatever." She lifted the dirty bags containing her cherished items and started walking to his car.

"There ya go, Girlie—go get 'em!"

Babs walked to the bow of the ferry as they approached Mount Haven. She watched as they passed the ancient Monument and veered in towards Nor'Easter Harbor and the Village.

"He better not be hiding anything from me," she said out loud, prompting a few people to look away.

Bob didn't want Stacy to stay in the hotel room. He thought that a love suite might be just the thing to woo Babs away from her suspicions. Carrying a couple large boxes, he passed Stacy in the street and said, "Have ya found a friend's place you can stay at? Huh?!"

"No, Bob."

"Well hurry up! Get on the phone there! I'll finish the packin'!"

She took out her phone and stared at it like a deer in headlights. It displayed her current life. She wasn't close enough with anyone on the island whom she could ask. She didn't want to go off the island and stay with her parents. Too many questions to field...

She felt a strong urge to call Todd—a really strong urge—but knew it was wrong. She'd heard that Manuel had left the island with a pile of IOU's to his landlord.

She stared at the phone with a glazed film over her eyes and felt more tears coming, but squashed them. "No. I'm not going to cry. I'm going to get through this." She dialed Kara.

Kara had accidentally left her phone sitting in Ziggy—each of the musketeers had left things, due to the unexpected way they had bolted onto the island amidst the distraction of Seth and crew.

Lillith was there and heard the phone. She extended a black energy streak and snapped it up, deciding to answer as Edna. "Helloooo?" she answered meekly.

"Um, hi? Is Kara there, please?"

"She can't come to the phone right now, dear, who's this?"

"I'm her friend Stacy from the See Food. Could you have her call me back?"

Lillith was a hand hiding under a stone abutment in the Inner Chamber, a guy standing outside a closed stone door, and a being from the earliest times of creation in a boat off Black Island. She quickly assessed that there was nothing about this call that could benefit her and dropped the phone onto the deck.

Stacy stood in the street, confused. "Hello? Hello?!"

Bob bounded out of the apartment with another load. "Find a place yet?"

"No, Bob."

"Well, hurry up! I gotta go pick up the bitch in a couple minutes!"

"How about *Todd?* I'll call *him*," she said, glaring.

"No, no, now wait a minute here... Okay, I got it! I'll drive all your shit to the See Food, and we'll put it in the storage shed out back. Then we can find someone at the restaurant to take you in. I'll *make* an employee do it! Now come on! Squeeze into the passenger seat. I'm gonna run in and make sure there ain't any evidence left!" he said while handing her a full metal bucket.

As he ran back in, she sat in the car and placed the bucket at her feet. One of the items inside it was her little white teddy bear, which always stayed on her bed wherever she was. She'd had "W'il Fluffy" since childhood. Bob had gotten a smudge of black goo on its right shoulder. It felt like she was looking at herself. She started crying.

8

Lillith couldn't do much as a hand. There were no eyes or ears. She could only scurry and try to mess things up.

She remembered what she'd seen of the Inner Chamber through Dan's eyes before the door had closed—that's how she was able to scurry into a hiding spot—but getting onto the controls of the Main Console was going to be a shot in the dark. She could feel the surface of what the hand touched, and hoped she'd feel the flesh of Olias or the pretty little thing.

Olias looked up at the main seat of this odd room. The captain's seat. "Watch for the hand, I'm going up to the Main Console and get this party started!"

"Alright, luv. I'll look for the Sun Collector thing!"

Olias jogged up the smooth stone ramp to the helm seat. Before sitting, he couldn't help but stare at the console. It was a huge stone desk, sporting myriad ancient symbols carved perfectly into the rock. Some were lit. Some were dormant. Some were flashing.

Kara searched for a sun symbol on the walls.

The hand bolted out of its hiding place and climbed toward the console. It darted onto Olias's leg and scurried up his body to his face. It tried scratching his eyes out. He screamed as he tried to bend its fingers back and get it off his head.

"Olias!" Kara ran up the ramp.

Olias was able to grab the lone hand with his two hands as it flailed. He pulled it off his face and started beating it on the rock chair. He broke one of its fingers, then two, then three— "Crack! Crack! *Crunch!*"

He threw it to the floor and started jumping on it— "Crack! *Crunch!*"

Kara stopped and watched Olias break its thumb and all its fingers, reducing it to a semi-lifeless shaking lump. It vibrated wildly on the floor.

He picked it up and threw it across the Inner Chamber. It hit the far stone wall with a "splat" and fell to the floor, lifeless.

"I won't make any Addams Family jokes if you won't," he said.

"No promises, luv!"

They hugged. She broke away and descended the ramp. "I have to find the Sun symbol on the wall!"

"Okay, luv. I will try and understand this console."

She needed help. "Gumtooo? Where is the Sun symbol on the wall?"

"Look where the ramp to the console starts, then from there to the wall, about head-high above the floor."

"I see it!!!"

"Push it!!!"

Kara pushed the Sun symbol.

The console lit up and a deep hum emanated from beneath them.

As Jon was running up the rocky hill, the ground shook, toppling him over. He regained his footing and saw a huge multi-armed rock tower rising slowly out of the thick forest. "Holy crap!!"

"I think it's working, luv!" Kara yelled over the growing noise.

Olias saw a huge diamond-shaped button—which he instinctively knew activated the Great Crystal's full power—and pressed it.

Small multi-colored lightning chains snapped around the console. He stayed in the chair as if melded to it.

Kara was standing by the wall with a huge smile of relief. She didn't notice at first, but her feet had left the ground. She was floating.

"I'm floating! I'm floating! Ohhhhhhh!"

She floated a few feet off the ground. She started laughing as though she were being tickled. "I can flyyyyyyy! I can flyyyyyyy!"

She pushed off the walls and floated around the room as Olias watched in awe.

"Look at me, luv... I'm flyyyyyyyying!"

CHAPTER 16:   Caretakers

1

Bob knew Todd was at the See Food, and didn't want him or anyone else to know that Stacy's belongings were being moved into the storage shed out back. Maybe if he'd had more time, he could've spun some lie, but this was all happening too fast.

He drove to the alley behind the restaurant and parked. Stacy sat in the passenger seat, quietly crying.

He hoped no one—especially Todd—looked out the back door. "I'm gonna go in the back and ask the dishwasher and maybe someone else to help us load your shit into the shed, then I gotta pick up the fucking bit—" His phone rang. It was Babs. He quickly answered while jumping out of the car and running away from Stacy's ears. Her crying erupted into loud, gulping sobs.

Babs was livid. "Bob?! Where are you?! I'm off the boat and standing here with my things, Bob!"

"Sorry there, babe, yeah, just had a restaurant problem here," he said as he unlocked the back door and walked into the restaurant so she could hear the kitchen sounds.

"Hurry up, Bob! I'm just standing here!"

"Yeah babe, yeah, I'm on my way!" He hung up on her and asked a couple kitchen workers to follow him outside.

Stacy saw them coming out the back and tried to stop crying. She couldn't. She took W'il Fluffy in her arms, got out of the car and started walking up the alley.

Bob was worried that someone would see her crying, and was elated when he saw her walking away. "These inbred island kitchen-worker hicks don't know it's *her* shit they're moving around," he thought. "Okay, fellas, unload this stuff into the shed. Now." They did as they were told.

2

Jon stared in wonder from the rocky hill as arcing rays of sunlight began to dance around the tips of the Sun Collectors.

He felt a vibrating hum inside the hill and continued his ascent. In two minutes, he reached the baobab. "Gumtooo, I've reached the baobab."

"The what?"

"The big funky freak-tree at the top of the hill?"

"Yes. That is Xlobost. It is an ancient being like me."

"Can I talk to it?"

"No. Xlobost is a watching sentinel for the Inner Chamber and can only communicate with someone sitting at the console."

"No way!"

"I would not lie to you, Jon. Now hurry."

Jon limped into the forest, making his way through the thickening trees as fast as he could.

"A little to the left, Jon."

He came to Gumtooo's clearing. "Gumtooo! Nice to see you again!" he said out loud.

"A little to the left will bring you straight to the barrier."

"Got it," he replied easily with his mind.

He made his way quickly toward the wall of black, passing over the ancient monument slabs. While crawling through a particularly dense thicket, he saw the wall. "How will I see in there?"

"There is some light in there now. Olias and Kara have activated the console in the Inner Chamber. But the other two men are unaccounted for and thus still pose a threat. Be careful. They will readily take a life."

"Great..." Jon half-stood in the bramble and ripped a dead branch off a tree. "I guess this is my big weapon." He got back down on his knees and kept moving.

He came to the wall and crawled through without hesitation.

He stood. It was still murky, but the created blackness was dissipating before his eyes, appearing more of a brown. He could see this brown getting lighter and lighter before his eyes, until the area was completely lit.

He could see everything! Not far ahead, across desert-like terrain, was a round stone structure, lit up and slowly turning. From its center, he saw the huge Sun Collector Tower stretching up and out of the Barrier. The sky above was starting to become visible as the light-absorbing particles of the Black Barrier were evaporating around him.

"Go to the round building, through the door and to the left. Be cautious!"

"Okay." He limped in a straight line toward the structure. As it turned clockwise, a deep hum emanated from within.

He ran around it in the opposite direction it was turning, and found the door. He jumped through, darted to the left and ran down the well-lit hallway.

"Slow down. Be quiet."

He slowed and turned the bend to see Seth standing and staring at a large door while Dan was on the ground, his arm crushed. They were both motionless.

"Gumtooo, what the hell should I *do?*"

3

Lights on the Main Console blazed as mini-rainbows flew around Olias's face.

Kara slowly floated to the ground and landed with ease as normal gravity was restored. "Can you get it to do that again, luv?!" she asked.

"I don't know. But this looks good! It looks like the sunlight is activating all the old systems and the Great Crystal is coming to life!"

The power of the Sun was collecting at the tips of the many-spired tower. More lights all along the Inner Chamber walls came to life. Olias and Kara took it all in, their eyes wide, their smiles involuntary.

A huge light on the console seemed to beckon Olias to press it. He did so without second guessing.

A recorded female voice spoke in an ancient language as a huge, cavernous "TWANG" cracked underneath them—the sound of massive electricity and energy.

"The Great Crystal must be on the other side of this wall!" Olias said.

"Can you get it to talk again?" asked Kara. "I almost understood that!"

"I don't know."

"Well, maybe you'll figure it out, Tine," she laughed.

"What?"

"My dream! You and I have been here before, luv!"

"Wow..."

"Good job, Kara. Good job, Olias."

"Thank you, Gumtooo!" Kara sent.

"Jon is out in the hallway, but so are those other two. You have to listen intently. It is time you both learn how to operate the Main Console."

4

Lillith saw that the Sun Collectors were gathering power, and felt the Great Crystal come to life. She knew that Olias and his friends had succeeded, and now had the full power at their disposal.

She knew that the ancient defenses would soon detect her cloaked presence right off the island, and might even detect the purple crystal floating next to her—her main power source.

She had known the whole time that it was going to be difficult to steal the ancient powers, and knew that it would be a very long, arduous process to change humans into Hybrids. Yet she had no choice but to try. She was simply a force of nature. Her dark, Underworld, uni-dimensional drive was solely bent on the destruction of the "haves"—which to her meant "having spirit."

She rocketed out of the boat and flew over the ocean in the form of a black streak. In the streak's wake could be heard the screams of souls she'd captured and imprisoned inside her. They gave her power. The more she captured, the stronger she became.

She flew at the speed of sound and quickly dropped into the well at her cottage.

As she passed into the earthen catacombs, all the tunneled wells and openings to the outside world from below were shut.

Once down there, she screamed—the most hideous sound in all of creation.

5

As Jon watched, Seth fell to the stone floor in a heap, unconscious.

"Gumtooo! Seth fell down and is out!"

"Approach with caution."

Jon walked up to them and poked the back of Seth's shoulder. No movement. He took Seth's pulse—healthy. He took Dan's pulse—barely there. "Gumtooo, they are both alive, but Dan is fading, and the door has crushed his arm!"

"Wait there. Kara?"

"Yes, Gumtooo?"

Jon heard Kara's voice in his mind. "Kara! I'm right outside the door!"

"Jon! We'll be out to help you. Gumtooo, what do we do next?"

"Olias, place a finger on the flashing representation of the Inner Chamber door, and turn it counterclockwise. This will deactivate the security protocols I placed into the system."

"Hi Jon! Okay, Gumtooo, doing it now." Olias turned the lit symbol.

The door opened. Jon jumped over Dan and landed in the Inner Chamber. Kara ran and hugged him. Olias jogged down the ramp and joined the hug. The musketeers were back together.

6

Stacy kept walking down the alley, squeezing "W'il Fluffy" in a vice-grip. All she knew was that she couldn't turn around. She tried rubbing off the goo smudge, but it was permanent.

She decided to walk to Todd's apartment, even though he was at the restaurant. She figured she'd wait there until he got home, and beg for his friendship, or something. She didn't know. She had nowhere else to go.

And Todd would be nice.

Part of her felt love for Todd. She knew he would take her in, and might even love her again, if she wanted him to. "But Bob has so much to offer..."

Just then, the sky over Mount Haven and the surrounding islands brightened. Some people didn't notice as they went about their mundane tasks, but most did.

Stacy stopped walking, looked around and looked up. "Why is it so *light* all of a sudden?"

All the island children noticed right away.

A sense of calm descended over the harbors, coves, stream beds, lakes, mountains, ledges and hearts of most people in the island cluster. People smiled involuntarily. Peace reigned for a moment.

Stacy knew in that light that she would be staying with Todd for a little while, and felt inner warmth at having a place to stay.

The light diminished back to normal. The Great Crystal was fully activated.

Bob never noticed the light. He kept throwing Stacy's things into the spider-ridden shed, hearing a couple things break. Once finished, he jumped into his car and raced to the ferry terminal.

He saw Babs standing with her arms crossed as he drove up. "How long were you going to make me wait, Bob?!"

"Babe, c'mon, I run a fucking restaurant, huh?!"

They gave each other a cold, utilitarian hug. He knew it was song and dance time. "Hey, it's good to see ya, babe."

"We'll see about that, Bob. Take me to your apartment. I have to use your facilities."

He knew she wanted to fully inspect the place for any evidence that he was cheating. "Yeah babe, of course. And I can't wait to show you our love suite!"

"Yes, that's nice, Bob."

He drove to the apartment. She beat him to the door and silently waited for him to unlock it.

"Babs, what?! You ain't talkin' to me now?! What's that about, huh?!!"

"Bob, I'd like to look around your apartment. You can't stop me."

"But, babe! C'mon babe, you know how long I been waitin' for some lovin' from my Babs?!! Wayyyyy too long! Isn't that why you came to Maine?!"

"But, Bob... you've been... distant."

"Look, you're feelin' insecure and maybe a little selfish about needing me so much. I run a restaurant! It's hard work! I got to be married to *it* as well!"

"Bob, you know I appreciate that, but... I just need to look around. For my own peace of mind."

"I got to say, babe, you're breakin' my heart with your distrust. Now *I'm* not in the mood."

"That's fine, Bob. Unlock the door."

He unlocked it and she walked in first—right for the bedroom. He silently followed, then veered off into the kitchen to show he wasn't going to take part in this. "You do what you have to, Babs," he said with disappointment in his voice.

She went right to the bed, took off the covers, jumped in and smelled. It was newly laundered. She wondered why she'd given him laundry-doing time. "That was stupid of me," she thought.

She was glad he hadn't followed her into the room. Nothing to distract her. She'd always fancied herself a sleuth like Nancy Drew.

He went to the fridge and grabbed a bottle of cheap champagne and two flutes. He saw that Stacy had left a bouquet of wild flowers on the kitchen windowsill. He looked in a cupboard and found a little glass vase. He rinsed it in the sink, arranged the flowers in it and placed it on the kitchen table between the flutes. He quietly filled a bucket with ice.

He was lucky that Stacy hadn't lived there long and had kept the place clean. Babs found nothing in the bedroom and marched to the sofa in front of the TV.

Meanwhile, he was waiting in the kitchen with his romantic display.

She went for the sofa fibers, looking for any hair that wasn't his. She found a long golden strand of Stacy's hair under a pillow and picked it up. Her heart sank, and her anger swelled. "Bob!!! Get in here!!!"

He jumped up and walked to the living room. "What is it now, Babs?"

She held up the golden hair. "Who is she, Bob?! Huh?! What's her name?!"

He looked down at his feet and laughed. "Ha ha! Oh Babs, that could be anyone's hair! Anyone from the restaurant! They all come over sometimes! We watch movies and sports, and I even have meetings up here with management."

She couldn't dispute this logic. "Oh... but, Bob... you've been so distant lately..."

"Babs, Babs, Babs. Look, you're just all stressed out from your trip. Come with me into the kitchen, I got somethin' to show ya!"

He walked to the kitchen and she followed. She saw the flowers and the champagne on ice.

Bob jumped in front of his display with the subtlety of a vaudevillian and thrust out his arms in a pleading gesture. "Huh?!! Huh?!! Who loves his Babs, huh babe?!!"

She smiled. "Oh Bob... you can be sweet... I've missed you."

"And that's why you came to Maine, right?! Huh?! Huh?!"

"Bob, I'm sorry..." She started to cry.

He jumped to her and hugged her. "There there, my Babs! Come! Sit!" He softly tugged on her arm in the direction of the chair. She went willingly.

"I'm being silly, Bob." She dried her eyes.

"Well hey baby-Babs, have some champagne!" He overflowed the bubbly into the flutes. "Drink up, my sexy wife! You know, Babs... I cleaned the bed, Babs..."

"Oh Bob!" She started crying all over again.

"C'mon now Babs, drink up!"

"I'd love some, Bob."

They sat and talked. They talked about their children. Their early days together. She drank and laughed at his jokes. Over the course of a half hour, he slowly moved his chair closer and closer, until their chairs were touching and they were looking into each other's eyes.

"Let's go to the bedroom Babs—the reason you came, Girlie..."

"Oh, Bob!"

"Get over here Babs!" He scooped her up with his meaty arms and bounced to the bedroom.

"Oh Bob!!! Oh ha ha haaaa!!!" She threw off her blouse.

He collapsed them onto the bed. They kissed as they undressed.

They had sex. Bob snorted.

Afterward, they held each other. "I'm so sorry I doubted you, Bob," she whispered.

"That's alright, Girlie," he whispered back, "you were just feelin' insecure 'cuz you were without your big man."

"My Bob," she peeped.

He held her tightly.

Their bodies relaxed. The high stress they each separately endured this day—helped by the catalyst of alcohol—started to find its yang. They fell deep asleep in each other's arms.

Babs woke first. It was night. As she lay in the dark, a few pickup trucks grumbled by on Main Street—their headlights temporarily lighting the room in a swirl of contorting light.

Bob was snoring. Loudly.

She looked at the clock and saw it was only eleven. She got out of bed, turned on a small lamp, pulled the shades closed, and started gathering her clothes. But she couldn't find her blouse...

She knew since the very first time they had sex—the night of her sister's wedding—that Bob could sleep through anything, so she turned on the overhead light and searched for the blouse. She remembered throwing it while he carried her to the bed. Throwing it toward the dresser. But she saw no blouse there. "Maybe it fell behind."

She got on the floor and peered under the dresser. There was her blouse, lying right next to a hairbrush. She squirmed on her stomach and grabbed both items.

She brought the hairbrush up to the lamp. From it hung a few long, golden strands. "Bob! Bob!!!"

"Huh?"

"Wake up, Bob!"

"Babe... relax. What time is it?"

"It's time for you to explain yourself! Whose brush is this?!"

Still half-asleep, he saw her holding up the brush. She looked like the Statue of Liberty. And he knew right away whose brush it was. "Babe, why are you holding up your hairbrush? Come back to bed, babe."

"Bob! Who is the blond girl?!"

"What? Who?"

"Get dressed, Bob."

"Babs, I'm disappointed in you..."

"Well then, where did this brush come from, Bob?! It has the same blond hairs I found on the sofa!"

"What? Maybe from whoever lived here before me, Babs. I've lived in this apartment for less than a year. I don't use girlie hairbrushes!"

"Bob, we're going to your restaurant—*our* restaurant—so I can see who you have working for you."

"Yes, of course Babs, relax already!"

"Oh I'm relaxed, Bob."

"Well stop it with the inspection stuff! What are you tryin' to say? Huh?! Huh?!"

"Do you love me, Bob?"

"...Sure I love you!"

"Take me to the See Food, Bob, *now.*"

They drove in silence.

The See Food was hopping. Loud music pumping. Main Street was full of cars on both sides—no spaces left. Bob parked in the walkway entrance.

She got out first. He quickly followed and ran ahead of her as she marched to the door.

"Babs, don't embarrass me in front of my employees and customers, you got it?!" he whispered emphatically. He plastered a smile on his face when he saw regulars eyeing his approach. They were drunkenly gathering to greet the happy owner as Bob and Babs came to the door. "Everybody loves me!" he briefly thought.

Babs was going for the door first, but when she saw the greeting they were about to receive, she adjusted her expression accordingly with a cosmetic smile of her own.

Bob reached past her and grabbed the handle. He wrenched the door open and put his arms up in a regal "hello" gesture. "Thanks for comin' everybody! We do this all for you, ya know!!!"

"Hi Bob!" and "Thank you Bob!" rained down on them.

"Everyone!!! I'd like you to meet my wife, Babs!!!"

"Oooooooooohhh!!!" An onslaught of drunken people descended upon her with outstretched hands. She'd already committed to her smile, and started saying hello to her new See Food friends, while stealing glances at the waitresses—looking for one with golden hair.

Bob wanted to make his getaway to the kitchen to check on the Stacy situation, but knew Babs would be suspicious if he did. So he waited, playing the role of devoted husband. He knew the drunks would keep coming—there were many in the wings waiting their turn. He bided his time. He kept animatedly looking at his employees throughout the restaurant to show the preoccupied Babs that he was concerned with employee performance. He pointed at a table of elderly people who were still waiting for their waters, then pointed at Romona and mouthed that their waters weren't on the table.

Babs was fooled, thinking Bob was truly concerned with restaurant matters. And he stayed by her side. The devoted husband in all his glory. Whenever her eyes went to him, he mouthed something to a waitress. And he stayed at her side.

The drunken fawners kept coming, declaring how happy they were to finally meet her and how were the children and oh wouldn't she love a drink?! One had already ordered a drink for her.

Bob finally found a time to break away and she watched him walk up to a young man who looked like the manager.

"Todd, buddy, thanks for staying for Stacy's shift! You're the best, buddy! I'm gonna have to give you a raise! Stacy isn't feelin' well."

"No sweat, Bob. Glad I could be helpful."

Babs answered questions about her children as she watched Bob walk away from the manager-looking guy and into the kitchen.

She couldn't follow him. She was swamped with an adoring audience.

He stomped to the office and found it empty. He looked around the kitchen for Stacy just in case she was there. She wasn't.

Around him, the kitchen staff hurried to and fro, calling out for items and help from one another—working as a well-oiled, end-of-the-season machine. He didn't notice.

He went out the back door and looked around. Stacy's belongings were in the shed. The place was deserted. "She better 'a found a place to stay," he thought, and quickly walked back in.

He hurried through the kitchen and stopped at the door to the house, turned and faced all the kitchen workers, and yelled, "Everyone! One moment, please! Stop what you're doing for one moment!"

Everyone stopped.

"You're all doing a great job tonight! *Two* shift drinks for everyone tonight!!!"

"Yay, Bob!!!" the kitchen staff cheered.

"Everyone loves me!" he thought.

He walked into the house to see that Babs had managed to break away from her fans and was fast approaching. "Mind if I take a tour of your office, Bob?"

"Not at all!"

He escorted her into the kitchen and stopped. "Everyone, this is my wife, Babs!"

"Oooohhhhhh!!!" The staff stopped working and approached Babs the way the drunk patrons had.

Meanwhile, Todd was very busy, but couldn't believe what he was seeing. Bob's wife! They didn't look like a couple getting a divorce... And where was Stacy? He figured maybe she was humiliated by the appearance of Bob's wife. Or maybe... He fought an urge to call her, having no idea she was sitting on his stoop, clutching W'il Fluffy. But he was too busy.

The kitchen staff surrounded Babs as Bob nonchalantly walked into the office to call Stacy. He kept the door open knowing Babs was watching. He jumped into his chair and started reaching for the phone.

His body froze. His eyes rolled up in their sockets.

The restaurant phone rang. Todd answered it. "Hello? See Food Restaurant."

"Oh my God! Is my daughter Babs there?! She must come home immediately!"

"Um, you are Babs Lianelli's mother?"

"Yes! It's an emergency! Is she there?! Is she *there?!!*"

"Yes, ma'am! One moment!" Todd ran into the kitchen. Babs, finished with her hellos, was walking toward the office. "Mrs. Lianelli! Emergency phone call from your mother!"

"What?!" Babs spun around as Todd placed the phone in her hand. "Hello?!"

All activity in the kitchen stopped. Everyone was staring at Babs. Her face went white. She screamed and dropped to the floor, wailing. "Oh God noooooooooooooo!!!"

Bob's eyes returned and he heard Babs yelling. He ran out to see her on the floor with all the workers circling her, dumbfounded. "Babs, what's goin' on?!!"

"Bob!!! It's Bob Junior!!! He's been hit by a car!!! He's in the hospital!!! In critical condition!!! Oh Bob, he's going to *die!!! To diiiiie!!!!*"

"Oh, God!!! C'mon Babs, let's go!" He took her shoulders and guided her toward the back door. Everyone watched them go. He said, "*Nothing* will happen to him, Babs!"

As they hurried to his car, he whipped out his cell. "Hi Chummy, it's Bob. I got a major situation here! How much gas you got in your plane?!"

"She's ready for the mail run tomorrow, Bob. What's up?"

"We need to get to the Bangor airport right away! Family emergency!"

"Oh shit... Okay Bob, meet me at the strip."

"On my way!"

Babs was wailing incoherently as he shuffled her into the car. He drove to his apartment and quickly gathered her things. He packed some of his own items—he was going too.

He ran back to the car with the luggage and floored it for the small island airstrip—a mostly-flat grass strip used only by the four-seat mail plane.

"Bob! *Why* did I come to Maine?! Will he be okay, Bob?!"

"Damn straight, Babs. He'll be fine. And we'll both be at his side soon."

Chummy lived right next to the little airstrip and was getting the plane ready as they raced up. Bob skidded the car, lifting a cloud of dust into the sweet air.

"C'mon Babs!" He jumped out and got their bags from the back seat. "Chummy, how we lookin'?!

"Good, Bob. So what's up?"

"It's our boy—he's been hit by a car in California!"

"Damn. I'm ready to go. C'mon!"

Bob handed Chummy the luggage and went to help Babs into the plane. He noticed an odd wooden structure lying partly on the runway. "Chummy, what is that thing lying on the runway? Is that in our way?"

"That's just the top of an old well, see the well over there?"

Bob saw an old well protruding from the scrub.

"That top was on there pretty firm. Probably some damn vandalizing teenagers did that. But don't worry, it's not in our way."

Chummy started the plane. The roar flooded the night, causing nearby owls to dart from their perches.

As Bob and Babs approached the plane door, Bob froze. Babs froze. Chummy froze.

As the loud prop spun, their eyes rolled up in their sockets. Soon, their eyes returned.

Chummy jumped in and checked the instruments. Bob helped Babs inside, but didn't get in himself. He shut the door and walked back to his car.

He waved as the plane raced down the grass strip and into the air.

Meanwhile, back at the See Food, there was only one topic of discussion—the Lianelli family crisis.

The phone rang. Todd answered. "Hello, See Food Restaurant."

"Oh hello, this is Babs's mother. Is Babs there? I need to talk to her right away!"

"No, sorry, they raced off when they heard the horrible news."

"But that's just it! Bob Junior is completely fine! It was a mistake by the police, they called the wrong house! Bob Junior just got home, he's fine! Oh, where is Babs?!"

"I don't know, try Bob's cell." Todd gave her the number.

"Thank you, my son." She hung up.

Todd told everyone how it was a mistake, and that Bob Junior was fine. Another round of drinks was needed to discuss this turn of events. Todd told the kitchen to shut down at the normal time. The kitchen workers had their two shift drinks with the drunk patrons, who still filled the restaurant.

Bob never returned. He stood by his car at the airstrip, staring at the sky in the direction Chummy and Babs had flown.

Todd had to yell "Last call!" three times. Eventually, he got everyone out and locked up. He went home.

And there she sat. Stacy. On his stoop, all cried out.

"Stacy! I wondered where you were!"

"Todd... Is it alright if I sleep on your couch tonight? Things aren't going well."

"Of course. Let me get you something to eat and drink."

He unlocked the door, poured her a glass of pinot grigio and made her a grilled cheese.

She told him everything. He consoled. She cried. They hugged.

"Todd, I should never have left you, you're so nice, and caring, and sexy..."

"Stace..."

They kissed.

"Oh, Todd..."

They made love.

7

Babs got a flight to California. It went smoothly. She took a cab from the airport to her house, where she found her mother watching TV with Bob Junior and his younger sister. "Hi, everyone!"

"Mommy!"

Her mother was startled and confused. "Babs?! Why are you back so early?!"

"I had enough fun seeing the restaurant, and Bob is so busy. I just wanted to get back home!" she exclaimed, an odd smile pulling at her face.

8

"You must bring Dan and Seth to the Pyramid Room."

"Where's that?" sent/asked Kara.

"It is far down the hall and to the left. I will instruct you as you go. But first, you will need a few floating devices. Look for a blue button on the wall."

She found the button. "I see it."

"Press it."

She pressed, and a small panel opened in the rock wall, exposing a shelf containing a few odd-looking items. "What do I take from here?"

"Take two of the blue bands. Put one around Dan's arm and one around Seth's arm. It does not matter which arm."

She did as she was told.

"Press the small blue button on the inside of the opened panel."

Jon pressed the button. Suddenly, the unconscious Dan and Seth floated three feet into the air and hung there, lifeless.

"This will help you move them."

"Holy crap, it sure will!" Olias said. "C'mon, Jon!"

The musketeers gently pushed the unconscious men down the hall. Dan's crushed, handless arm was bleeding profusely. Seth's thighs—where the badgers had ripped out chunks of his flesh—were also leaving a trail. Olias, Kara and Jon didn't talk; they took it all in, wide-eyed.

After a couple minutes, they came to the door. *"Put your palms up to the door."*

They did, and it shot open—much faster than the first door had, since the Great Crystal was now fully activated.

They pushed the floating bodies into a huge pyramid-shaped room.

"Lay them down on the flat slab."

They floated Dan and Seth to a large, smooth rock slab. Kara softly pushed them downward. They gently floated to the surface.

"Go to the console, all three of you."

They jogged up the ramp to the Pyramid Room's console.

"Press the big white-lit button on top."

Jon pressed it. A huge beam of blinding light shot down from the top pinnacle of the pyramid into Dan and Seth. They stopped bleeding. A recorded female voice spoke from the console in a language they didn't understand.

"It says there is a part missing."

"His hand!" blurted Olias. "I'll go get it!" He ran out of the room and back to the Inner Chamber.

He found the beaten, lifeless hand against the wall, fought a queasy feeling, snatched it up and ran back. "Here!"

"Place it at the end of his arm."

Olias put the hand at the end of Dan's arm.

"Go to the console."

Olias rejoined Kara and Jon.

"Press the blinking red button next to the big white one."

Kara pressed it. A second beam shot down from the top of the Chamber, this one so bright that the musketeers had to look away. In no time, Dan's hand was reattached to his arm. The arm and all broken fingers were healed.

The light beams ceased and the room became quiet.

"Press the green flashing button."

Kara pressed it, and mini-bolts of lightning appeared underneath Dan and Seth, quickly moving around their bodies. The lightning slowly moved to their heads, where it pulsated for a few minutes, then disappeared.

Silence.

"Is it over?" Jon squeaked.

"Remove the blue bands from their arms."

They jogged to the slab. Kara removed the bands.

Seth's eyes opened, then Dan's. "Where am I?" asked Seth.

"That's a long story, my friend," Jon said.

Dan and Seth sat upright. "I... was showering in my apartment..." Dan stammered.

Kara took over in a soothing voice, talking slowly. "Hello, my friends. You are fine. Everything is okay. We'll explain what happened to you. Do you feel alright?"

"Yes," they chirped.

"*Everyone: Please go back to the Inner Chamber, where you will be given the knowledge of the ancient Rescue Souls.*"

Dan and Seth could hear Gumtooo.

"Who said that?!" Seth asked.

Kara replied in a continued soothing tone, "That's Gumtooo, he's our friend. He speaks in our mind. He's outside this building."

Dan started to hyperventilate. "Who are you people?! What am I doing here?! Where is this place?! Am I dead?!!"

Kara hugged him. "Dan, just trust this, please. Trust *me*. I don't understand what is going on here either, okay? None of us know exactly what's happening, and Gumtooo wants us all to learn together. Can you come with us to the learning room? Please?"

Dan didn't mind a gorgeous girl hugging him and blushed. "I can."

"*Please everyone, go to the Inner Chamber.*"

"You got it, Gumtooo," Olias sent. Everyone heard. "Let's go, everyone!" he said out loud.

Dan and Seth walked normally, even though their minds were still in shock. The five made the trek back to the Inner Chamber.

"*Somebody close the door with your palm and fist.*"

Olias did.

"*Okay, all. It is time you learned of your past, present and future.*"

Kara, still holding the two blue bands, plopped down on the floor right where they were standing. "This works for me!"

Olias laughed and sat next to her. The others followed suit.

Gumtooo started to place images in their minds. "*Can you all see these images?*"

"Woah! Look at that!" cried Jon. He could see the early Earth forming from gravitationally attracted elements.

They all followed with a "yes." The images moved on to a now-formed Earth that had a Saturn-like ring. The beginnings of life, which started in the ocean, were shown. The evolution of that life was rapidly shown, and then Gumtooo began.

"In the beginning, this planet was only relegated to the natural process of evolution. There was a burgeoning number of evolving animals across its one continent, which some refer to as Pangea. The higher order of beings—what a human might call 'God'—wanted it to stay a sanctuary for those animals, and asked all beings in this region of space to please not go from their higher dimension into this thick, simpler one.

But one of them, an overly curious being named Lillith, wanted very much to experience this world. Lillith went against 'God's' word and forced her spirit—her very being—into one of these four-legged animals. An ugly, distorted hybrid was created—half human-looking and half four-legged—a being screeching in agony, flesh pulling at itself. The simple structure of the animal's body could not contain the higher dimensional spirit of Lillith. She was in anguish.

A male counterpart of Lillith's named Joshua entered an animal in an attempt to help her, but was also struck with extreme pain.

The rest of us—yes, us, for your spirits witnessed all of this as well—looked down from the higher dimension in confused shock at what was transpiring for Lillith and Joshua, but no one went down to help, because they didn't want to get similarly trapped. They didn't want to 'eat the apple.'

Lillith and Joshua slowly adapted to their new bodies over the years, and gave birth to other beings, also Hybrids.

Meanwhile, all of us still in the higher realm watched and tried to come up with ways to help the Hybrids. Through a very complex process, the Rescue Souls were created, and entered this world. They were human looking— 'in God's image', if you will—and brought with them the power of the higher dimension. They erected the Great Crystal of Atlantis—where you sit right now—and created healing centers—pyramids—where Hybrids could go, and through a process that took years, have their bodies changed to human.

But Lillith had given birth to many Hybrids, and felt pride over her brood. She hated the Rescue Souls and their attempt to change the world she had created. She is the enemy you fought today. She is the energy that controlled Dan's and Seth's bodies."

"What?!" Dan blurted. "You mean, Mrs. Black?! She's... Lillith?!"

"Yes, Dan. Lillith was in Seth's boat, right off this island, until Olias and Kara started the Sun Collectors. She escaped to her catacombs under Mount Haven, where she has since locked herself in, such that we cannot penetrate her defenses. But, she is contained."

Kara had so many questions. "What happens now, Gumtooo? What is required of us?"

"What is specifically required of you is unknown. We must let the world determine that. For now, you must be the caretakers of this ancient technology."

Olias asked, "Gumtooo, was this island once a desert mountain peak?"

"Yes!" answered Kara. "It was!"

"Kara is correct. All the islands off Maine used to be mountain peaks, much taller than they are today. But there were three main destructions of Atlantis, caused by selfish mistakes of the Rescue Souls when they became too much a part of this thick world.

Lillith was responsible for the first destruction, but the Rescue Souls themselves were to blame for the final two destructions, which raised the oceans, split Pangea into sections, and killed many."

Jon needed more. "Gumtooo, we were told by Old Man Cranchet that we don't have to go back to our jobs. But what about our homes? What about money? What about our lives? What about food? Bathrooms?! How will we live?"

"That is up to you. We must keep the Great Crystal a secret, only to be revealed in a worldwide catastrophe.

You are now the caretakers of the Great Crystal. Food must be obtained the regular way—from local markets. A garden could be built on the island, with a greenhouse. There are bathrooms in this facility. I am sure you will find them to your liking. They are coupled with many sleeping chambers.

You have no more need of your jobs. You will indeed need money, and there is a gold-producing room in this structure called the Alchemy Chamber, which will provide you with gold in any shape or form you wish to use in exchange for currency.

These two issues are absolutely critical: YOU MUST BLEND IN WITH SOCIETY, AND YOU MUST NOT ABUSE THE VAST

POWERS YOU ARE INHERITING. Now you may explore your new home."

The five stood and walked through the hallways and doors, exploring the structure and its odd rooms, staying in contact with each other by talking with their minds.

Kara walked back to the brilliantly lit Inner Chamber, picked the blue bands off the floor, put one back into the compartment in the rock wall, and put one on her left arm.

She pressed the blue button and slowly floated up and around the room. "Wheee heee heeeeeeee!!!"

9
A spider had spun a web between Bob's nose and chin as he stood motionless for hours at the airstrip. His body finally loosened, and he looked around. "Hmmmph!"

He got in the car and drove back to his apartment.

As he walked in, the phone rang.

"Must be Babs. I hope she found a flight to California. Hello, Babs?"

"Hello son, it's Edna Black."

David Forbes Brown, from the 4500 islands of Maine.

Black Island II is completed and will be available soon.

My novel **Adventures with George**, about a time-traveling Babe Ruth, is also set on the Maine islands, and will be available soon.

My book **2000 Band Names** took over two decades to write and is currently available.

To baseball fans: I write a **Red Sox Report** blog for every game of the season.

Go to davidforbesbrown.com for all my links and stuff:
http://davidforbesbrown.com/

Made in the USA
Charleston, SC
05 December 2015